THE CLOCKWORK MAGICIAN

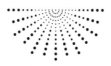

ELDRITCH BLACK

The Clockwork Magician

PUBLISHED BY:
Eldritch Black
Copyright © 2019

http://eldritchblack.com/

To our cat Bing, who was and will always be Happiness

CHAPTER ONE

Mortaphir hung in the night sky over London like a dark, ancient bat. The demon twisted his head back as bittersweet scents of coal smoke and gunpowder filled his nose. Scraps of conversation hummed in the air, bursts of laughter, raucous shouts and the clatter of horse hooves on the cobblestone streets below.

So many distractions.

The temptation to swoop down was almost unbearable. How he yearned to unleash horror and hellfire upon that mass of petty fools. To liven this bitter cold night.

Mortaphir turned to his partner in crime who sputtered behind him, the twin umbrellas strapped to his back twirling and creaking as they propelled him through the air. Kedgewick, that strange, absurd man of clockwork, brass, and servitude. That man with a borrowed life.

"Have you seen anything?" Kedgewick's gloomy voice was low beneath the din of his umbrella's rasps. He swayed uneasily while he waited for Mortaphir's response.

"Flight doesn't become you," Mortaphir said. "And neither

does stealth. Hold still and quiet, I'm listening." He narrowed his eyes as a sudden volley of fireworks burst into vivid colors upon the starry sky, then glanced to the rooftops below. Countless columns of thick chimney smoke streamed into the night, obscuring his vision.

Something shifted in the darkness; another shadow for his master's collection. This one was a girl, sitting at the edge of the roof, hunched in a threadbare shawl, her eyes bright with the fireworks. Mortaphir could sense her gift; a perception beyond mortal sight. Thankfully her exhaustion, coupled with the fireworks, was overwhelming her senses. He pointed a black, scaly finger. "There."

They dove toward the rooftop, Mortaphir fleeter than the man of brass.

He let forth a battle cry, his bright eyes shining like rubies as he tensed his claws and grinned, revealing a sickle of white spiked teeth.

JAKE STOPPED RUNNING. He leaned down, rubbed his calves and caught his breath. His body ached, making him feel far older than his thirteen years. It took a moment for the sheen of sweat plastering his disheveled hair to his forehead to cool.

He pulled his coat tight as the bitter cold air seeped through each of the holes in his ragged clothes. The street seemed to stretch on for miles, each of its huge white terraced houses like a miniature palace. Fireworks crackled and roared overhead, but Jake had no time to watch them. "They're not for me," he murmured, "just like everything else in this rotten old city."

How far had he run since leaving The Tattered Crow? Three miles? Four?

He pulled out the thick beige envelope Silas Grumble had ordered him to deliver to the old crone and gazed at the slashes of black ink scored upon its surface. What did they say?

How he'd love to open the envelope and decipher the message inside. To know what dark business Grumble had with that hideous witch. But he couldn't read.

Jake ran his finger over the glob of scarlet wax sealing the envelope, before thrusting it back into his pocket. It would be dark news for someone tonight, that much was for certain. He just prayed that someone wasn't him.

"Why does he always send me to her after dark? Can't she go out in daylight? Is she a vampyre as well as a hag?" He shivered as he thought of her cold, calculating eyes, and the darkness that writhed about her like a spectral cloak. "Still, the sooner I get this delivered, the sooner I'll be free of her." And maybe, if he hurried, he'd have time to visit Nancy and Adam afterwards. To while away a few idle moments with his friends.

Jake ran on and ducked down a short passage that emerged into a deserted square. People stood behind their tall shiny clean windows, watching the fireworks burst across the sky. "Look at you," Jake said, as he passed the homes that could house dozens, and yet occupied so few. "With your safe, easy lives. Not a care for anything or anyone but yourselves." He allowed his anger to build. Anger was a much better companion on this dark winter's night than fear. But as his eyes strayed to the alleyway ahead, he couldn't help but think of the letter's recipient once more.

Jake ran faster, hoping to leave his growing dread behind,

and burst from the alleyway into a spectacle of light and sound.

Lanterns and torches lent the night an otherworldly glow. He paused to drink in the scents of roasted meat, ginger, caramels, spices and wood smoke. The fair stretched across Primrose Hill, its lights twinkling and illuminating the black expanse.

The profusion of sights and noises overwhelmed Jake as he strode towards the festival. Barrel pianos, riotous trombones and hurdy-gurdys combined to create a strange soup of sound. A firework struck the street and burst before him like a fallen star, its edges glowing bright orange. The sight of it entranced Jake so much that he failed to look up and he stumbled into someone.

A man wrapped in a dark blue cape with a shiny silver badge towered over him. A top hat bathed his rugged face in shadows and the nearby gaslight's reflection played across the thick round goggles obscuring his eyes. He turned to regard Jake and Jake caught his own pale narrow face and mop of hair reflected back.

He looked so small. So inconsequential.

The Inspector stared in silence.

Jake swallowed. His friend Fat Henry swore the Inspector's goggles could see into a person's very soul. Right now, Jake could believe it.

Two more police officers appeared by the Inspector's side.

"Trouble?" one asked, a tone of eagerness in his voice. Neither wore goggles and their hard, narrowed eyes swept over him like he was something unfortunate they'd trodden in.

Another flash of light played over the Inspector's goggles

as he leaned down and prodded Jake in the chest. "What business does an urchin like you have at the fair?"

"I came to see the fireworks, sir," Jake lied. The envelope in his pocket felt as heavy as a stone, and he imagined its words and letters crying out as if desperate to be heard.

"Looks like a thief to me," one of the officers snarled.

"A rag-tag scrap of dirt and moth-holes," the other added.

The Inspector inclined his head. "Have you been around magick, boy?"

"No," Jake said. "I don't know my letters, sir. And I can't spell, let alone cast one. Besides, I thought magick was against the law."

"Yes," the Inspector said, "it most certainly is. Which is why-" He stopped as a scream rang out below a boom of fireworks. "Stay here," he ordered Jake. "I'll be back for you." He bounded off into the fair, the two officers flanking him.

Jake waited for them to disappear, before slipping between two stalls. His stomach rumbled at the sight of the hot golden-brown gingerbread biscuits, spice-cakes and Chelsea buns displayed so temptingly. The stall's owner, a plump old lady in a knitted shawl, took one look at him and folded her arms.

Jake's mouth watered as he turned to the next stall. There were platters piled with ham sandwiches, hot green peas and smoked mutton. "Can I help you?" the vendor asked, his round spectacles perfectly framing his withering look.

"No. Not unless you take pocket fluff as payment."

"I don't."

Jake nodded. It was going to be another hungry night, unless Silas Grumble gave him whatever greasy scraps might be left over at the Inn.

"So are you just going to stand there gawping? Or were you devising a plan to steal my wares?" the vendor pressed.

Jake didn't grace the question with an answer. Instead, he made his way through the sea of walking canes, finery and thick winter coats.

A man on stilts strode by, dressed like the grim reaper. He grinned as his eyes crawled over Jake from below his hood. A jester followed the reaper, carrying a salamander that belched bright blue flames into the night, and a bearded lady stomped behind them, leading a great muzzled black bear on a leash.

As Jake moved through the fair, he spotted various patrons from The Tattered Crow, each plying their nefarious trades. There would be many people leaving the fair tonight with their purses and wallets gone and their evening ruined.

"What are you doing here, Jake?" Mr. Bellows asked as he appeared out of the crowd. He wore a military outfit that clung tightly to his corpulent frame. Rows of war medals decorated his chest, each one purchased or pilfered rather than earned.

"Evening, Mr. Bellows." Jake wondered how he'd failed to spot the portly confidence trickster. He was one of Jake's favorite customers from The Tattered Crow, for not only did he slip Jake pennies when Silas Grumble's back was turned, he also took the time to teach Jake new words. Or improve Jake's vocabulary, as he put it. For Mr. Bellows often proclaimed that words were far keener than daggers and, unlike daggers, they'd never rust.

"It's Admiral Werthington, actually." Mr. Bellows tapped the side of his nose. "Tonight at least. So has Silas Grumble finally given you an evening off?"

Jake gave a short, bitter laugh. "You're jesting, surely? No, I'm here on one of his errands."

"Well I won't keep you." Mr. Bellows waved his hand. "Besides, a decorated hero such as myself shouldn't be seen keeping company with a lowly guttersnipe like you." He winked and handed Jake a few pennies. "Buy yourself something to eat, lad."

"Thank you." Jake was about to continue when he stopped. "Um, Mr. B... Admiral Werthington. Have you seen Mrs. Wraythe tonight?"

Mr. Bellows stiffened and a grimace darkened his jovial face. "What on earth do you want with that old witch?"

"Grumble's given me a message to take to her."

"A fouler toad than your master I should never hope to meet. It's a great pity you fell into his service, Jake. Dreadful man. I can't believe he sends you to see the likes of her, and after dark!" Mr. Bellows shook his head. "She's set up some sort of service for bereaved parents here, but God only knows what she's really up to. Still, if you must find her, then look for a large grey tent that's about as far into the shadows as you can get."

"That'll be about right."

"Do you want me to come with you?"

Jake was tempted, but with Mr. Bellows' great lumbering gait it would take forever to get up the hill. "No thanks. But I appreciate the offer, Admiral."

Mr. Bellows sighed. "Be safe, Jake. Stay in the light if you can. That witch's heart is chillier than a January midnight."

CHAPTER TWO

J ake checked the time on his tatty old pocket watch, a relic he'd recovered from the mud flats along the Thames. The case was tarnished, dented and scratched but somehow it kept on ticking and had become Jake's most prized possession. Even more remarkable was the fact that Silas Grumble had taught Jake how to use it. But only after moaning, *"Illiterate serving whelks are one thing, tardy whelks are quite another!"* for at least the hundredth time.

It was just after eleven o'clock. Jake ran up the hill and carefully threaded his way through the crowd. He did his best to stay focused on his errand, rather than the lights, colors and succulent scents of cakes and treats perfuming the air. Thankfully, Bellows' directions were good, and it didn't take long to find the large, grey tent nestled in deep shadows, its opening a vast mouth with tiny flickering lanterns for teeth.

Jake's heart raced as he peered through the gap. The figures looming inside were as still as statues. Dolls. Although to Jake's mind, they always looked more like ashen faced girls in black mourning dresses. Girls suspended in time with glassy lifeless eyes that stared right through him.

Something rattled within the tent, and he heard a rustle of skirts. "Mrs. Wraythe?" Jake's voice broke. "Are you there?"

He shivered as he saw her standing deep within the shadows. How long had she been watching him?

She snaked towards him, her pale face an oval in the gloom. Tonight she wore a thick fur coat, the dusty, mottled remains of some long-dead animal. Ragged peacock feathers topped her bonnet, crowning her cadaverous face. Her piercing green eyes flitted over Jake and he forced himself not to wince. She grinned, and foul, sour breath issued between the cracked brown teeth nestled in her blackened gums.

Jake fumbled for Silas Grumble's envelope. His hand trembled as he held it out to her, wanting all the while to throw it into the tent and race away as fast as he could.

Mrs. Wraythe stopped mere feet from the entrance. "Come, child." She waved toward a chair and gave him a thin smile as cold as a winter's breeze. "Now."

Jake stumbled into the tent leaving the music, lights and colors of the fair behind. The silence inside felt cloying and haunted, as if he'd entered a world far removed from London. The air was icier than the wintry night beyond the fabric walls and the smell hanging over the place reminded Jake of stale tea, thunderstorms, and rot.

Something shuffled at the back of the tent.

Jake jumped as Mrs. Wraythe's voice cut through his thoughts. "Give me my message, Jake." Her sing-song voice was like a little girl's, a stark contrast to her haggard face.

He continued to hold the envelope out, but she ignored him. "Here," he extended his trembling hand. "Please take it.

I've got to get back to the inn, or Mr. Grumble will have my guts for garters."

"What a thoroughly interesting idea." Mrs. Wraythe snatched the envelope from his hand. "My, my, how your hand shakes, child."

"It's the cold."

"Of course it is."

"Can I go now?"

Mrs. Wraythe shook her head. "Not until I see those eyes of yours." She grabbed Jake below the jaw with strong, bony hands.

"I really must-"

"You really must do as you're told." Mrs. Wraythe glanced away as a wretched squawk came from the shadows.

Jake knew exactly what it was; her foul cockatoo with its greasy, shabby feathers. No doubt watching from its gilded cage as it perched on gnarled feet over a bed of petrified droppings.

"Quiet, Ozirious. Be silent for Mother, for she's with the boy now. The special boy. Come closer child, stop trembling and show me those wonderful eyes."

Jake fought the urge to shove the old witch away. Her touch made his skin crawl but he kept calm. She'd tire of her game, sooner or later. He glanced away from her gleaming bloodshot eyes to the billowing, canvas ceiling.

"Ah, there they are. One nut-brown, the other as blue as sapphire. Pretty little jewels."

She'd said the exact same thing the first time she'd met him. It was only a few weeks ago but somehow it felt like months.

"You see more than most, child," Mrs. Wraythe said.

"Although you don't know it. But I've seen something too, my dear. This very night. The three are hunting. One with wings as black as tar, one more automaton than man. And the last..." Her eyes clouded over, and she gave a slight shudder. "The last...is a great wave of darkness such as I've never seen. Mark my words, London will fall." Her eyes grew fearful.

"That sounds most awful, Mrs. Wraythe, but I really need to be on my way. Mr. Grumble told me once I delivered your message, I had to be back to the Crow as quick as lightning."

"Silas Grumble is a fool. Leave him and work for me. I'll pay you a pretty penny."

"I can't, Mrs. Wraythe. Silas Grumble's my master."

"You could be your own master. You have magick within you. Faint and weak perhaps, but it might be the first buds of something powerful. You have the sight, my child."

"I don't think so. Anyway, magick's against the law."

Mrs. Wraythe laughed. "And what do you know of the law?"

"Enough to know that I want to stay away from magick."

Mrs. Wraythe shook her head. "I'll give you one last chance. Join me, or drown with the rest of them."

Jake had no idea what she was talking about. "I can't, Mrs. Wraythe."

She sighed. "Go back then, idiot boy. Back to your den of cutthroats, larcenists, pickpockets, footpads and fences! But don't dare come crying to me when The Tattered Crow becomes a noose around your neck. That's if it's even standing by the end of this year. For the city is going to fall." She led Jake further into the tent. "I'll release you, but before you go I want you to meet my new addition. She's still waiting for her new parents but alas no one's come to my tent tonight. Asides from you."

Mrs. Wraythe lit a candle and dragged Jake by his wrist. The doll standing before them was as tall as Jake, and so life-like! If she were alive, they'd be the same age.

Jake shuddered as the candlelight gleamed in her pitch black eyes and a flash of blue-white light passed across her form.

"I call her Sally Sixpins." Mrs. Wraythe's voice was laced with sadistic amusement.

"Please..." Jake tried to break her grasp.

"Don't be coy, Jake. Give her a kiss."

The tent walls felt as if they were closing in, like fabric lungs billowing with breath. Jake tried to fight his rising panic as he struggled in vain to shift his gaze from the doll and the faint blue glow highlighting her pallid features.

Her hand twitched.

Jake howled, and wrenched himself from Mrs. Wraythe's bony fingers. She seized him again, pulling at his hair. "Just a lock or two for remembrance." Mrs. Wraythe cackled as he jerked away. "Run now Jake, run as fast as you can. Flee, for the devil himself will be at your back!"

Jake darted through the tent opening, which had narrowed to little more than a sliver. Mrs. Wraythe's mocking laughter rang out behind him as he pitched himself out onto the hill, half expecting to feel the clasp of her hand on his shoulder.

He ran, cutting through the long rows of tents as a sound of skittering came from the darkness behind him. Jake yelped as his foot struck a tent stake and he found himself tumbling through the air.

Fireworks exploded silver and green above him and his breath was snatched from his lungs as he hit the frosty ground.

His tortured scream became a strangled rasp when he saw

13

the huge gleaming beetle, easily the size of a hound, whirring towards him.

"No!" Jake cried as the creature clicked and clacked, its great mandibles slicing the air as it drew ever closer.

CHAPTER THREE

M rs. Wraythe remained inside the gloom of her
tent as another round of fireworks exploded
overhead, coloring the canvas roof with garish
colors. It seemed apt. Soon there would be plenty of
explosions in London.

She glanced at the lock of hair clutched in her hand.
"You're a foolish boy, Jake Shillingsworth." He would have
been useful, that was for sure, but he was just the same as all
the others out there. Lost to the world beyond their senses,
lost to a higher calling. Compliant. Yet he had so much power
at his fingertips, such a gift. She'd known it the first time she'd
peered into his mismatched eyes.

The boy saw things, that was plain. Things others couldn't
see. He'd have made the most marvelous divination tool,
revealing magick wherever it thrived, and most importantly,
exposing those who wielded it.

"But it's all a bowl of sour milk now," Mrs. Wraythe
muttered. Things were set in motion now, things she couldn't
stop even if she wanted to. The boy might be lost to her, but

he'd make the perfect gift for her new business partner. A show of good faith.

Mrs. Wraythe stepped outside, took a small copper whistle from her pocket, placed it to her lips and blew. No sound came forth, at least none she could perceive, but then the whistle wasn't made for human ears.

She shivered as she thought about the creatures who might answer its call and glanced up at the starry sky. Soon, something would eclipse the stars and block them from her view. A thing of wings, claws and pure evil.

CHAPTER FOUR

P ain stabbed through Jake's ribs as he struggled to
push himself away from the giant beetle's mandibles.
Panic clouded his mind as the beetle's feet whirred,
clicked and marched steadily closer and a din of clockwork
clanked and rang in his ears.

Someone had chosen to build the horrible creature!

"Help!" Jake cried.

A whoosh of air flitted over his face as the mandibles
sliced and slashed. They were so close now...

Jake backed into the taut canvas of the tent behind him. It
left him nowhere to go as the beetle skittered onward at a
relentless pace.

"Please!" Jake cried, "Help-"

He glanced up as a man bounded from a nearby tent and
hopped over the campfire muttering "Fiddlesticks!" as he dove
to the ground, seized the beetle and struggled to keep hold of
it. "My, my," he growled. "This is an adversary and a half! Flee,
boy. Flee for your life. I don't know... if... I... can... stop... it...
in ...time!"

Jake staggered to his feet as the man clasped the beetle to his chest, its legs kicking against the air. "I can't contain it for... much longer!" the man gasped. He wrapped his arms around it, restraining its thrashing limbs, his face growing red with exertion.

Jake watched, impressed until he saw the slight smile on his *savior's* lips.

After a moment more of the farce, the man set the beetle down and flicked a small lever on its abdomen. Its mandibles and legs slowed, and a great whine issued from its shell. The man stood and nodded to Jake.

He was a strange looking cove, possibly thirty years old, or maybe even older. His reddish-brown hair looked as if it had been hacked into shape by a lunatic barber, yet his goatee beard was clipped with keen precision. His long coat was the exact shade of bottle-green as his waistcoat and this, coupled with his chocolate brown trousers made him look a bit like a tree. That was if a tree wore a top hat strapped around its chin.

The man bowed with a flourish. "Fear not, young sir, the beast has been bested."

"Was that supposed to be funny?" Jake spluttered. "That thing nearly took my head off!"

"Trust me; it wouldn't have touched a single hair on your tousled head. The mandibles are merely for show. The moment they detect anything solid, they stop moving."

"Well that's a comfort." Jake could barely contain his fury. "What is it anyway? Some sort of assassin?"

"I call it the Chronophasm. It's made from clock parts, and a tiny engine I-"

"I don't care how you made it. What's it for?"

"Primarily, light cleaning duties. Yes, the Chronophasm is

a foe of dust and fluff! To use it, you simply switch it on, and off you go. Maybe for a walk in the park, or a punt on the river, and by the time you arrive home; your carpets and rooms are spotless! At least in theory. Would you be interested in acquiring one? Once it's finished, of course."

"I don't have *rooms*," Jake said. "I have *a* room, and not much of one at that." Jake was about to make his way back to the path, when the man darted forward and offered his hand. "Professor Thistlequick, otherwise known as the clockwork magician, at your service. I'm glad to make your acquaintance."

Jake shook his hand. "Jake Shillingsworth. And I'm not sure I'm glad to make yours."

Professor Thistlequick tugged the tip of his beard. "My, oh my. What curious eyes you have."

Jake shrugged. "So I'm told."

"I believe I detect a note of anger in your voice. Are you still troubled by your encounter with the Chronophasm?"

"No." The Professor's interest in Jake's eyes reminded him of Mrs. Wraythe. He glanced at the shadows flickering on the surrounding tents. "I need to be on my way."

"How about a nice cup of tea to settle your nerves?"

"No thanks, I'm late enough as it is."

"Where are you going?" Professor Thistlequick asked.

"St. Giles. I should have been halfway there by now."

Jake was about to set off when the Professor pulled a knife from his pocket. "Give me your shoes, Jake Shillingsworth!"

Jake was stunned. "Are you robbing me for my shoes? They've got more holes than soles and they smell like dead pigeons."

"I'm not robbing you, I'm assisting you. It's my fault you've been delayed, and for that I apologize. Unreservedly. Now, hand me those shoes and let me help you make up the lost time."

Jake's curiosity got the better of him, so he kicked off his shoes and held them out. If the Professor noticed their stench, he hid his displeasure as he spun his knife around and used the hilt to knock the heels. "Perfect!"

"Perfect for what?"

"I'm going to affix a device to these shoes that will allow you to run at twice your normal speed, and leap higher than a flea on fire. Bear with me, it will take no time at all." The Professor vanished into his tent. A din of sawing and hammering came from within, followed by a great hiss.

Jake glanced into the tent. Old tools and all manner of strange items hung from the ceiling. A black metallic lion stood in one corner, and perched upon a bench before Professor Thistlequick was a small tabby cat. It glanced at Jake as something sizzled and sparked a flash of bright light.

Professor Thistlequick emerged from the tent holding up Jake's shoes. Two blocks were attached to the soles and they were held in place by thick black straps.

"What have you done to my shoes?"

"Modified them. These blocks contain springs that will allow you to run and jump at an amazing pace!"

"Is this another one of your inventions?" Jake asked, gazing at the inert Chronophasm.

"Sort of. I got the idea from a rather unpleasant encounter with a chap in Gloamingspark Yard. The fellow the newspapers christened Spring Heeled Jack."

"You met Spring Heeled Jack?"

"In a manner of speaking. But listen, by my calculations, my modification will have you back in St. Giles in half the time it would have taken you otherwise. Which means if you leave soon, you won't be a moment late, and the unfortunate encounter with my cleaning machine will be of no consequence at all. Except to your rattled nerves perhaps."

Jake put the shoes on as the Professor placed a steadying hand upon his shoulder.

"I only ask one thing," Professor Thistlequick said, "which is that you remove the springs the moment you arrive at your destination. Here, take this tool, you'll need it to disengage the blocks. See here; unscrew these first and then remove the straps. And make sure you dispose of everything once you are finished." Professor Thistlequick handed Jake a long-tipped tool.

"If they're so good why do I need to throw them away?"

"Well, they're not quite ready. They still need some... adjustments. The last pair exploded actually. It was quite a mess, I can tell you! Had I been wearing them at the time... well I might have lost the use of my legs altogether."

"That fills me with confidence," Jake said.

"It should! My invention will be perfect for a brief journey like yours. I fitted a modified version to a shire horse and it bounded along quite happily for ten miles straight with no problems at all."

Jake checked his pocket watch. He didn't have time for debate. Any damage the shoes might do was nothing compared to Silas Grumble's temper.

"Please. Take this before you go." Professor Thistlequick fished into his waistcoat and produced a curious looking card. Its coppery surface gleamed in the firelight as he handed it to Jake.

"I created that alloy especially," the Professor explained. "You see, I seem to have a gift for giving my business cards to the unluckiest of souls. You'd be astonished if I told you how many people have lost my cards to fires, floods and hurricanes."

"I see." Jake had a very good idea why people might lose the Professor's cards. Who in their right mind would want to keep in contact with the lunatic? He peered at the glistening golden script upon the card, pretending to read it. When he looked up, he found the Professor studying him carefully.

"Professor Thistlequick. Number thirty-three Brightstar Terrace, Primrose Hill."

"I can read it for myself," Jake snapped, trying to ignore the hot flush spreading across his face.

"My mistake. I thought perhaps... with the lack of light-"

"Course you did." Jake tied his laces. "Well, I'll be on my way then."

"You certainly will. Just be careful; those shoes are very springy."

Jake stepped forward and bounded into the air, barely avoiding the campfire as he landed. "Well, they definitely work!"

"Quite," Professor Thistlequick said. "Now, you know where to find me if you have any issues removing the springs. Or if you run into any other problems, for that matter."

"Sure. See you later then." Jake jumped down and vaulted up. He let out a yell of excitement as he bounded back down, and lurched up again.

"Safe journey, Jake!" Professor Thistlequick called, as Jake leaped through the gap between the tents and out into the night.

CHAPTER FIVE

Mortaphir sprang from the cold London cobblestones and soared into the sky. The fireworks still whizzed and roared around him like the phantoms of fiery dragons.

"I don't think we should stray too far," Kedgewick said, as he buzzed behind Mortaphir. "The rookeries would make a better place to hunt. Few are missed in the slums."

For once, Mortaphir found himself agreeing with the clockwork man. The night was still young but dawn would soon follow like a malignant sore. They still needed to find more servants for the master and there was no time to waste.

Mortaphir scrutinized the people threading through the filthy streets below. Each had their head tilted up, their eyes on the fireworks. They were such an ignorant species, their senses as dull as mirrors coated in mildew. And yet, they were fascinating. Mortaphir often wondered what it felt like to be so fragile, to have skin as thin as paper, and bones as soft as chalk.

He slowed to a hover as a screeching whistle came from the north.

Someone was calling.

The demon wheeled around and shot through the air. "Keep up, Kedgewick."

"Where are we going?"

"We've been summoned. Now hurry!"

"GET OUT OF THE WAY!" Jake bounded through the bustling crowd. He'd never run so fast in his life, and even if he'd wanted to stop, he had no idea how to. With each step, the springs compressed and launched him back into the air.

His initial fear had worn off, but it soon returned as he spotted a flash of electric-blue lights. The Inspector who had detained him earlier was patrolling the road ahead with his officers. "You boy!" the Inspector boomed. "Halt!"

"I can't!" Jake's shoes took him blundering on.

The police fanned out to block his way as Jake flew up and landed with a thump, spattering them with mud.

He propelled himself through the air, sailing over their heads and outstretched hands. Then his shoes took him careening down the road as police whistles filled the night behind him.

Jake wound through the streets, leaping over pillar boxes and piles of litter. His teeth snapped hard as he landed on the cobblestones and a surge of numbness shot through his legs.

People gasped and spluttered as he bounced past them, weaving in and out of the gas-lamps. "Forget Spring Heeled Jack," he cried. "Meet Spring Heeled Jake!"

The streets whizzed by in a blur of brick, soot and smoke.

Soon the buildings grew taller and wider, and Jake found himself joining the throngs in Tottenham Court Road. Elegantly dressed theatre-goers shot nervous glances at him before going back to pretending not to notice the knots of beggars in their midst.

A delicious scent of roast chestnuts wafted through the air as peddlers huddled around the fiery coals of their braziers. Jake's stomach rumbled as he bounded into the center of the street and weaved through carriages and omnibuses. All eyes seemed to be on him as he waved to lords, ladies, and tramps alike.

~

THE EARTH RUMBLED as the beast thudded into the ground before Mrs. Wraythe's tent.

She fought to contain a sliver of dread as his eyes flickered like red lanterns and his two leathery wings stretched out from his back. The demon was shorter than Mrs. Wraythe, but it gave her cold comfort. While she'd consorted with demons and all manner of black-hearted beings in the past, this one was different. He possessed a savagery she was certain could never be tamed, at least not by her.

A spluttering, whining drone filled the air as the clockwork man, Kedgewick, flew down, landing between Mrs. Wraythe and the demon. His heavy brass suit reflected the fireworks as the twin umbrellas attached to the pack upon his back ground to a halt. His eyes were cool and appraising as he gazed at her. "You summoned us," he said, in his rich Irish accent.

"It better be important," the demon added.

Mrs. Wraythe held up the lock of hair she'd yanked from

Jake's head. "This belongs to a boy who I believe will be of great interest to your master. I heard he's seeking talent as well as mindless slaves."

"Indeed," Kedgewick agreed.

"Good." Mrs. Wraythe held the hair out to the man, but the demon snatched it, his claws raking her hand.

"This better be useful," the demon said. "For your sake." His grin revealed long wickedly curved teeth. She shuddered. It was surely only a matter of time before he succumbed to his appetite for bloodshed..

"Now, now, Mortaphir," Kedgewick said. "We must show civility to Mrs. Wraythe."

"Indeed you should," Mrs. Wraythe said, determined to hold her own. "For your master needs me as much as I need him. Now go, find the boy."

The demon's eyes glowed as it leaped into the sky.

"Until next time." Kedgewick pulled a lever, and the machine on his back began to rumble. A dull groan stirred as the mechanical umbrellas upon his back spun, lifting him up into the air.

Mrs. Wraythe watched while they rose into the darkness beyond the glare of the fireworks, sticking to the shadows. Hidden for the time being, but soon the city would see their faces before it fell.

CHAPTER SIX

J ake shot by Trafalgar Square before making his way towards the ramshackle warrens of St. Giles. He slowed as a bright yellow light engulfed the street ahead.

A heavy rumble filled the air as HMS Watcher descended over the city like a great steel leviathan. It dwarfed the buildings and blocked out the sky as it hummed across London, leaving a trail of steam in its wake.

The nose of the craft gleamed like a bullet in the moonlight as it descended. Jake could see the people standing in the central cabin situated in the belly of the craft. They gazed from the windows and manned the searchlights. The ship was so large and so close he could see little else; even the aft of the ship was obscured by the bulk of its colossal frame.

Jake shuddered. According to Mr. Bellows, the craft carried at least four spotters; psychics who scoured the city for traces of magick. Legend said they were hideously thin and pale, with telescopes affixed to their eyes. The mere thought of them made Jake want to be far away.

Steam hissed from the airship as a smaller hornet-shaped craft detached from its hull and swept down toward the street. It buzzed past Jake and headed for the row of houses illuminated by HMS Watcher's searchlights. The hornet landed and police officers and Inspectors rushed from the craft and gathered before the tenement building. Each brandished a rifle, which meant some sort of magickal raid was in progress.

One of the Inspectors glanced at Jake and strode over.

Jake bounded away and cut through a short passage leading to a desolate street. He stopped to check his pocket watch. He had thirty minutes before he was due back at The Tattered Crow; just enough time to visit his friends.

He ran on, making his way through the alleys and pitch black streets toward the old ironmonger's shop. It had been abandoned and looted long ago, and now served as a Night House; a place filled with mean-eyed drinkers and barrels of illicit beer. Jake had ventured inside on an errand for Grumble on one dark rainy night, and that visit had been more than enough for him. But the rooftop was usually quiet and empty, which made it the perfect place to meet his friends.

Jake cut through the weeds and broken glass and flew up a flight of steps, taking them three at a time.

MORTAPHIR WHEELED over the bright streets toward an altogether darker knot of roads and passages. The air changed, carrying the stench of decomposition, sewerage and rot. A din rose up, cries and threats, screams and high, manic laughter. It was the sounds of suffering, madness and despair. Mortaphir drank in the chorus like a fine wine.

"We should be careful," Kedgewick said, as he sputtered through the air. He nodded to the great steel airship hovering less than a mile away.

"I'm not afraid of them." Mortaphir raised the lock of hair to his slitted nostrils and sniffed. He gazed down, searching for a matching scent in the city below.

"I'm not afraid of them either but the master was most specific when he said we're to remain unseen. If you want to raise his ire, then so be it. But keep me out of it."

Mortaphir cursed in his native tongue but paused as a breeze brushed his wings, bringing the boy's scent. "This way," Mortaphir said, and dove towards the roofs below.

JAKE SLOWED as a figure appeared at the top of the rickety staircase, blocking his way.

"Who goes there?" Adam demanded in a gruff voice, but his scowl turned to a grin when Jake passed through a patch of moonlight. "Jake. What-"

"Out of my way!" Jake jumped down on the springs and flew past his friend, bounding and landing in the middle of the roof.

Jake grabbed a chimney stack to steady himself and flashed a smile at Nancy, pleased to have a chance to impress her. She sat on the edge of the roof peeling an orange, stolen no doubt. Her messy blonde hair strayed from her hooded cloak and her face was pale but for her rosy red cheeks. She grinned at Jake, her worn smile making her seem older than her fourteen years and looked as if she was about to say something, before she glanced down to his shoes. "What on earth have you got on your feet? And why are you late?"

"Actually," Jake said, "I'm early, considering how late I nearly was. I thought I was going to miss you."

"Why? And what are you looking so happy about?" Adam asked, his breath frosting the air. "I went to the Crow looking for you, and Mr. Whitlock told me old Grumble had sent you on an errand to that witch you're always moaning about."

"Yeah, she was at the winter fair... with her dolls." Jake pulled the collar of his coat tight around his neck.

"I hope I never have to meet her." Nancy's fingers trembled slightly as she handed Jake a segment of her orange. "What was she doing bringing her dolls to the winter fair anyway? Surely no one would want to buy such things?"

"Someone must be buying them," Jake said. "Apparently she makes them for grieving parents so they can remember their daughters. But they're not like any dolls I've ever seen." He lowered his voice. "I swear I saw one move tonight."

"Forget the dolls," Adam said. "I want to know what the bleeding hell those things on your shoes are."

"I got 'em from an inventor," Jake said. "He was a proper weird old cove. He put those blocks on my shoes and now I can run and jump really fast. He told me he got the idea from Spring Heeled Jack himself."

"That's a barrel of lies. No one sees Spring Heeled Jack and lives to tell the tale," Nancy said, with her usual steely conviction.

"Well, I believed him, even if he was an old toff." Jake was unsure why he was leaping to the Professor's defense. But he'd liked him, even if he'd easily been the most ridiculous man he'd ever met.

"A toff!" Adam laughed. "He must have been proper high and mighty if posh Jake calls him a toff."

"I'm not posh." Jake felt his cheeks blaze, as he ate the orange. "I've just been taught my words by Silas Grumble and Mr. Bellows."

"*Taught my words*," Adam mimicked. "Don't try and talk like us, Jakey. We like you well enough without it." He nudged Jake in the ribs. "Anyway, show us how high you can jump."

Nancy and Adam huddled close to Jake. He placed his hand on Nancy's shoulder to steady himself and prepared to jump. "Right then." Jake bent his knees and leaped up.

He came down on the shoes with his full weight and shot into the air, jumping high over his friends' heads. "See, I-"

Jake froze mid sentence. Ice-cold dread passed through him as he caught a glimpse of black wings, blazing red eyes, and a mouth filled with fangs. Whatever it was, it was coming right at him...

Jake ducked and the creature shot by, missing him by inches.

But it didn't miss Nancy.

A bloodcurdling scream rang out as the creature scooped Nancy in its scaly arms and hovered over the rooftop. Its wings blotted out the stars as it gazed down.

"Nancy!" Jake glanced around for a weapon, anything to throw at the hellish thing in the air above them.

"Bring her back! Right now-" Adam stopped as a strange, whirring sound drew closer.

Jake looked up as a man flew over the roof. Two umbrellas spun above his swarthy blue-tinged face. They were attached by tubes to a box strapped to his back and moonlight glinted off the thick brass encasing him like armor. In the center of his chest was a glass porthole and behind it, an eerie red lump of flesh beat with mechanical precision, assisted by tiny cogs and springs.

"Help us mister!" Adam called out. But as the man soared down, it became obvious his intentions were far from heroic.

"Run, Adam!" Jake leaped aside as the man swooped towards him.

The man snatched Adam, before turning his flint-black eyes on Jake. "It's you we want." His accent carried a strangely mournful lilt. "Come with us and I'll release your friend." One of his hands inched to the rifle at his side. "Listen boy-" The man stopped as bright yellow searchlights swept across the rooftop, and HMS Watcher wheeled in the air overhead. "Go!" he shouted, and soared up into the dark sky with the winged creature by his side.

Jake glanced to HMS Watcher, praying it had witnessed the event, but it continued banking north as it rose up over the city. And then he watched as the monster and the mechanical man bore his friends away, Nancy hanging limp in the creature's claws. Within moments, they'd be lost amongst the plumes of chimney smoke.

He glanced across the street to the crooked sloping rooftops.

If he could make the jump...

Jake looked to the hard frosty cobblestones below and took a good deep breath of wintry air. His heart hammered as he fixed his eyes back to the rooftops ahead. "I can make it," he told himself. "I have to!"

CHAPTER SEVEN

J ake backed far away from the roof's edge before taking another deep breath and sprinting towards the gap as fast as he could. Just as he reached the edge, he jumped down and sprang over the street.

He sailed over lines of washing and the hard icy cobbles below, keeping his focus fixed on the rooftop ahead.

Jake landed with barely an inch to spare and grabbed a rusted weathervane, wincing as the cold hard metal bit into his palms. But as he spotted the glint of the brass man and the creature's beating wings, he put the pain from his mind.

The hem of Nancy's cloak fluttered like rags as they flew over the distant roofs. Jake clambered up the sloped roof, his shoes slipping on a dusting of frost. He fell hard, grimacing as his frozen fingers sought purchase in the cracks of the weathered rooftop.

Slowly he crawled to the apex of the roof, using a chimney stack to pull himself to his feet, glad for its warmth.

Nancy and Adam were even further away now.

Jake gritted his teeth and raced down the roof, his shoes

hard on the worn slates, his heart beating hard. He leaped over a dark yawning gap, and clattered upon the next roof. He ran, emptying his mind of fear and doubt, filling it with cold, hard determination.

The thrill of danger and excitement blazed through him as he propelled himself from rooftop to rooftop. "I'm the hunter now," he spat, his eyes never leaving his quarry.

Soon the distance between them closed.

Jake scampered up a sharply sloped roof, spluttering as he broke through plumes of thick grey smoke. He grabbed the chimney and stopped as the brass man vanished behind a long flat roof across the way.

The street between the buildings looked impossibly wide, but Jake ran toward the chasm. He jumped up and brought his weight down on his shoes. The springs creaked and catapulted him out over the street, his hands wheeling through the air.

His heart skipped as the road blurred below, and for a moment, he was certain he'd fall. The tips of his shoes only just found the level roof beyond the street and he skittered across it, grasping a flagpole to slow himself.

Jake's mouth fell open as he gazed down to the courtyard below.

In the middle of the yard was a giant craft shaped like a great brass fish. It was huge, easily the size of a house, and flashes of blue light played across its surface until they slowly faded.

A deep rumble came from within the craft, causing the eaves below Jake's feet to shake. Clouds of steam burst from the row of wicked looking spines set upon the fish's back, and moonlight glinted on the two enormous panes of glass forming its eyes. Its mouth hissed open, revealing vicious, jagged metallic teeth that glinted in the gaslights lining the gangway leading down into its throat. Jake tensed as he heard someone weeping inside the craft.

It sounded like a child.

The winged creature and the brass man entered the fish's mouth, carrying Nancy and Adam as if they were sacks of coal. Nancy cursed and kicked but the demon ignored her. A cloud of steam poured from the fish's mouth as its jaws slid shut.

Jake scoured for a way down to the courtyard.

He reached for a drainpipe running from the roof to the yard, but it came away in his hands. The windowsills below were no better. Their weather-beaten ledges were splintered and rotten. He glanced around for another way down and spotted a ladder on the other side of the roof.

Jake started towards it but froze as he caught sight of a man standing behind it.

The man wore a long winter coat and a tall, elegant top hat rested on his head. He was hunched over, his back to the courtyard and Jake, as if oblivious to the giant mechanical fish below.

Jake strode towards the ladder, keeping his eyes on the man. There was something jarring about him.

The man continued to lean over a net, whispering to something caught within its mesh. A raven. The bird squawked and feathers flew from its thrashing wings. Moonlight glinted on the short, thin knife in the man's black gloved hand as he cut the netting and tucked the bird under his arm.

Jake gazed from the man to the shadows behind him where a pair of black boots jutted from the darkness. A body lay there, as stiff as a board. Jake looked closer, and spotted a police officer's blue uniform. A gun lay on the ground before the officer's splayed fingers.

The man rose up, far taller than he'd first appeared. He still had his back to Jake as Jake made his way to the ladder, but then he turned.

Jake's cry caught in his throat.

The man's expressionless face looked like something from a nightmare, a fairground automaton that had crept from some terrible netherworld. His eyes were as hard as iron and crueler than the plague, and his lips were pursed into a line. He threw up a gloved hand to cover his face, but it was too late, Jake had seen it and they both knew it.

The man's eyes flitted to the gun on the ground. Jake bolted forward and seized it. It felt cold and heavy in his hand. "Please!"

"Please?" A smile danced across the man's lips. "You're the one holding the gun. That makes you a somebody now, doesn't it. Or are you?" His accent was curious, well spoken, yet with a hint of the street below its rich cadence. "What's it going to be, boy? How much courage do you really have when it comes down to it?"

"I don't want to hurt you," Jake said as the man stepped closer, his unrelenting stare fixed on Jake. The gun seemed to grow heavier as Jake's finger curled around the trigger, but he couldn't pull it. Couldn't take a life, even one as monstrous as this nightmarish man looming over him.

"Then you will die," the man said. "That's your destiny. You and the rest of the souls trapped in this infernal place."

"Why?"

"Because the slate needs to be wiped clean. We need to build anew. But you won't see the new city's glory. You should have made better decisions, boy. You should have attempted a modicum of bravery. You should know showing mercy is always worthless. You chose poorly."

The man released the raven. It flew at Jake in a whirl of black wings. He backed away but it was too late. Before he could move, the man seized Jake's wrist in his gloved hand, and took the gun.

Jake tried to run but his legs were as weak as jelly.

"The end I'm going to grant you will be quicker than the one the city would have given you," the man said.

"Please!"

The man's finger curled around the trigger. There was a flash of light and a roar of thunder. The bullet slammed into Jake's chest knocking him onto his back.

He lay there, sprawled and motionless as slowly the stars above blurred and winked out.

CHAPTER EIGHT

J ake woke to an agonizing, exploding pain in his chest. It felt like he'd been kicked by a horse. The pockmarked ceiling of his room wasn't there, and neither was the scratch of rats in the rafters. Instead he saw twinkling stars and frost glistening on the roof around him.

"What am I doing here?" Slowly, Jake sat up, nursing his ribs as another bolt of pain shot through them.

A chain of memories flashed through his mind. Nancy and Adam. The man of brass, and the winged demon. A giant bronze fish and the man in the top hat. The man who had held a raven, and then a gun, his face expressionless but for that malicious cruel stare.

Jake massaged his chest, expecting his fingers to come away warm with blood. Something hard and sharp bit into his thumb. He reached into his shirt pocket. It was Professor Thistlequick's indestructible calling card, and smack in the center lay a charred mangled bullet.

Jake flinched as a mechanical roar echoed from the courtyard below.

He crawled to the roof's edge as dry, acrid steam billowed up and the building shook and rattled like a speeding railway car.

Jake coughed and clamped a ragged sleeve over his nose and mouth.

The fish-like craft rose through the mantle of steam and smoke, and its jagged teeth interlocked as its mouth slammed shut with a great clang. The window-eyes glowed yellow in the murk, framing the silhouette of the tall thin man in the top hat. He glanced out from the craft, his hands clasped behind him with an air of command.

Jake rolled onto his back and played dead, peeking through his narrowed eyes as two colossal wing-like fins lowered from the craft. One caught the roof across the way, and tore through it like it was made of butter.

Slates and bricks tumbled and clattered to the ground as the craft turned and steam poured from the line of spines along its back. Jake sat up as a blue halo of light played across its riveted hull and a heavy, low rumble roared across the city. The craft hovered, tensing like a cat hunting for prey, and its shadow fell upon Jake, engulfing him in cold darkness.

Far off in the distance, HMS Watcher patrolled the city, its great searchlights sweeping over west London. If only it would turn...

The craft gave a heavy metallic boom, before climbing into the sky.

"Nancy, Adam-" Jake clambered to his feet, forgetting the springs attached to his heels. They took him lurching perilously close to the roof's edge.

He fell to his knees to stop himself from falling as an earsplitting whistle whined through the air. The craft ascended and shook as it climbed higher into the sky.

As the ship spun around, Jake saw the black figure in its window.

Surely the Devil himself, and London his playground.

CHAPTER NINE

A wave of energy pulsed through the air as the craft sailed away. The din of its engines faded as it glided towards the great dome of St. Paul's Cathedral where it ascended, its hull a mass of bright blue fizzles.

Jake glanced down from the rooftop to see if anyone else had seen the craft. A few windows opened and people gazed out toward the sky but none seemed to focus on the rising ship.

"It's right there!" Jake pointed. An irritable looking man followed the path of his finger, before snapping his window shut.

A crack of thunder boomed across the city as the craft shot up into the sky. It soared away until it was so tiny Jake could barely see it amongst the goose grey bank of clouds.

And then it was gone, taking Nancy and Adam with it.

Jake's nails sunk into his palms as he clenched his fists. "I'll find you, Nancy!" he shouted. He descended the ladder. A heavy scent of burning coal filled the courtyard as the last of the craft's steam vanished in the breeze.

He hurried out into the street, and ran, the springs on his heels taking him back to The Tattered Crow.

JAKE STUMBLED down Crow Alley and forced himself to stop in a shop doorway. He kicked off his shoes and stashed them inside his coat, and decided to wait to remove the springs once he was out of sight of his master's malicious gaze. Jake pushed The Tattered Crow's sturdy worn door open, and made his way through the Inn, keeping his head down.

Despite the late hour, the Crow was heaving with customers. A crowd had gathered around the dark oaken bar, their chatter and curses echoing along the low beamed ceiling. The tables were piled with empty tankards, and a few slumped drinkers watched Jake with bleary eyes. The knot of people sprawled before the fireplace demanded more drinks but Jake pressed on through the cloud of smoke, grog and sweat.

He'd almost reached the staircase leading to his room, when a heavy hand clamped down on his shoulder and he cried out as sharp fingers dug into his collar bone.

"You decided to come back then, boy?"

Jake did his best to mask his discomfort as he turned to face his master.

Some people claimed Silas Grumble was part toad, that somewhere in his lineage, an ancestor had hopped from the muddy banks of the Thames and had been transformed into a man. Some said it was down to the kiss of a witch, some a blessing of the devil. The resemblance was there in the cunning line of his thin wet lips, which seemed forever on the verge of a conversation that never began, and in that thick, flabby throat.

Silas Grumble flicked his lank hair from his shoulders and jammed a finger into Jake's chest, just where the bullet had struck him. "Well?" he demanded.

"Please," Jake couldn't suppress his pain. He flinched and tried to pull away from his master's liver-spotted face and the tufts of hair trembling in his long nose.

Grumble rolled his pale, red-rimmed eyes. "Enough of the crocodile tears and hokum, I barely touched you, you fiend! I should smash, bash, and thrash you. That's h'exactly what I should do."

Silas Grumble often added h's to words that didn't need them. He believed it made him sound like 'a proper gent', and supported his plans to take The Tattered Crow 'upmarket'. For it wouldn't be long, he vowed, before he'd rid the place of riff-raff, and turn it into a 'quality h'establishment'.

"I'm sorry I'm late, Mr. Grumble." Jake tried not to pay attention to the spit dripping down from Grumble's lips to his mottled chin.

"Sorry! You're sorry! I'm sorry. Sorry for all the pots I had to clear tonight. Me and I, the master of this domain cleaning up after drunkards like a dust monkey! Grubbing my fingers in drool and ash. The very duties I employ you to fulfill, you revolting little carbuncle!" He snarled, revealing yellow and black teeth squashed together like ancient gravestones.

"Something happened, Silas-"

"What?" Grumble's eyes bulged with fresh anger. "Are you referring to me? *Silas* is it now? Like we're fond old friends on a pleasant outing to the zoo? I'm Mr. Grumble to you, you fetid pimple."

"I'm sorry, Mr. Grumble. Really I am." Jake did his best to

placate his master as he tried to squirm from his rough grip. "I took your errand to Mrs. Wraythe like you asked, and then everything went wrong. I bumped into Nancy and Adam-"

"Bumped into them did you? By chance and fortune?"

"Yes sir, Mr. Grumble. But then they were taken"

"Taken?" Grumble's eyes grew wider. "How, pray tell?"

"By a vampyre. Or maybe it was a demon… and there was a man, all in brass and he had these umbrellas that made him fly. And then him and the other thing took Nancy and Adam to a giant flying fish. And I was shot… and I need your help. Please, I have to find them!"

"It's always the stories with you, boy. Is this a follow-up to your Halloween tale? The one about the ghost in the attic?"

"There is a ghost in the attic. And it's not alone-"

"Then as I've said before, tell your ghost it owes me rent and I want it backdated. Now get to work before I fetch my cleaver, smite off your head, and leave it for the rats and gulls."

"But I need help. Nancy-"

"I told you," Grumble pinched Jake's shoulder hard. "I don't want any more stories. You're a liar, a fantasist and a flaming ne'er do well! You, Jake Shillingsworth, will never h'amount to h'anything! Your one purpose in life is to clean tables and pots. So go and do that, before I fetch my stick and thrash you. But know that if I do, I'll take no pleasure in it on h'account of my spirituality. Still beat you I will, with vim and vigor!"

Jake swallowed his response.

Grumble released him. "Now, it has been a long devilish night, so I'll take to my bed forthwith. You'll make up for your idling by turning out the roustabouts in the bar and cleaning every last inch of the Crow. And not a word or whimper will you make."

Jake nodded and set to work. He could barely remember a time when he'd felt so weak or alone.

It was hours before he finished. His chest ached, his fingers were sore and chilled to the bone. Swirls of anxiety clouded his mind as he wondered what had become of his friends, and how, or if, he'd ever get them back.

CHAPTER TEN

Dim dawn light colored Jake's tiny room as he scrunched up his coat and set it in the middle of the warped floorboards. He took a ratty woolen blanket from the corner, and smoothed it out. This stained, moth-eaten scrap had resided in The Tattered Crow even longer than Jake, but he laid it over the splintered floor, wrapped himself up in it, and rested his head on his coat.

Thoughts jumbled through his mind, holding sleep at bay. Nancy on the roof. Adam swept up by the man in the brass suit. And then the man with the cold white, empty face.

Jake ran his finger over the lump on his chest. It still ached and stung.

The window rattled. Was it the wind, or that winged creature? The demon... he'd been told such things were faerie stories. Cautionary tales to make children behave, and yet he'd seen it with his very own eyes.

He had to tell someone. He desperately needed help. But from who? Grumble didn't believe him, and the police were unlikely to listen to his story. For while they ruthlessly tried to quash all forms of magick, their main concern seemed to be protecting and serving the high and mighty.

Adam's house was only a few streets away... Maybe, Jake thought, he could go there and speak with Adam's father, even though it was likely he was locked up in a dank cell in the debtor's prison. Or maybe he could go to see Nancy's mistress, but then he recalled she was away painting volcanoes in Italy.

Jake sighed, and turned over. "I'll find you Nancy," he whispered. "And you Adam, I swear it."

~

TWO EPIC THUMPS shook the door, jolting Jake from his sleep.

"You better be dressed, Jake Shillingsworth! I've no wish to see your chicken bone legs at this ungodly hour, or any hour, for that matter." Silas Grumble threw the door open and took a deep sniff. "Why does your room smell like the inside of a toadstool? What have you been doing in here?"

"There's tiny mushrooms growing on the walls," Jake said. "They're always about at this time of year."

"Well you can't say I don't offer you bed and breakfast. And... oh-" Silas Grumble's eyes grew wide as he clutched his chest.

"What's wrong?" Jake grabbed the pitcher of water from the corner and held it out to his master.

Silas Grumble clutched his left arm. He gasped and his face turned a shade of burgundy. Tears spilled from his eyes. "Think... it's... my... heart!"

Jake was about to scurry from the room to fetch help, when Grumble released a belch like a clap of thunder. Jake winced as a smell of rotten pilchards and sour milk settled over the room.

"Oh my Lord!" He belched again, and grasped Jake's shoulder. "I thought it was my heart. Finished off by the sight of your wretchedness at this fragile time of day!"

Like you have a heart, Jake thought. Even believing himself on the verge of death, it seemed Silas Grumble's final words would be insults.

"Well," Grumble said. "That's put paid to my morning constitutional. I'll have to lie down now and let nature takes its course. You'll need to go out boy, and fetch my findings."

Silas's *findings* consisted of fresh vegetables, but unlike most inns and restaurants, Silas Grumble didn't shop for them at the market. Instead, he found them by the roadside, dropped by delivery carts bringing them to be weighed and sold at Covent Garden.

Each morning, Grumble would follow the carts like a hound, patiently waiting for their wheels to hit pot holes, or one of the many well placed obstructions he'd laid out in their path. Then, as quick as a magpie, he'd snatch them up within the folds of his grubby coat.

"Be quick, Shillingsworth. The carts will be rolling to the market by now. Or would you see me do the rounds, crippled and stricken as I am? Go. Leave this room of fungus and unspeakable odors. Fetch a sack and fill it with rich and varied findings. Quick, before you put an even bigger strain on my ailing heart!"

"Right, Mr. Grumble." This was his chance. As soon as he filled the sack, he'd find the nearest police officer and tell them everything that had happened the night before. For while Jake had little faith they'd listen to him, there was no one else to turn to.

CHAPTER ELEVEN

Crow Alley, which was more of a dingy street than an alleyway, was awash with people. Traders traded, people perambulated, and stall holders hawked. Jake weaved past a rotund pie seller barking invitations to taste his golden-brown pies. The pies looked and smelled delicious, but Jake knew their meat was of dubious origins so he left them well alone. The next stall was laden with moldy apples, oranges and pears, and their aroma grew pungent in the crisp December air.

Throwing Grumble's vegetable sack over his shoulder, Jake crossed the street to avoid Mr. Gabling's hot eel soup stall for its reek was so bad it could turn a pig's stomach.

A bookseller's cart stood at the end of the way and an elderly couple, dressed in finery rarely seen in Crow Alley, stood before it. They looked sickly and gaunt with dark smudges below their eyes. "These are far too expensive," the old lady pointed her gloved finger at a pile of grimoires.

"The price reflects the rarity of the book, madam, as well

as the chance to browse such contraband in safety," the bookseller replied, his voice laced with impatience.

It was true. Crow Alley was a place ignored by the eyes of the law, which made it perfect for shopping and trading in nefarious and magical items. The police had tried to restore order to the alley in the past, but they'd been chased from St. Giles by the worst of its denizens, and left bloodied and broken. Now it was a place they largely *forgot* to patrol.

Jake grinned as he spotted a mousy looking girl playing with a gaggle of kids on the street corner. He raised his fingers to the corners of his lips and gave a shrill whistle. The girl broke from the group and skipped towards him.

"What do you want Jake Shillingsworth?"

"Morning, Becky. How are you?"

"Fine and dandy until you interrupted me." She regarded Jake suspiciously.

"Well I suppose we can leave out the pleasantries, eh. Have you seen Fat Henry?"

"I might have. What of it?"

Jake produced a chipped coin from his pocket and smiled, knowing the half farthing would sway Becky. She reached for the coin, but Jake snatched it back. "Do you know where Fat Henry is?"

Becky's eyes remained fixed on the coin. "He said he was on his way to meet his boss at the Cheshire Cheese on Fleet Street."

"Thanks." Jake gave Becky the coin. He'd make his way to Fleet Street as soon as he filled the sack with whatever vegetables he could scavenge.

He hurried on, eager to finish his chore and find Fat Henry, who was his last option before resorting to visiting the police.

~

JAKE WEAVED through the growing tide of people shuffling across the icy pavements, and scoured the gutters. He'd already found plenty of turnips and potatoes, and while most were scuffed and encrusted with mud, or worse, they'd make Grumble happy. Jake was about to pluck a handful of carrots from the mire, when a nasally, high pitched voice cried out, "That's the way to do it!"

He glanced up at the bright red and yellow awning of London's most infamous Punch and Judy show. Infamous not for its humor and satire, but for how poorly the plays were produced. The puppeteer only ever showed one character at a time, thus Punch would appear with his string of sausages, duck down, and then his wooden dog would jump up. Next would be Judy, who would harangue an empty stage, before being replaced by the screaming baby.

The performance was legendarily bad and yet it always drew a crowd, usually composed of somber adults rather than children, and not one of them ever laughed.

Most of the time Jake ignored the show, but today something caught his eye; a flash of blue-white light in the alley, just behind the show's awning. The exact same light that had surrounded the flying craft. He was about to examine it further when heavy footsteps clomped behind him and a shrill shriek rang from the crowd.

CHAPTER TWELVE

J ake froze as four Police Constables and an Inspector burst through the crowd, scattering the audience. Blue light fizzled across the Inspector's goggles, matching the glow shining behind the Punch and Judy show's awning.

The Inspector ripped open the back of the tent and pulled out the puppeteer.

Or was it *puppeteers*?

It took Jake a moment to understand what he was seeing… a man with two heads. One face was pale, the other a livid shade of purple. One hand clutched a Punch puppet, the other tossed a wooden board to the ground that skidded across the icy cobbles and came to a rest before Jake. Letters and numbers covered the wood, as well as symbols of the sun and moon.

Jake recognized it at once.

It was a Ouija board.

He backed away as a Constable pulled a woman from the alleyway behind the red and yellow awning. Her black clothes stood out in stark contrast to the stall's garish colors and as Jake glanced at her mourning clothes, he began to understand.

She hadn't come for the Punch and Judy show, she'd come to make contact with the other side. The show was a sham. It explained why the puppets only appeared one by one; the puppeteer had been conducting a séance at the same time.

"Move along!" one of the Constables barked. "There's been a highly illegal use of magick in this vicinity meaning the area's infected. So clear it now or face a spell in prison."

Jake followed the dispersing crowd as a Constable gingerly scooped up the Ouija board. The blue-white light glowing upon its surface was fading, but it was definitely the same shade as the light he'd seen on the craft that had taken Nancy and Adam.

Fury blazed through Jake as he watched the police lead the mourning woman away. She'd come for help, not to cause harm, but they didn't care. They just followed their stupid laws, and that was that.

None of it boded well for what he had to tell them.

St. Paul's Cathedral's dome loomed pale and ghostly as Jake hurried down Fleet Street. He ducked into an alley, stopped outside the gloomy exterior of Ye Old Cheshire Cheese, and peered through the window.

Jake scoured the crowd until he spotted Fat Henry standing before the crackling fire lighting the dark tavern. His hands were a flurry of movement as he spoke to a well dressed man with skittish eyes, mostly likely the reporter Henry ran errands for. As if sensing Jake, Henry half turned and nodded to him. Then he said something to the man, and made his way through the pub.

Fat Henry was the opposite of his nickname. He was tall, thin and as frayed as a length of string. His gaunt, grubby features and hollow cheeks made him look half starved and in need of a hot meal, as well as a good bath. Henry appeared before Jake and doffed his cap. "Alright Jakey?"

"Sort of."

"Good good. So what can I do for you, me old chuckaboo?"

Jake swallowed. It often seemed with Fat Henry's job at the newspaper, that he knew everything there was to know in London. But that also meant he wasn't the best person to share secrets with. Still, what choice was there? "Something bad happened last night, Henry. Did you hear anything?"

"I've heard more interesting things this morning than I can shake a stick at, which means you're going to have to be a bit more specific. Spit out your ails and troubles, and be quick about it." Fat Henry patted Jake on the head and messed up his hair.

"Did you hear anything about... about a flying ship that looks like a giant fish?"

"There are lots of weird things flying around the city these days, but I haven't heard tale of anything like that. Although that's not to say I won't. I can ask around for you, if you like, but I'll need more information. Tell me everything that happened, Jake, and don't skip a single detail."

Reluctantly, Jake began his story.

"WELL THAT'S a tale and half, Jakey!" Fat Henry said as Jake finished. He fixed him with an appraising glare. "Are you selling me a dog?"

"No! Why would I? They took Nancy and Adam… I swear it!" Jake gazed up at his friend carefully. "Are you sure you don't know anything?"

"Nothing like you mentioned. But people have been muttering about hearing strange noises across the city for awhile now. They say it's like a great booming. Like a thunderstorm, but with no lightning."

"It's not thunder. It was the ship!"

"Right," Fat Henry nodded. "So just to be clear, you're telling me Nancy and Adam were kidnapped by a demon, and a man who flies with a pair of umbrellas. And they were taken aboard an airship that looks like a great big fish that hovered right over London. And no one, apart from you, saw any of it? I think Silas Grumble's been working you too hard, Jakey."

"I didn't make it up! It happened."

"Okay," Fat Henry said. "Me and you go way back, so I'll ask around and see what I can find out for you, okay?"

"Thanks, Henry. But… but please don't mention me in any of it. Alright?"

"Course not." Fat Henry slapped Jake on the back. "I'll keep you well out of it, don't worry. And I'll let you know as soon as I hear anything, alright?"

"Sure." Jake gathered up his sack of fallen vegetables and nodded to his old friend.

As he made his way back to The Tattered Crow, he passed a pair of Inspectors, and for a moment he was tempted to stop and tell them his story, but he didn't. For he was sure Fat Henry would discover far more than they ever could. "I'll do it my way," Jake muttered, "just like I always do."

~

THE REST of the day passed without incident and Silas Grumble was so pleased with the mud-soiled *findings* Jake had handed over, that he sent him off to bed just after midnight.

Jake lay on the boards and was right in the middle of a rare deep sleep, when the room began to shake and tremble. He glanced up as a low pitched whine came from outside and dust fell from the ceiling. Jake jumped up and peered through the window.

The view through the dusty glass was obscured by plumes of chimney smoke, but he still managed to spot the flash of blue-white light before a metallic form materialized in the night sky.

The brass fish was so close to Crow Alley that he could hear the hum of its workings, and the rumble of its wings made the very roof tremble.

Jake clambered out of his window and reached for the eaves sloping down over his room. He pulled himself up and scrambled onto the roof.

The craft's glass eyes seemed to gaze back as it turned slowly in the air, revealing the man framed in its window. The man who had shot him, and left him for dead. He was gazing down into the street, as if searching for something.

"Where's Nancy and Adam?" Jake yelled. "Let them go!"

If the man heard him, he showed no sign. He lifted a hand, as if signaling to someone, and the craft moved off, swimming through the smoke as it vanished into the gloom.

The people passing through the street below gazed dumbly into the night sky as HMS Watcher's great beam swept over the rooftops, scouring for the source of the disturbance. But the craft was gone.

CHAPTER THIRTEEN

J ake cleared the Inn's tables as he waited for word from Fat Henry. He used his growing frustration to savagely scrub at the ash, beer, drool and occasional spatter of blood encrusting the tables. His arms ached and his hope wore thin as he peered through the window for what felt like the hundredth time that morning.

Crow Alley was the same as ever. The traders traded their illicit goods, and the hawkers continued to hawk, as if nothing had changed. Like a giant craft hadn't hovered over the rooftops outside mere hours before.

There was no sign of Becky on the street corner. Jake wondered if she'd seen Fat Henry yet, and if he had any news. It felt like Nancy and Adam had been missing for weeks, rather than days.

"Enjoying watching the world go by, are you boy?" Silas Grumble stood at Jake's shoulder. "Perhaps you should put your feet up while you're at it."

"Sorry. I was just-"

"Dreaming of more ways to bring shame upon the head of your master, no doubt."

"What?"

"Don't what me, or I'll what you, and it will hurt." Silas Grumble grabbed Jake by the ear and kicked him up the backside, sending him sprawling to the floor. "That's it, take a seat."

Silas Grumble grabbed a newspaper from the bar, unfurled it, and shook it with such intensity Jake almost expected inky letters and words to tumble out. "Do you know what this is?"

"It's a newspaper. Unless I'm mistaken." Jake regretted his sarcasm as Silas's face turned the color of a putrid radish.

"Why did I expect anything other than witticism from the bard of St. Giles?" Grumble asked. "Clearly a civil answer would be far beyond your newfound standing in the world. Jake Shillingsworth... from pot collector to scribe. Such a heartwarming transformation!" Grumble prodded Jake in the chest. "You've certainly put the Crow on the map this time, boy."

"I'm not sure I follow, Mr. Grumble." But as Jake glanced at the newspaper, he thought of Fat Henry and a sick, queasy feeling spread through his stomach.

"Well let me h'enlighten you." Silas Grumble placed his ancient pince-nez glasses on his nose and began to read out loud. "The case of the sinister flying craft, and the missing children. An h'exclusive by Ernest Gumblegabe."

Jake slumped to the cold, dusty floor.

"An h'enthralling development occurred yesterday in the heartbreaking saga of London's missing. This astounding new information came straight from the lips of an h'anonymous source who contacted The Times with a highly bewildering tale.

According to our secret confidant, a most sinister plot is in play. One that concerns a flying man, a winged demon from the very pits of Hell, and a strange invisible craft that hovers over our fair city in the blackest depths of night.

In this h'exclusive report, our source revealed a bizarre tale told to him by one of his oldest friends; a poor, forlorn boy with mismatched eyes who dwells in the seedy labyrinthine streets of St. Giles. A wretch whose urchin friends were kidnapped by wicked devils in a most diabolical manner, just two nights ago. Our intrepid child pauper dashed across London's rooftops to desperately try and save his friends, only to witness them being bundled into a giant mysterious craft that resembled a great bronze fish!

The boy witness, who cannot be named, told how he was shot at point blank range by a man with a ghastly pale visage and terrible, empty eyes. Thankfully, by chance and good fortune, the valiant child escaped death, but was forced to watch wounded and helpless as the perpetrators flew away with his friends in a behemoth craft of brass and steam. A great swordfish that was said to have sliced through London's skies.

Could this craft be the source of the low rumbling sounds so many terrified Londoners have reported during these dark winter nights? Could it be linked to the mysterious case of the poor unfortunates, still unidentified, who fell upon the dome of St. Paul's Cathedral?

One thing is certain; something dark and diabolical is taking place in London, and people are going missing. The only question now is whether this new development is the work of malicious forces, or the ramblings of a young mind filled with fantasy and phantasmagoria." Silas Grumble slung the newspaper across the bar. "So now you fraternize with men of ink!"

"Men of ink?"

"Writers, tattlers, practitioners of print! Gossip hounds, nosy beasts, truth avoiders. Spreaders of muck and falsehood!" Grumble's face turned a dark shade of violet.

"I didn't tell no one nothing. I swear it, Mr. Grumble." *But I know who did.*

"This is h'exactly the same web of lies you spun the night you were out gallivanting! The night you were supposed to come straight back after delivering my message to Mrs. Wraythe. The very same night you claimed to have been shot in order to obscure your nocturnal dilly-dallying. Don't think I forgot. Don't take me for a fool!"

"I *was* shot. You saw it."

"That was a bee sting, not a bullet wound! But that's beside the point, do you realize what you've done, Shillingsworth? You've shared your ridiculous story for the whole city to read! Even now there's no doubt a procession of the curious, aimless and idle beating a path to St. Giles. Seeking the teller of this tallest of tales. *A poor wretched boy with mismatched eyes.*"

"But-"

"Tell me, how many other whelks do you see gadding about the streets of St. Giles with unseemly, queer colored eyes?" Grumble slammed his hand on the bar. "So cleaning tables isn't enough for you? You're forsaking the Crow for the literary world now, are you?"

"I didn't ask them to print that story," Jake protested. "I-"

"Picture a great filthy anchor covered with barnacles, seaweed and vile crustaceans. Imagine it chained around your throat, because that's what I'd strap to you if I could! And then I'd cast you off into the middle of the good ship Crow, tethered to your duties forevermore," Grumble snarled. "But sadly I have no such anchor. Yet it will feel like I do, Shillingsworth. Mark my words."

Jake nodded. He knew better than to argue. The more bizarre Grumble's threats became, the hotter the coals of his temper burned.

"You'll remain within these walls for the foreseeable future, boy. There'll be no more deliveries, no messages or missives. No taking to the great outdoors. You'll remain here, where I can keep my eyes on you. And if any seekers of tattle or gossip enter the Crow, I'll repel them back outside into the muck and mire. This Inn is a refuge for those who wish to evade chatterboxes, police and other such uncouths. A sanctuary from the law, not a place for you to air your fetid laundry." Silas Grumble dropped his voice. "Do you think the regulars will thank you for blabbing, and running to the newspapers? Or perhaps you want to end your days floating in the Thames with your throat cut?"

Jake shook his head.

"Not that it would bother me if you were found face down in a puddle with your bloody particulars strewn amongst the horse leavings. And do you know why it wouldn't bother me, boy?"

Jake nodded. He'd been told often enough. "Because you can replace me quicker than a flash of lightning."

"Yes! I can. Were I to throw crumbs outside the window this instance, I'd chance upon a gaggle of whelks only too h'eager to work at the Crow and find a roof over their bony little heads."

"I know, Mr. Grumble. I'm very lucky."

"Indeed. And the only reason I don't cast you out to a life of pox and famine, is on h'account of my spirituality. The lord sent you to me, Jake Shillingsworth, as a trial and tribulation. And I shall pass his test, just you wait and see! And when I'm at the pearly gates there'll be a fanfare of the type not heard since the saints themselves ascended. Do you understand?"

"Of course, sir." Jake chanced a quick look at his master. Thankfully Grumble's face had turned from violet to its usual shade of porridge gray.

"Get away from my sight Shillingsworth. Go to the kitchen at once! There's a sack of vegetables to wash and peel, though the lord only knows why I bother! It's not as if the ne'er do wells around here h'appreciate the gourmet foods this fine establishment has to offer. Now get to work you vicious little pustule!"

"Yes, Mr. Grumble." Jake scurried away as fast as his aching feet would take him.

CHAPTER FOURTEEN

M r. Spires sipped tea from a china cup as he gazed through the window. The rising sun painted the clouds below in a sea of swirling salmon pinks, and bloody reds. It was a vision worthy of a canvas, had any of the painters been left alive.

The raven squawked from its perch upon the bookcase and still hobbled from where it had been caught in the netting.

Mr. Spires set down the cup, stood and stroked the bird's head. It regarded him with beady black eyes as he smoothed its ruffled green-black feathers. They scrutinized each other for a moment until the raven looked away.

The knock on the door was both firm and cautious. It was a knock that knew it was intrusive, and yet needed to be answered. "Enter, Kedgewick."

Kedgewick carried a folded newspaper below his great brass arm. His eyes gleamed in the morning light below his tangled, black and silver mane of hair. Mr. Spires gazed through the porthole in Kedgewick's chest to the maze of clockwork within and noted the gears were slowing. They'd need winding. "What is it, Kedgewick?"

"I brought the deliveries from the warehouse." Kedgewick said, in his lilting Irish voice. "And a newspaper." He unfurled the paper and traced its headline with his brass finger. "You'll want to read this."

Mr. Spires eyes swept over the newspaper, devouring the words and implications. His mind whirled with the information. There were many choices, but only one outcome would suffice.

"I believe it was the boy from the rooftop that spoke to the papers," Kedgewick said.

"I left him for dead."

"I know."

"I'm not sure I like the accusation in your voice."

Kedgewick lowered his eyes. "I... I don't like seeing children harmed."

Mr. Spires laughed. "We're all children, Kedgewick. But some of us are a little older than others. Do you think I derive pleasure from causing harm? No, I do not. But learning is all we have in this life. And to truly learn, we must take things apart and examine their every facet. It's the same with the city. We have to turn it to rubble so it can be rebuilt with a better new founding vision. A freer place for all."

"Indeed," Kedgewick nodded dutifully.

"And as of last night, we're well on course with those plans. We almost have enough capable, pliable minds to allow us to start afresh with our new city. Are the arms ready?"

"The weapons were delivered this very morning. They're on the docks, waiting to be despatched."

"Good, good. So for now we have but a single fly in the ointment; this boy who should have died. I need him to stop telling tales. Indeed I need him to stop speaking altogether. Our foes cannot be alerted to our presence until the final hour has arrived." Mr. Spires's eyes narrowed as he stared at Kedgewick. "Where's Mortaphir?"

"In the city awaiting nightfall."

"Fetch him."

"It's daylight, and HMS Watcher is patrolling. It's not a good time for-"

"Don't whine, Kedgewick. Whining is for the living, not for you." Mr. Spires felt his pulse twitch as slow anger simmered in his veins. He glanced at Kedgewick's hands and saw how his fingers were curled into fists.

"I cannot deny that you're still a behemoth of a man," Mr. Spires said. "One of London's greatest fighters. Kedgewick; snapper of necks, gouger of eyes, and shatterer of limbs. Snuffing opponents like candlewicks. Or at least you did while you lived. But here you are now, standing in thrall to me. I imagine that causes you great anguish."

"No, sir, I'm here to serve you. As we agreed." Kedgewick's fingers unfurled.

"Yes, we did agree. So if you want me to continue turning the clockwork that keeps you in the land of the living, you'll go and find Mortaphir this instant. Bring here him, and together we will decide the best course of action for our new predicament." Mr. Spires smoothed over the newspaper. "For as minuscule as the boy is, he's managed to capture the whole of London's attention, and that simply will not do."

CHAPTER FIFTEEN

The very moment Jake scrubbed the last of the muck from the vegetables, Grumble summoned him to work in the bar. The Inn was already busy with patrons, many of whom cast withering glares at Jake as he gathered up the empty tankards. Some even held up their newspapers with contempt, just in case he needed a reminder.

Each time the creaky, warped door swung open Jake would flinch, half expecting to see the man in his brass suit or the demon standing there. Or worse, the man in the top hat with the blank face, and wicked cruel eyes.

Jake threw himself into his work, scrubbing, cleaning and fetching, trying anything to put the terror swirling through his mind to rest. He couldn't believe he'd trusted Fat Henry, for he was known for having morals looser than a prizefighter's teeth. But who else could he have turned to? Silas Grumble had mocked him, and the police weren't there to help people like Jake, Nancy and Adam.

A sick, bleak feeling enveloped him as he wondered what

had befallen his friends. He glanced up as the door swept open, jolting him from his thoughts.

A crisp breeze blew a handful of curled, dead leaves in, as Mr. Whitlock entered The Tattered Crow. He was a small, powerfully built man with long grey hair and a full tangled beard. He'd been a regular who had been frequenting the Crow long before Silas Grumble had owned it. Yet still, after all this time, no one knew what Mr. Whitlock did for a living, or even where he lived. He was cordial and utterly inscrutable but it only took a single flash from his dark eyes to send the largest thugs cowering. Now those dark eyes rested on Jake as he sat at a table by the fire. "Come here, lad."

"Do you want a pint of your usual, Mr. Whitlock?"

"Yes, in a moment, and bring a cup of brandy too. Its been a wearying day." Mr. Whitlock gave Jake a slow, appraising look. "I read about your adventures in the paper this morning."

"I never said any of it. At least not the way they-"

Mr. Whitlock raised his hand. "I believe you. You're a good lad and you know very well that whatever's discussed within these walls stays within these walls. And anyone I've met today who's said otherwise has been... corrected. You'll get no trouble, at least not from people in these parts. But there's been an outsider asking after you."

The hairs on the nape of Jake's neck prickled. "Who?"

"A vicious little weasel from the East End, goes by the name of Arlington. Do you know him?"

"No. I've never heard of him, Mr. Whitlock." Jake's eyes flitted to the window as the lamplighter's staff clinked against the glass and the gaslight cast shadows in the darkening alley across the way.

"Said he was offering a fair price if I could help him find a lad 'round here with mismatched eyes. So I took Arlington for a walk, to a nice quiet spot by the Thames. Asked him what business he had with such a lad. It took a little persuasion, but he coughed up in the end and said he'd been paid a small fortune to find the boy from the newspaper."

"Who... who paid him?" Jake's throat felt tight and dry as he tried to swallow.

"He wouldn't say." Mr. Whitlock lowered his voice. "So I made firmer inquiries, but he still wouldn't budge, no matter how hard I pressed him. Said he'd take a knife to the heart before spilling his secrets, that anything was better than *facing that devil.*"

"Devil?"

"Aye, devil. That's what he said. I've seen fear in the hearts of men plenty of times before, Jake. But not like that. This was stone cold terror. Anyhow, I told him to stay out of St. Giles, and he agreed, in amongst spitting out great swallows of the Thames. He won't be a problem now but there'll be others. I'm certain of it. Someone means to find you, and if they inspire greater fear than I do in a creature like Arlington, then God help you, boy."

EVENING DREW IN, but Jake was so busy, he barely noticed. The Inn was crammed with customers. More than a few made rude, mocking remarks to him, as they ordered tankards of rancid smelling beer. Silas Grumble did little to help. Instead, he held court with his regulars, the king of his squalid little castle.

"Quick," the cook yelled, as she held out two steaming bowls of leek and potato soup in her doughy hands.

"Grumble's insisting that the customers have been waiting for their food since before time began." She gave Jake a knowing look as she handed him the food.

Jake's mouth watered at the delicious scent of soup and the chunks of warm bread resting on the rims of the bowls.

"Who are these for?"

"Two gentlemen in the passage."

Jake's heart sank. *The passage* was a dark, narrow section at the back of the Inn. No matter the hour it was filled with gloom, even on the brightest summer's day, and only the more dangerous of the Crow's clientele ever ventured back there. Thieves, highwaymen, murderers and mercenaries. London's damned, stooped over their pints with grim, roving eyes.

Tonight, the passage felt chillier than ever. And quieter too, with most of the cutthroats seeking solace around the fire.

Two men were huddled in conversation at the end of the passage and as Jake approached, they cast wary glances at a frail old man sitting a few tables away. The old man was hunched over his glass of sherry, his face a mess of deep lines illuminated by the soft candlelight before him. He gazed into the shadows, as if searching for something he'd forgotten.

Jake shook his head. The man's neatly cut tweed suit was completely out of place in The Tattered Crow. Who was he, and how had he missed him when he'd come into the Inn? More troubling was the question of why the man had chosen The Tattered Crow in the first place, and how he'd survived the mean, narrow streets of St. Giles in order to get there.

Jake set the soup on the table before the two men and walked away. As he passed the old man, he thought of offering him a seat closer to the fire. Jake was about to speak, when the old man regarded him and his lips curled into a strangely unpleasant grin.

An icy shiver ran through Jake, as a curious thought came to him. That nestling behind the old man's insincere smile were teeth as long and curved as a wolf's. Jake hurried on, until a thin rasping voice called out, "Excuse me, young man."

"Sorry?" Jake forced himself to turn back. "Can I help you?"

The old man's papery hair was gathered into a ponytail that glistened in the candlelight and his hooked nose twitched like a dog sniffing for scraps of food, while his eyes...

Were too large.

And too black.

Where were the whites? A glint danced deep in their dark centers, a spark that did not belong to the candlelight.

"Is-" Jake froze as the man's thin lips slid down to his chin, then slithered back up into place.

Surely a trick of the light?

"Come closer."

"Would you like a bowl of soup? Or perhaps another glass of-"

"I said come closer." The man's voice slipped from a weak, hoarse whisper, to something deeper. Something feral. He cupped a hand to his mouth as if trying to contain the *other* voice, but Jake had heard it.

The man cast a glance to the men at the table behind him. Neither paid Jake or the old man attention as they ate their soup and continued their hushed conversation.

Jake tried to walk away, to return to the warm light of the Inn, but it seemed so distant now. And somehow, with every step he took he found himself moving closer to the old man. As if his aching feet had been bewitched by the will of someone else entirely.

He tried to look away from those deep, black eyes, but couldn't. The darkness spilling from them threatened to engulf the entire world.

"Please." The gloom swallowed Jake's words and The Tattered Crow flickered from view.

It was just the two of them; Jake and the old man stranded in a pocket of night, the candle flame the last light in the world.

"What?" Jake watched in shock as the old man's face transformed. His thick white eyebrows slid up to his forehead and became lost in the thicket of his hair. His thin lips and long hooked nose slipped down his chin and vanished within the folds of his shirt as the black pools of his eyes grew larger and blazed with fire.

Horror engulfed Jake as the darkness around him thickened.

The demon had found him.

CHAPTER SIXTEEN

J ake's feet felt like they were glued to the cold
flagstone floor.

A cry cut through the darkness, and it took him a
moment to realize it was his own.

Time ran still and Jake's thoughts turned as thick as tar
until finally, he broke the demon's gaze.

He glanced into the gloom billowing around them like a
curtain. The Inn was gone.

"You're in my domain, Jake Shillingsworth. Now you will
play by my rules."

Jake screwed his eyes shut, but a touch, like the lightest of
fingers, tugged at his eyelids. Slowly, it prised them open.

"Look at me, and this will end," the demon said.

Jake's eyes darted wildly, gazing anywhere but into the
demon's eyes.

Was the darkness surrounding him lightening? Just a
fraction? Was the demon losing his grip?

"Look at me!"

Jake used the last of his willpower to keep his eyes away

from the black holes tugging at his gaze. The ghostly forms of the two men from the Inn drifted back into view, distant and hazy, as if obscured through a veil of thick smoky black glass. They sat like two spirits huddled in conversation, oblivious to the nightmarish world rolling around them. Jake watched as one of the men slurped soup and lifted the salt cellar, sprinkling it over his bowl. The other took a long, slow draught of his pint.

"Help!" Jake's voice echoed, as if he were trapped inside some long abandoned well. The Tattered Crow faded and the flickering candle became the last light in the haunted nightscape.

The demon stared, but Jake still refused to meet his eyes. He tried calling to the men, but this time his cry faded into the velvet black surrounds.

"Don't waste your energy," the demon said. "You won't be heard, not from here."

"Where are we?" *Had they crossed into some terrible underworld?*

"A place between your city and the realm I was summoned from. A limbo, a refuge from the stench of your tired old world. This is where I bring dying things. Can you feel them watching from the shadows?"

Jake shuddered.

"Look at me, and it will be over. Your heart will stop, your breath will fade, and your worries will cease. There's no price for crossing over, boy. I've already paid your toll."

Jake's eyes shifted slowly, as the demon's will tugged at his gaze.

"It won't hurt," the demon promised. "Indeed, this will soon feel like the only place you ever really belonged. Just let go and be at rest."

"Why are you doing this?"

"It's the master's orders. He doesn't like to be seen."

"I won't tell anyone about your master. I didn't even really see him, I-"

"But you did, Jake. And you spoke about it." The demon rapped his nails against the table. "Of course, I could just take your eyes and that one fleeting memory of my master. That would satisfy him, but it has been many moons since I've fed." The demon's lips crawled back up to his face. Now they were different; wide and thin and stained inky black. The demon licked them with a long roiling tongue. Then he reached up and ripped the paper white pony-tail away, and with a swift wet tearing sound, the old man's features slid from his head.

"You can see my true face now. Look at me."

Jake flinched as a clawed hand grasped his palm.

The demon drew his mouth open so wide it would surely split his head in two. "Look at me!" His voice echoed around them in the cavernous darkness.

Jake jerked his hand away.

The Tattered Crow reappeared in a sooty haze, as if the demon's transformation had weakened his powers.

Fangs flashed in the darkness and a blast of noxious air broke from his mouth. "Look at me!"

Jake refused. Instead, he focused on the distant smudges of the two men sitting at their table eating. If they'd be the last thing he'd ever see, then so be it. Better them than the monster before him.

A sharp slow clatter rang out, and it sounded as if it were a thousand miles away. Jake watched the man's back arch as he reached for the salt cellar and knocked it over. Its contents scattered across the table. The man swore, his voice low, thick and muffled as if coming through a vat of treacle.

The demon reached out, his claws slowly arcing towards Jake's throat. Tears blurred Jake's eyes, but he refused to let them fall.

A claw tickled his throat and time slowed further, as if forcing Jake to live through this horror over and over again.

Dimly, he watched as the man gathered the salt from the table and slowly raised his hand, before flinging it over his left shoulder.

Each tiny salt crystal glimmered like a star in the darkness.

The demon's talon punctured Jake's skin. He closed his eyes, and waited for the end.

Then, a guttural scream broke through the air.

A scream that wasn't his own.

The demon writhed before Jake, his face contorted with agony as he clawed at the salt crystals gleaming on his scaly arms.

The Inn rematerialized around them.

"The spell's broken." Jake's words were his own once more. "The salt..." Jake grabbed the shaker from the table and held it up.

"No." The demon hissed as he writhed and howled. The men behind jumped up and moved away. "Please!" the demon begged.

"Please?" Jake laughed. "Please? You want me to pity you? You were about to tear my throat out. To hell with you." Jake poured the salt into his hand as the creature scattered chairs in his bid to stumble away.

"This is for Nancy." Jake flung the salt at the demon's face."And this…" Jake poured the last of the salt into his hand. "Is for Adam." He let the salt fly.

Blisters broke upon the demon's skin as he clawed at his

face. He shoved the table, knocking Jake to the ground as he ran past.

Jake grabbed another salt shaker and chased the demon through the Inn, racing past a blur of befuddled faces. Steam enveloped the creature's head and a stench of putrid meat wafted across the Inn as the demon wrenched the door open and stumbled into the night.

Jake slipped out the door as Silas Grumble growled behind him.

A terrible, agonized shriek echoed across Crow Alley.

The demon stood in the middle of the empty road. He hissed and bared his teeth, pulling at the remains of his tattered clothes and sloughing off the last of his disguise.

Jake slowed as he approached the creature and its narrow, hate-filled eyes found his. The demon spat curses, unfurled his wings and flew up, the *whoomph* of his leathery wings like a starched sheet being beaten by the wind.

"What the bloody hell's going on?" Silas Grumble's voice quivered as he seized Jake by the neck.

"Look," Jake pointed up, "The demon-"

But it was gone.

"Demon, my eye!" Silas Grumble roared. "Let me tell you what I saw. A patron running in agony. Staggering from my Inn as if Old Nick himself were at his heels! What did you do to him?"

"That wasn't a patron. It wasn't a man!"

"Granted he was disfigured," Grumble conceded. "But were I to bar the ugly and unseemly from the Crow I'd be a pauper. Now, enough rot about demons. There's no such things!"

"Look at my throat," Jake pulled his shirt back from his neck. "He cut me."

"Pah! You've been scratched by a cat, or a bird. Or a rat. Or all three for all I care. I've had enough of your tall tales. First it's a bullet wound for a bee sting and now its demons. What next? Are you going to tell me the Crow is infested by supernatural weevils? A pox upon your preposterous stories!"

"But-"

"But nothing. I'm not going to take this nonsense and shirking of duties lightly, Shillingsworth. No I will not. There will be no meals or sustenance for you tonight. And don't even think about touching the mushrooms growing on your walls, because I've counted every last one! And one more thing…don't ever use the word demon in my h'establishment again!"

"We're not in your establishment. We're in the street. And it was a demon!" Jake's face burned with fury.

Silas Grumble grabbed him and pulled him close. "I told you boy, there's no demons in London! And we'll never talk of such things again. Now get back inside and get on with your work before I do you some proper mischief!"

CHAPTER SEVENTEEN

J ake shivered and pulled the tatty old blanket up to his chin as an icy draft swept through his room. The salt cellar resting on the floor beside him brought back the previous night's events and the dark dreams that had followed them. Nightmares of fiery red eyes, glistening claws, leathery black wings and a cloud of gloom that had extinguished every last light in the world.

He had no idea how he'd survived the night. He'd kept watch as long as he could, certain the demon would appear at his broken window to finish his task. But he hadn't. And now it was dawn and the common lore said demons despised sunlight, or so he'd been told.

"I've got to get out of here." The thought of leaving the Inn for good was terrifying, for as much as Jake hated the scant musty room, it was home and it was safe. Or at least it had been, until the demon had found him. "I'll find somewhere better," Jake whispered unconvinced. "Once I've found Nancy and Adam." He grabbed his clothes from the corner and dressed, before prying up a loose floorboard.

The meager possessions he'd salvaged from the mudflats were just where he'd left them. It was a sad collection: a tin soldier with a missing arm, a clutch of green rusted coins, and the pennies Bellows had given him over the years. Nothing much. Certainly not enough to feed himself for more than a week or two. No, if he was going to strike out on his own, he'd need proper funds and the so-called wages Silas Grumble had been 'saving' for when he was older. Like he was ever going to hand the money over willingly...

Jake was about to replace the floorboard, when something glinting in the early morning light caught his eye. He reached in and lifted out the Professor's calling card, still bent and warped from the bullet. Beside it was the tool and springs that had been affixed to his shoes.

"Professor Thistlequick," Jake murmured. It seemed like an age since the fair, and as he recalled that night he remembered the Professor's offer to help Jake, should he ever need it.

"Maybe..." No. The man was clearly as mad as a hatter, and what use would a toff like him be against demons? Still, the man knew about machines, so he might know something about flying crafts. As well as how they might turn invisible to everyone's eyes but Jake's.

Jake slipped the card into his pocket. It had brought him luck once, perhaps it would again.

The corridor outside was mercifully empty. Muffled voices came from the bar below and a smell of frying food wafted through the cracks in the floor. It was breakfast time.

Soon, Silas Grumble would be sitting down in front of a hot plate stuffed with bacon, eggs, and mushrooms sliding in a sheen of grease. Holding court with whichever addled subjects had spent the night at the Inn. He'd be occupied, which meant now was the perfect time for Jake to take back what was rightfully his.

Jake tiptoed along the long hallway to Silas Grumble's room.

He'd only ventured inside once before, when Grumble had been laid up with a 'malady of the innards'; a reeking sickness whose stench had filled the entire room.

Jake recalled how Silas had reacted when he'd brought him a jug of water. How his wretched eyes had traveled around the room, as if checking everything was where it should be. Jake was fairly sure he'd been glancing at his hiding places; the secret areas where the old miser stashed his money and precious things.

The door handle turned. It was unlocked! "Careless, Mr. Grumble," Jake whispered. "Very careless h'indeed!"

The room was as warm as an August morning. Flames crackled and spat in a fireplace and the walls, Jake noted, were perfectly free of pockmarks, damp, and mushrooms, while the carpet was free of rain spots. Fancy red drapes covered the windows and a four-poster bed took up most of the floor.

"It's alright for some, isn't it," Jake spat. For a moment, he considered climbing upon the bed and jumping up and down for the sheer hell of it. But instead, he checked the first place Silas Grumble's oversized eyes had strayed that day. The bedpost closest to the window.

Jake knocked on the carved wooden support. Sure enough it was hollow. He unscrewed the finial to find a rancid sock inside. Inside were enough coins for Jake to live off for months, maybe even years. "Thanks for saving my wages for me, Mr. Grumble." Jake was about to stuff the sock into his pocket when a thump came from the staircase at the end of the hall.

Jake shoved the sock back into the hollow. He could barely screw the bedpost back in place for his shaking fingers.

A loud creak came from the stairs. Grumble would be in the corridor within moments. Jake's heart beat hard as he closed the door, ran down the hall and ducked into his room.

Seconds later, a thunderous pounding rattled his door.

"Are you up, you unsightly muck-snipe?"

"Almost," Jake called.

The door lurched and Grumble entered the room. "Almost, my eye. You're up and lurking and no doubt plotting."

"Plotting?" Jake felt his cheeks redden.

"Plotting to rob me."

"Rob you?" Jake's voice trembled.

"Of time. I don't pay you to idle, Jake Shillingsworth. No, today's going to be a proper day of toil for you. No half measures. And-" Silas Grumble belched, filling the room with a sulfurous stench of eggs. "My digestion's giving me the devil of a time this morning. I need to lie down, which means you're going to have to do some real work for a change."

"Right." Jake's spirits sank. If Silas Grumble lounged in his room all day, there would be no chance of getting to the sock.

"Yes. I want the place spick and span. Sleaford and his mob were in last night, so you can imagine the state the place is in. I've seen cleaner slaughterhouses. Anyway, I want it sorted before noon."

"Why Mr. Grumble? Are there h'important people visiting The Crow today?"

Silas Grumble stared intently at Jake. "Are you mocking me, boy?"

"I'd never mock you, sir. Never."

"And you better not, you ferocious little pimple!" Grumble pinched Jake's ear, before exaggeratedly snatching his hand back. "Forgive me! I forgot I was addressing the Bard of St. Giles! Jake Shillingsworth, bearer of bullets and slayer of demons." Grumble laughed at his own malicious humor, before a slow spiteful grin slipped across his lips. "H'actually, if you must know, I need to have The Crow ship-shape by noon because you're going to be out all afternoon."

"Really?"

"Really. For even though I'd sooner keep you where I can see you, I have an urgent errand that needs taking. One that's just for you."

"Where?"

"Highgate."

"Right you are." Jake felt a swell of relief. If he was fast enough there might be enough time to get to Primrose Hill and visit the Professor.

"I wouldn't sound so pleased. It's freezing out and the roads are thick with ice, so you'll have to leave early. But you're not to deliver the message until five thirty. Five thirty on the dot."

"Understood. Is it for anyone I know?"

"Why, yes it is, now you come to ask." Silas Grumble gave Jake a bilious smile. "It's for your dear old friend, Mrs. Wraythe."

CHAPTER EIGHTEEN

By the time he finished scrubbing the pans, Jake's fingers were red raw, and he ached all over, even in his bones. But at least Silas Grumble had remained in his room all morning.

He pulled the Professor's battered metallic card from his pocket again and wondered, not for the first time, if the Professor really had been sincere in his offer of help. Or had it just been a figure of speech?

A bell rang, jarring Jake from his thoughts. The cook glanced up from the stove and nodded to Jake. "You better take yourself up to the master's room and see what he wants."

Jake's spirits dampened as he climbed the rickety steps.

Silas Grumble's room reeked of vinegar and sulphur, and things Jake tried not to think about. Grumble lay spread-eagled across his bed, his face the color of turned milk. "Is the bar spick and span?" he demanded, as he wiped his forehead with an ancient-looking rag.

"I can see my face in the tables, they're that clean."

Grumble sat up with a grimace. "You may think I miss

your vicious little witticisms boy, but each and every one is duly noted. And when, or if I ever manage to stand again, I'll fetch my stick and thrash the lot of them out of you."

"I merely sought to entertain you Mr. Grumble. To lift the burden of your malady." Jake chanced a quick look at the hollow bedpost. "Do you think you'll be up and about presently?"

Silas Grumble stared at Jake with rapt concentration, before letting forth a monstrous belch. "Enough questions, Shillingsworth. Don't think I don't know what you're doing."

Jake swallowed. Had Silas seen him looking at the bedpost? "I'm not sure I catch your meaning, master."

Silas stabbed the air with his finger. "You're stalling so you can soak up all the heat in my room to roast your greedy little bones. Now, take that envelope from my desk and be on your way. Get to Mrs. Wraythe's house on Tyburn Street. It's the last house on the right, the one with the yew tree in the garden. Five thirty sharp, no sooner, no later. Mrs. Wraythe was most exact about that detail, and you'll observe her requirements. Now, enough dithering and heat thieving. Be on your way!"

Jake picked up the envelope. A scarlet wax seal, like a drop of blood, marked the back, and the front was covered in a black spidery script. Jake didn't need to read it to know whose handwriting it was. "I'm confused, mister Grumble…"

"This isn't news to me, Shillingsworth. A pigeon could confuse you, you buffoon."

"Yes, but… this is Mrs. Wraythe's handwriting. So why has she sent a message to herself? And why-"

"Take that letter and be on your way. And not another utterance!" Silas Grumble shrieked, before collapsing back onto his bed.

Jake scuttled from the room, closing the door on the stench and curses within. He descended the stairs fast, the envelope weighing heavily in his hand.

∽

A CRISP BLUE sky greeted Jake as he emerged from the shadows of The Tattered Crow. He pulled his scarf tight against the wind biting through his thin, ragged coat. The ground gleamed with thick layers of ice and sunlight played across frozen puddles. Jake slipped on the ice almost immediately. Releasing a puff of white air he grabbed onto a lamppost, wincing as the cold metal stung his fingers.

The conditions demanded a gingerly pace so it took what seemed like forever to reach Charing Cross Road, which was noisy and crowded. People slipped and slid past him as they did their best to maintain their composure against the elements.

"Riots at the docks!" a gangly girl cried as she thrust out a fan of newspapers. "Riots at the docks!"

Jake stood at the edge of the road. The traffic passed by in a trundling river of horses, carriages, and hansom cabs. Drivers gazed from the folds of their great coats and blankets, searching for prospects. A four-wheeled brougham rolled towards Jake, the driver in deep conversation with the spotty footman sitting by his side. Neither noticed Jake as he ran behind them, leaped up to the back of the carriage, and clung on for dear life.

"Oi!" the ruddy faced man steering the hansom cab behind them shouted, but the driver of the brougham didn't hear. Jake grinned and waved to the snitch as they turned off the thoroughfare. The brougham headed north, exactly where he needed to go.

Jake held on tight even though his fingers ached with cold.

When they reached Camden Town, he leaped down and stumbled onto the pavement. He thrust his hands into his pockets to warm them, his mood darkening as they brushed the envelope. Highgate.

Jake had been there once. He recalled huge white intimidating buildings and a great cemetery filled with ivy-choked graves. It hadn't been a place he'd ever wanted to return to.

He shivered as he thought of Mrs. Wraythe's yellowy black teeth and the way her long nails bit into his shoulders as she examined him with those piercing green eyes.

Perhaps he could just drop the envelope through her door, and be done with it.

Except Silas Grumble had been most specific in his instructions.

Jake checked his pocket watch. There were still a couple of hours left before he had to make his delivery to Highgate. He half ran, half slid through Camden Town and headed for Primrose Hill.

The hill was empty now, the fairground long gone. A few charred fireworks littered the pathways and a clutch of rubber balloons hung from the bare branches of an old oak tree. Jake paused as an old couple doddered towards him. The lady was swaddled in furs, and her companion wore an expensive looking coat with a top hat crowning his dour face.

"Excuse me, Sir. Madam."

The old man's fingers tightened on his walking cane. "What is it?" he demanded.

"I'm looking for someone who lives around here." Jake held

out the Professor's battered card. "I believe he said he lives in Brightstar Terrace?"

The old man gave Jake a look of disgust and stepped away. "And what business do you have at Brightstar Terrace? "

"I'm delivering a message. To Professor Thistlequick."

Their faces fell even further. "Him," the old lady said. "Of course. Who else would bring the likes of you into our neighborhood?"

Jake ignored his anger and forced a smile. "I take it you don't get on with the Professor?"

"He's a dreadful man," the lady muttered.

"Indeed! Wanders around with a cat balanced on his hat, if you please." The old man's bones cracked as he clenched his cane ever tighter.

"And then there's the clamor and commotion. And explosions!" the old lady added. "At all hours. One of these days he'll destroy us all with his ridiculous experiments, you mark my words!"

"Yes. And what kind of man invents long-johns for horses, pray tell?" the man asked.

"He sounds proper barmy," Jake said. "But I might have good news for you," He pulled back his coat, revealing the envelope in his pocket. "This here letter comes from a law firm that specializes in evicting poor unfortunates who are behind on their rent."

"Really?" The elderly man almost smiled. "Perhaps Christmas has come early this year." He clasped Jake's shoulder and pointed along the street. "Brightstar Terrace is the third on the left. Thistlequick's house is halfway down. Number thirty-three. Now stop loitering, and be on your way".

Jake bit back his response and hurried off.

Brightstar Terrace was a short road lined with cottages. The gardens were neat, orderly and filled with foliage and exotic looking herbs. Jake pinched a sprig of rosemary and took a deep sniff, savoring the aroma. He glanced down as something brushed against his leg.

It was a cat, and it might have been the one he'd seen in the Professor's tent on Primrose Hill before, only now it was wearing a pair of small round spectacles. "Hello!" Jake called.

It was a dainty little thing with chocolate brown fur spotted with random marmalade-orange smudges. Bright green eyes flashed behind the spectacle lenses as Jake stooped to pet it, but before he could reach it, the cat arched its back and scuttled off into a garden. "Good afternoon to you too!" he called, as the creature vanished under a hedge.

The cottage the cat had emerged from was covered in ivy and a single window on the ground floor had been left ajar. A crashing din of clanking metal came from inside.

"This has got to be the place, surely." Jake unlatched the iron gate and stepped across the short graveled path. He grasped the door knocker and was about to knock, when a hideous, blood-curdling scream came from within.

CHAPTER NINETEEN

The scream stopped just as abruptly as it had started. Jake glanced around Brightstar Terrace. Apart from the odd twitching curtain, it was deserted. He checked the rooftops, half expecting to see the demon, but they were as empty as the street below. He took a deep breath and tried to calm his rattled nerves.

The scream came again, from the window just above him.

It sounded like someone was being murdered.

Jake's mind whirred. The closest police station was all the way back in Camden Town. By the time he got there, whoever was inside would surely be dead. He glanced at the open window, and considered climbing through.

The shriek stopped, leaving Jake in a silence almost as frightening as the screams.

As he leaned down to peek through the letterbox, the door jerked opened. A pasty white face appeared through the crack and a pair of wide brown eyes watched him intently.

"Hello?" Jake said.

The door opened a tad wider and a lady appeared. Thick

white makeup coated her face and her cheeks were spotted with two bright red circles. Long, fake black eyelashes curled from her eyes like dead spider's legs as she blinked at Jake. He gazed, entranced by the lofty tower of blue-black hair teetering atop her head, emphasizing her ghostlike complexion.

"Hello?" she whispered. "Hello?"

"Are you okay?"

The lady blinked rapidly. "I am now. No thanks to *him*. This is the second time this week I've encountered that ghastly device. They say the third's a charm, but it could well lead to my death. My heart just can't take it anymore."

"I'm sorry to hear that, Mrs..."

"Harker. Now, please rest assured, there won't be another uproar from these quarters today." A thin smile turned her berry-red lips. "I've caught it, you see, so he can't wind the beastly thing up again. Its days of prowling are finally at an end, and peace shall prevail. Now, good day."

The door slammed shut. Jake stared at it for a moment, before knocking.

Mrs. Harker opened the door, her eyes wide and quizzical.

"I'm looking for Professor Thistlequick. Does he live here?"

Horror passed like a cloud across Mrs. Harker's doughy face. "Professor Thistlequick resides with me, but we are in no way, shape or form *together*. He's a lodger. His rooms are situated on the ground floor whilst I live, quite separately, upstairs."

"Right you are," Jake said, bemused by the strange flood of information.

Mrs. Harker glanced up and down the street, before continuing. "Although I'll confess the Professor and I meet in the kitchen to dine, on occasion. He's most particular to a Sunday roast, you see. And I quite enjoy the custom myself. Besides, if I don't cook, he forgets to eat and he needs meat on his bones. But other than occasional meals, we live entirely separate lives."

"So you said. Look, would it be possible for me to speak with the Professor? I'm in a hurry."

Mrs. Harker seized Jake's wrists in her chubby fingers and led him into the house. "You must forgive my prattle. My wretched encounter with that... clockwork fiend has set my nerves on edge."

Jake found himself in a wide hallway. The walls were papered with a mauve and red flower pattern and a pea green door stood before them. Mrs. Harker knocked upon it, before hastily walking up a flight of steps. "Good luck," she called, before vanishing into shadows.

A muffled thud, a clatter, and a yelp came from the room. Moments later the door swung open and the Professor appeared.

Somehow he looked even odder than he had on the night of the winter fair. His auburn hair was wild and the only thing seeming to keep it contained was a pair of goggles.

"Ah." Professor Thistlequick whipped a paisley handkerchief from his coat pocket and wiped a dark smudge from the side of his face. "I apologize for my state of disarray. Had I known a man-child was going to visit..."

"Man-child?" Jack asked.

"Are you a man? Or a child? What are you?" He gave Jake a long, bewildered look. "We've met before, haven't we? Kew Gardens? Three or four years ago? A wet afternoon with a hint of autumn in the air, if I remember rightly."

"We met at the fair a few days ago. You gave me-"

Professor Thistlequick held up a hand. "No. Wait. It's coming to me. Ah, yes, Jake." He pointed at Jake's shoes. "I see my springs didn't leave you with any physical impairments. Thank goodness for that! So you must be here on a separate matter altogether. Come in, come in." The Professor swept his hand towards the murky room behind him. "I'll put the kettle on and make some tea, for I find myself more thirsty than baffled. Are you?"

"Baffled?" Jake had never been more baffled in his life.

"No, parched. And here's another question. Have you seen a cat? She may or may not have had a clay pipe clenched between her teeth. It's my favorite pipe, and it's missing."

"I didn't see a cat with a pipe, but I saw one wearing spectacles."

"Hmph! They're not hers either. Still, she won't get far. I made them for near sighted felines, whereas Happiness is relatively far sighted."

"Happiness?"

"The cat who stole my pipe. She's my cat, in as much as a cat can belong to anyone. Anyway, does nettle tea sound alright?"

"Sounds lovely," Jake lied, wondering if nettle tea could sting. "Only if you've got time?"

Professor Thistlequick followed Jake's gaze to the coat he was wearing. "Oh! I'm not going anywhere. I wear my coat indoors more than out." He pulled it open, revealing a number of pockets. "It's far more portable than a tool case and I can carry almost everything I need. Anyway, come in." The Professor grinned, and guided Jake into the strangest room he'd ever seen.

CHAPTER TWENTY

The Professor's rooms were almost as Jake had imagined them, but while he'd pictured the tools and clutter, it was nothing like the scale of chaos he saw before him.

Every available surface was covered with things. Telescopes, keys, journals, clockworks and cogs of all shapes and sizes. There were automatons, combs, coins and lots and lots of smoking pipes, and everything was partially obscured by a rich nutty blue smoke that reminded Jake of burning bread.

Tall towers of stacked books leaned precariously and some were so high they reached the sooty, pockmarked ceiling. Objects hung from taut brass wires; puppets, wooden hares and rabbits, and bunches of keys. Each swung in the breeze issuing through the open window.

A tiny silver hot air balloon flew around the book towers. Miniature people peered over a woven basket as tiny flames propelled them up through the smoke.

The half-built figures standing in a row against one wall

were almost as tall as Jake; soldiers, sailors and even a knight. They gazed lifelessly down to the large threadbare Turkish rug strewn across the wooden floor. Jake shivered. The figures reminded him of Mrs. Wraythe's dolls.

"Yes, it's gotten decidedly colder, hasn't it?" Professor Thistlequick said. "I left the window ajar to clear the smoke from my new toast machine. Once it's ready, it will construct buttered toast soldiers who will march from the device leading a carriage containing a perfectly boiled egg. Unfortunately, I became distracted by an errant clockwork toad, hence the fog of burnt bread. Anyway, come and sit by the fire, and I'll close the window. Happiness can knock with her tail if she needs to get back in."

Jake meandered through the piles of books and stood before a cheerful, crackling fireplace and warmed his hands before the blaze. Above the mantelpiece was a weather-beaten scrap of paper mounted and framed behind heavy glass. Jake wondered what the large blue elaborately curled letters said.

"You can have my seat, and I'll take the one reserved for Happiness." Professor Thistlequick gestured for Jake to sit in one of the armchairs set before the fire. It looked like it had rarely been used, whilst the other held a plump velvet cushion covered in a dusting of chocolate-brown fur. "I'll fetch refreshments, and then you must tell me all about your troubles."

"How do you know I've got troubles?" Jake asked. And then he nodded. "Oh, you read about it in the newspaper. I never said hardly any of those-"

"I've precisely no idea what you're talking about," the Professor called as he vanished behind a mountain of books. "I only subscribe to the papers for the moon cycles and cricket results. No, it's clear you're in trouble; those bags under your eyes are darker and far more pronounced than they were when we first met. Clearly, sleep has been a stranger to you these last few days."

Moments later the Professor returned with a tray. It held a battered old tea pot, two chipped cups and a tin of sardines. Jake's stomach rumbled. He hadn't eaten since that morning.

"It's a simple refreshment, if it can be described as such. Happiness and I usually share something around this hour, but she won't be a party to it today seeing as she's absconded with my favorite pipe. Do you like sardines?"

Jake gave what he hoped was an enthusiastic smile.

"And as for pudding..." The Professor rifled through his pockets and set something upon the tray. "I thought we could share a mince pie. What with Christmas almost being upon us."

"That's most generous," Jake said. As he glanced around, he became acutely aware of the worlds separating them. Of his ragged clothes and common accent, compared to the Professor's warm, posh tones.

"It's nothing really. You look famished. Had I known you were calling, I'd have asked Mrs. Harker to prepare one of her fabulous roast dinners. Now, tell me of your woes while I pour the tea. And please, explain why you believe I might be of use to you."

The tea in Jake's cup was stone cold by the time he finished his story.

The Professor had listened in silence, his face impassive, except for a brief moment when a flicker of... something, passed across it. But immediately after, his look became inscrutable once more as he rested his chin upon his steepled fingers. "Well that sounds like a rum turn of events."

"Do you believe me?" Jake hated the desperation in his voice.

"I do. I can find no reason why you'd make such a story up and it's plain by the haunted look in your eyes that you're deeply distressed."

"I just want to get my friends back."

"Of course you do." Professor Thistlequick gazed into the fire. "A demon, eh?"

"I swear it!"

"I've no doubt. There's magick and all manner of dark wonders running rife in this city, despite what our betters tell us. And you haven't gone to the police?"

"What's the point? They're not going to listen to me."

"Maybe, maybe not. You said you were the only one to see the flying machine that took your friends away? Are you certain no one else witnessed it?"

"Yes. But I don't know how anyone could miss it. It was huge and the whole thing was glowing with blue light."

"Interesting. I wonder..."

Jake waited for the Professor to finish his thoughts but he remained silent, his eyes reflecting the flames in the grate.

"So can you help me?" Jake asked.

"Help you? Against demons and suchlike?" the Professor shook his head. "I'm afraid not. That would be well beyond my paltry abilities. No, the only course of action I can suggest is that you go to the authorities."

Jake's heart sunk. "You said you'd help me."

"I can help with attaching springs to shoes, or keeping a hat on your head during the fiercest of storms. I can even assist you with breathing underwater for great lengths of time. But demons and kidnappings are not my bailiwick."

Jake's face burned with anger as he stood. "Thanks for the tea. I've got to go."

"Listen, I truly wish I could help you with your woes, Jake," Professor Thistlequick said as he set his tea cup down.

"Don't worry yourself getting up. I'll see myself out," Jake said as he stormed across the room.

CHAPTER TWENTY-ONE

J ake wound through the book towers until he came upon a door. He wrenched it open, but it wasn't the way out; it was a cupboard, empty but for a broom and painting of two foxes dressed as gentlemen dueling with ancient guns.

"Let me show you the way." The Professor appeared behind Jake. "That is... if I can find it myself." He smiled, but as he glanced at Jake, his expression turned somber. "I really am sorry. I wish I could be of use, but this business sounds like it has more than its fair share of dark magick. And for now, I must keep my head down as far as such things are concerned. Especially after my encounter with Spring Heeled Jack. It was a close shave, you see." Professor Thistlequick tapped the side of his head. "But my cogs are turning. And if a solution arises to your travails, I'll be sure to share it with you."

"That's so kind of you," Jake spat, as he finally found the right door and barged through it into the murky hallway. "But I doubt I'll be around for much longer."

"The darkest of clouds can only last so long," Professor Thistlequick said. "Eventually dawn will gobble them up."

"Maybe in your world." Jake tried to open the front door. It was jammed.

"Your problems will be resolved, Jake. I'm sure of it." Professor Thistlequick reached past Jake and pulled the front door open, admitting a cold blast of air.

"Thanks for your wisdom, I'm sure it will be a big comfort the next time the demon finds me. But maybe I can pass your advice on to Nancy and Adam, if I ever see them again." Jake glanced at the stairs. Someone was standing in the shadows. It took him a moment to make out Mrs. Harker's towering hair. "I hope you've enjoyed listening in to my problems, Mrs. Harker."

Her doughy face was riddled with concern as she stepped from the gloom. "Are you leaving already? I have some chicken soup on the hob-"

"Yes, I am. I should never have come here in the first place." Jake shot the Professor a venomous look. "Well, Professor, if you ever get tired of reading about moon cycles and cricket results, you'll probably find my name in the obituaries. Although I doubt I'm anywhere near important enough to make them."

Jake slammed the door on the Professor's response and shivered in the cold night air. He wrenched the Professor's metallic card from his pocket and tossed it into a rosebush, where it caught upon the thorns.

CHAPTER TWENTY-TWO

I t was night by the time Jake reached Highgate, and his mood matched the darkness. He still had no idea why he'd believed the Professor's offer to help him had been genuine. The man was privileged and soft. There were no grey clouds in his sky, and that was how he wanted things to stay.

"I have to get my money from Silas," Jake muttered. "Then I can find Nancy and Adam on my own." But before that, he had one last errand. He checked his pocket watch. It was almost five thirty.

Jake slowed as he spotted a Police Officer gazing wistfully at a grand house, no doubt dreaming of being inside its warmth and light. He cocked his head as Jake approached, like a dog assessing an intruder. "And what brings a young man such as yourself to a place like this?"

Jake swallowed his first response; it would only serve him a thick ear. "I'm looking for Tyburn Street, sir. Do you where it is? I've a message to deliver to a lady." Jake pulled the envelope from his pocket and held it up, making sure the Officer saw the official-looking red wax seal on the back.

"Right." The Officer's brow knitted and he gave a sharp nod. "Turn left at the end of this street. Tyburn's the fourth on the right."

"Thank you, sir."

"I patrol Tyburn, boy, so I best not find anything amiss."

Jake nodded and ran on.

Tyburn Street was dark, narrow and tree lined. Moonlight glinted on the frosty pavement, and dead leaves and branches rustled in a biting gust of wind. Jake blew into his cupped hands. His fingers were chilled to the bone.

He found Mrs. Wraythe's house at the end of the row with a sprawling yew tree growing in its tangled front garden, just as Silas had described. Behind it, the steep sloped roof and tall pointed tower in the center of the house rose high above its black spiky limbs.

Jake's heart thudded as he caught a flicker in the ox-eye window and saw a heavy curtain fall into place, obscuring whoever had been watching. He walked up the stone path, past the granite gargoyles looming on either side, and climbed the wide frosty stairs leading to the front door.

The envelope fell from his pocket as he reached in to check his watch. It was just after five-thirty. His fingers trembled as he scooped up the letter and seized the lion-shaped door knocker. He paused, and considered thrusting the envelope through the door, even if it would risk Silas Grumble's ire. What was one more beating before he left the Crow for good?

The letterbox was cold and heavy as he pushed it open and he almost had the envelope through, when the door opened.

Mrs. Wraythe's high-necked black dress melted into the

darkness behind her and her ghost-white face seemed to hover in the doorway as she glanced from the envelope to Jake. "The last time we met you ran from me."

"My apologies Mrs. Wraythe. It was the dolls. They-"

"You're an incredibly rude young man, Jake Shillingsworth."

"I'm sorry. Really, I am. I'm just here to deliver this message from Mr. Grumble." Jake's tongue felt as if it had swollen to twice its size as she stared at him. "Please take it."

She made no move to take the envelope.

"Please, Mrs. Wraythe. I have to give you this letter so I can return to The Tattered Crow, begging your leave."

"Begging is for dogs. Now come inside whilst I draft my response."

Jake took one last look toward the street as he stepped into the house, silently praying he'd make it back out with his sanity and wits in one piece.

Mrs. Wraythe closed the door and snatched up an oil lamp. A slight grin played on her withered lips as she produced a key and locked the door, turning it with a savage twist. "Now we won't be disturbed. Follow me." She pocketed the key and glided along the hall, with Jake following close behind.

The walls were lined with sconces. Most were empty but here and there candlelight punctuated the gloom, revealing tapestries and oil paintings. Ghostly faces stared at Jake, their expressions drawn and cruel. They wore fine clothes that were very old-fashioned, and the backgrounds surrounding them were stark and empty.

"Could this place be any more nightmarish?" Jake whispered.

"What did you say?" Mrs. Wraythe demanded.

"Those paintings... the people look familiar."

"They're my dear, deceased family. Perhaps you see a resemblance?"

They passed a flight of steps leading up into darkness. Something rustled in the gloom above and Jake almost bumped into Mrs. Wraythe as he hurried to keep up.

How could she live here? Surely the cemetery would be cozier.

"Your thoughts are so frantic, Jake, I can almost hear them." She pushed open a door, and entered a long, high-ceilinged room.

A fire burned in the grate, the coals glowing bright, and yet somehow the sparsely furnished chamber was icy cold. Heavy black drapes covered the windows, but a tiny crack of moonlight slipped through, a tantalizing reminder of the world beyond this haunted place.

Mrs. Wraythe eased herself into a high-backed chair set before a writing desk. She lit a candle, and glanced from Jake to the grandfather clock beside the fireplace. "Hand me the letter."

Jake flinched as her bony fingers brushed the envelope and a quiver ran along his back as something skittered across the ceiling. Had he really just seen a long, black, spidery leg unfurling among the shadows?

Mrs. Wraythe took a dagger from the drawer and sliced open the back of the envelope. When she removed the letter, Jake knew without doubt that the handwriting was hers. The loops of the letters looked like a hangman's noose, the words black hacks and slashes.

She nodded as she read. "Most enlightening!" Then, she crumpled the letter into a ball and threw it upon the fire. She smiled at Jake as she picked up her quill with great deliberation and dipped it into the inkwell.

The scratch of the quill's nib on the parchment set Jake's teeth on edge and a shudder passed through him as he turned away and spotted the doll standing in the corner. She stood facing the wall, as if in punishment, and a blaze of firelight from the burning letter illuminated one side of her porcelain face.

"Bloody hell!" Jake shouted as a shrill cry filled the room.

"Silence Ozirious," cooed Mrs. Wraythe. "Mother's indisposed." She snapped her head to Jake. "And if you utter another curse word in my house, you'll pay a dearer price than the one you have coming to you." She turned and glanced at the clock.

It seemed she was waiting for someone. Jake crossed his fingers he'd be long gone before whoever it was arrived. He had no wish to meet anyone that would call upon Mrs. Wraythe. Especially after dark.

The ticking clock seemed to slow as she filled page upon page with the scratch of her black letters. Now and then she paused to offer Jake a thin, barren smile. He looked away, unable to meet her eye.

What was she doing? Jake had watched Grumble writing letters, and even though it was always a ham-fisted display, at least there was purpose. This was different. Mrs. Wraythe's hand moved slowly, ponderously, as if she were more preoccupied with biding her time than with the letter.

"I'm sorry to interrupt, Mrs. Wraythe," Jake said, a light tremble in his voice, "but Mr. Grumble told me not to dither because he wants me back at the Crow to attend to the evening service. I should have left here ages ago."

"You'll be on your way soon enough." Mrs. Wraythe set

down the quill and gave Jake a strange, sad smile. "I had high hopes for you, Jake Shillingsworth. You see things... interesting things. But now your talent will become another's gain."

Her words held a horrible finality.

Jake fought to take a breath. It felt as if the room had run out of air.

As the grandfather clock chimed six, a muffled thump came from above.

Mrs. Wraythe scrunched up the pages she'd written and threw them on the fire. "Exactly six o'clock. He's the very paragon of punctuality, is he not?"

"Who, Mrs. Wraythe?"

Her laugh was high and cruel. "A man who's dying to meet you once again."

CHAPTER TWENTY-THREE

J ake gazed at the ceiling as a second thump came from
above.

"So, what will you do?" Mrs. Wraythe's smile was
thin and cruel. "Fight? Run? Resign without fuss or
drama? The last would be the easiest, for why prolong the
inevitable?" She pursed her lips. "Such a talent, such a waste. I
offered you a chance but you scorned me."

Jake ran, slipping out the doorway into the hall. The
candles in the sconces stretching before him blew out one by
one, leaving him in total darkness. He threw out his hands as
he sought to navigate the pitch black corridor.

He found the front door and wrenched its handle but all
hope melted away as he remembered how she'd locked it. Jake
beat his fists against the wood.

A loud creak came from upstairs and then the squeak of a
window sliding open. Fingertips brushed his cheek in the
darkness with a touch of gnarled skin like dead winter leaves.
Jake cringed as Mrs. Wraythe gave an almost girlish cackle.

He darted back toward the hall, remembering the tiny

sliver of moonlight that had appeared through the drapes. He'd throw himself through the windows if needs be. Straining his eyes, he searched for the glow of the fireplace but he could see nothing in the impenetrable darkness.

Something struck his foot and he fell forward, only just stifling his curse as a solid edge smashed into his chest, winding him. Jake reached out and felt the sharp angles of the stairway.

"Clumsy child." Mrs. Wraythe's voice was close behind him.

He gritted his teeth and pulled himself to his feet. Her breath was warm on the back of his neck as she goaded him on, herding him like a lamb towards the darkness above.

A bony finger jabbed his back. Jake threw out his hand, finding the cold, damp wall.

He stumbled up the stairs, praying whoever was above hadn't reached the landing. Every step creaked and moaned below his feet, but it didn't matter. He was certain Mrs. Wraythe knew exactly where he was, that she could see just as well in darkness as daylight.

A heavy footfall rang out from one of the rooms above. Jake strained to listen.

Silence followed. And then a loud screech.

Jake's heart thumped madly.

"Quiet, Ozirious," Mrs. Wraythe's voice chirped behind Jake. "He hasn't come for you dearest. He's come for the boy. That little shadow of what might have been." She poked Jake in the back again.

He bolted, taking two steps at a time, running his hand along the cold pitted wall to guide himself. A metallic clatter came from above, followed by a curse in a thick, familiar Irish accent.

"Take care, sir," Mrs. Wraythe called. "There's no hurry. The boy's coming to you. Climb Jake, climb!" The clap of her hands was like a whip crack.

Jake fell onto the landing. He pulled himself up and stumbled forward, throwing out his hands, trying to avoid potential obstacles. Heavy footfalls came from behind him and a cloying reek filled the air. It was the stench of rot, death, and flesh long since withered.

"Damn this darkness," the man growled.

"Very well," Mrs. Wraythe replied.

Something brushed past Jake's arm and then a dozen gas lamps burst into light, burning with vivid orange blue flames and illuminating the hallway. Jake screwed his eyes against the glare and ran toward the nearest room.

"Confound it, you idiot woman. Are you trying to blind me?" the man emerging into the corridor ahead of Jake demanded. He could see him now, a blur of glowing brass and black.

"My apologies Mr. Kedgewick," Mrs. Wraythe called from behind them.

Jake's flailing hand found the door handle. He twisted hard and the door opened. The giant thundered towards him, his mechanical heart pounding behind the murky glass portal in his chest. Jake ducked into the room, stumbling as he rushed to slam the door behind him.

"Leave me alone!" Jake wheeled around with his back against the door, and searched for a means to block it.

A scrape of icy dread ran across the nape of his neck as he glanced past a pair of flickering candles to the sea of china-white faces and dead black eyes gazing back at him.

CHAPTER TWENTY-FOUR

The door thundered in its frame, breaking Jake's attention away from the dead-eyed dolls' paralyzing gazes. He spotted a short wooden bookcase crammed full of heavy-looking books against the wall. Using all his might, Jake dragged it in front the door. With every blow of Kedgewick's fists the bookcase juddered and the books flew from the shelves and crashed to the floor like dead bats.

With a booming crack, Kedgewick's huge brass fist smashed through the wooden panels. A reek of putrefaction issued into the room and Jake's gaze fell upon the porthole set in Kedgewick's armored chest. His dirty-red heart thumped wildly behind the glass, enmeshed in a snarl of copper tubes and cogs. "Let me in boy." He sounded almost reasonable, as if he were merely asking the time of day.

"No! Where are my friends?"

"They're safe. They're working with my master, and once they're finished, he'll set them free. I can take you to them, Jake. Let me in."

Jake wedged the top of the bookcase under the door handle and stepped back. "How do you know my name?"

Kedgewick laughed. "We know everything about you, son. Just open the door and we'll be on our way. I won't harm you. I don't harm children, I swear it." He pushed his brass fingers through the hole in the door and pulled. Cracks ran through the wooden panels.

Jake backed away and cried out as he collided with a doll.

He spun around. They stood right before him, their glassy eyes boring into his. Had they crept forward?

Jake flinched as Kedgewick punched the door again. There was no anger in his actions now, just cold, measured precision. Jake searched the room and his gaze fell on the dusty black drapes behind the horde of dolls. Perhaps they concealed a window…

The door splintered and rattled in its frame. Jake wound through the huddled dolls, fighting to avoid their staring eyes. At any moment he expected them to turn their heads and lunge at him.

Kedgewick roared as the door smashed from its hinges. He kicked the bookcase aside and stormed into the room. "I told you to come to me, boy."

Jake shrieked as frosty fingers brushed his palm. A doll stood right beside him, one that definitely hadn't been there moments ago.

Jake recognized her from the night at the fair.

Sally Sixpins.

He wrenched his hand from hers and the dolls sighed as one, the sound soft and low.

Horror cut through Jake like a knife as Sally turned to watch him and the others crowded behind her. Their heads were cocked to one side, as if listening.

Jack glanced back to find Kedgewick standing in the middle of the room, his dim blue face creased with confusion. And then his bewilderment became frustration as the dolls formed a barricade between him and Jake.

"Get out of my way!" Kedgewick demanded as he barged through the horde. They cried out as one, their shrieks deafening.

Jake threw back the drapes. There was a window! It was fogged over, making the street lamps thick orange circles below the blurry stars. He pulled at the window sash, as the dolls crashed to the floor behind him.

It wouldn't move.

Kedgewick roared.

Jake's fingers shook frantically as he wrenched at the latch. Finally it shifted. He shoved the window open and clambered out onto the sill.

"Stop!" Kedgewick demanded.

Jake looked back.

A few dolls still stood between them, but the rest were sprawled like corpses upon the floor. As Mrs. Wraythe appeared in the doorway, they screamed louder than ever. Kedgewick clamped his hands to his ears, his eyes blazing with fury. "Shut up!"

The icy air drew around Jake, chilling him to the bone. He glanced to the yew tree below and back to the room as Kedgewick lunged for him.

He leaped.

The tree rushed up toward him.

Jake grabbed a branch. It held for a moment, before snapping. "No!" He cried out as he tumbled through a thicket of twigs and limbs, howling in agony as springing branches pounded his ribs and slashed at his face.

He reached out, searching for anything to slow his fall but then the branches vanished, leaving nothing between him and the ground.

Time slowed, and for a moment the frost on the grass below glittered like thousands of tiny jewels.

And then he slammed into the ground.

Jake pushed his hands against the ice-cold grass and dragged himself to his feet. Pain burst through his hands and legs as he staggered away. He glanced back as an explosion of glass shattered from the house behind and the window frame toppled to the garden.

Kedgewick stood in the hole in the wall, his face grim as pale white fingers grasped at his legs. The twin umbrellas on his back sputtered to life and he glided up and over the yew tree. His eyes locked upon Jake's as he dove down.

Jake stared dumbly before dodging away.

Kedgewick shot over a low wall and rose back into the air.

"Oi!" someone cried. It was the Police Officer who had questioned Jake earlier. "What do you think you're doing?" he called as he stood in the street watching the spectacle, no doubt drawn to the din.

Kedgewick gave the man a murderous glare.

"What the devil are you?" the Officer asked. He raised a whistle to his lips and blew. A high, shrill whistle pierced the silent night.

Seconds later, another whistle answered, and then another.

Jake fled, slipping and sliding on the icy pavement. When he glanced back, the Officer was standing dumbstruck, gazing up at the empty sky. The flurry of whistles converged. Jake limped as fast as he could through the network of narrow passages running between the houses.

Finally, he stumbled out onto a high street and joined the bustling crowd, glad for their cover. He took a moment to orientate himself, before limping after an omnibus and pulling himself up onto the rail above its wheels.

He didn't care where it was headed. Anywhere was fine, just as long as it was away from that terrible place.

CHAPTER TWENTY-FIVE

Professor Thistlequick settled back in his chair. He watched the glow of ashes in the hearth for a moment, and then his eyes strayed once more to the letter above the mantelpiece. He'd read it so many times he knew its words by heart, but tonight his uncle's letter seemed to hold a fresh meaning.

Happiness growled in the chair beside him, flexing her claws as she dreamed. The unsettling sound only added to the general sense of disquiet that had dogged the Professor since Jake Shillingsworth had left. He glanced up as someone knocked lightly on the door, disrupting his thoughts.

Mrs. Harker stood in the hall, holding a glass of drinking chocolate. "I thought you might like a nightcap."

"I wouldn't usually, but I will tonight. Thank you." He took the glass and was about to bid her a good evening, when she sighed. "Is something troubling you, Mrs. Harker?"

Her towering hair wobbled as she nodded. "Actually, yes. There is." Her voice quivered, but she straightened and met his eye. "I couldn't help but overhear your conversation with the boy. Or at least the final part, where he mentioned being in mortal danger."

"Well, I'm not sure-"

"And I can't stop thinking about it," Mrs. Harker continued. "It's been turning around and around in my head like a snake."

"A snake-"

"I'm haunted by the vision of that poor child leaving the warmth of this house, treading into the dark night alone. I tried to sleep, but it was impossible. And may I say, you do not seem to be your usual restful self either."

"No, I'm not. And I share your concerns. I've been mulling-"

"Mulling will not do, Professor. You need to resolve yourself and fix that poor boy's woes. Whatever's happened to you of late? Where did the clockwork magician we all know and admire go? As much as your madcap misadventures shred my nerves, I've been more unsettled by your lack of oomph, Professor. You've festered in this house for far too long."

"I've been trying to remain inconspicuous. I won't horrify you with the details, but suffice to say I had a fairly close encounter with the authorities not so long ago."

"Well stop it. Please. Inconspicuous doesn't suit you. You've become a fish out of water, and as wretched and dull as a rainy Tuesday afternoon." Mrs. Harker glanced up at him. "Go after the boy at first light. Help him. Please."

Professor Thistlequick nodded. "I'll give the matter my full consideration, Mrs. Harker. Now, may I bid you a good night?"

"You may," Mrs. Harker said, as she made her way back up the stairs. "But just remember what I said."

"Very well." Professor Thistlequick returned to the fireplace, eager to escape the dark questions springing up in his mind like ragwort.

CHAPTER TWENTY-SIX

The Tattered Crow was filled with a swell of noise as Jake wound through the raucous crowd and made his way toward the kitchen.

"You look like you've been to hell rather than Highgate." Silas Grumble fixed Jake with a suspicious look. "What was the problem this time? Vampires? Ghouls? Do tell."

"I took your message to Mrs. Wraythe." All Jake wanted to do was get upstairs, break into Grumble's room and take the wages that were rightfully his. And then he'd be gone, into the night, leaving The Crow behind for good.

"And dilly-dallied on the way back no doubt."

"Can I be excused, sir. I'd like to wash and-"

"You'd like to be h'excused? Why of course. Perhaps I can run a bath for you as well? Put your feet up lad. Let me do all the work." Silas Grumble twisted Jake's ear. "There's a mountain of dirty plates and a small country of leftovers for you to sort in the kitchen. Save what you can, we'll use it tomorrow in the mulligatawny soup." Silas Grumble whispered this last instruction out of earshot of the regulars as he shoved Jake behind the bar toward the kitchen.

Jake stood by the stove for a moment, before ducking upstairs.

His heart beat fast as he tip-toed along the hall, praying Grumble had left his bedroom door unlocked. As Jake grasped the door handle, he screamed.

It was red hot.

He shook his fingers as tears of agony blurred his eyes.

Footsteps thundered up the stairs and Silas Grumble appeared, wearing a devilish grin of satisfaction. "Caught you!"

"My fingers-"

"Don't think I didn't notice you looking at my valuables this morning, you fiend! No, I saw you, and I knew you'd be back." Grumble laughed and slapped a hand against his thigh. "I wedged a poker in a bucket of hot coals and leaned it against the door handle. I had to climb out of my own window like a cat burglar after I'd set it up, but it was worth it to see the look on your thieving face!"

Jake winced as blisters spread across his fingers.

"You could say I caught you red-handed!" Grumble crowed. "Boy thief! Child sneak!" He grabbed Jake by the scruff of his neck, dragged him along the hallway and shoved him into his tiny room. Grumble's eyes gleamed madly as he loomed in the doorway. "There's a bucket of ice in the corner for your hand, although why I went to such thoughtful measures to ease your pain, I have no idea. The greed and ingratitude I get from you! I saved your scrawny life. Did you know that?"

Jake knew it perfectly. He'd been told enough times.

"Found you at an auction when you were just a tot, I did. You were up for sale like a custard cake, though a lot less sweeter, and far more vinegary. Sold by a she-witch you were, and had I not paid for you, she'd have snuffed your life out like a dying star."

"Thank-"

"Don't thank me, boy. Not after you tried to rob me blind."

"I was just trying to collect my wages. There's people after me Silas-"

"Silas! Mr. Grumble to you. Mr. Grumble!"

"I have to leave. I've got to find Nancy and-"

"No more." Silas Grumble clutched his chest. "You'll bring on another heart attack. If there's anything left to attack that is, for your recent devilry's sunk my heart into a black soup of despair and shattered it like glass." Grumble stabbed a finger at Jake. "This is it for you, boy. The straw that twisted the camel's spine. You'll remain here, incarcerated while I decide what to do with you." The door slammed, sending fungus raining down from the wall. Moments later there was a banging din as Silas Grumble hammered nails into the door, sealing Jake in.

"Please, Mr. Grumble!"

"Don't you Mr. Grumble me," he called through the door. "Our days of familiarity and friendship are gone. Smashed like a china plate under the hammer of your treachery. This is your final night at The Tattered Crow. Tomorrow, I'm taking you to the poor house. Who knows, I might even get a bent penny or two for you if they're feeling charitable!"

Jake ran to the window. It had been nailed shut. He felt sick as he realized Grumble must have been planning this all afternoon. And that no matter how many threats Grumble had given Jake over the years, this time it really seemed he meant what he said.

Jake's days in The Tattered Crow were truly at an end.

CHAPTER TWENTY-SEVEN

P rofessor Thistlequick gazed out of his window at the bright blue December sky. "It looks frightfully cold," he said to Happiness. Her tail and whiskers twitched as she glanced at him, a sure sign of irritation. "You stay here by the fire," he continued, "I'll leave some jam and pilchards for you. Not that I advise you mix the two."

Happiness yawned, licked her paw, and curled into a ball.

Professor Thistlequick sighed. The prospect of leaving Brightstar Terrace was not a happy one. The world outside seemed troubled enough, without him adding himself to the chaos. "Plus I still need to finish off those self-heating slippers," he muttered. "And yet I promised Mrs. Harker I'd do something to help the boy, and I know better than to break my word to that dear lady. For to do so means being deprived of Sunday roasts and baked delights." He glanced at the parchment above the fire. "Yes, yes. I know, Uncle Claudius. You're right of course." The Professor wound through the towers of books. He paused by the door, pulled on his paisley scarf, strapped on his top hat, and left the house.

The streets were busier than he'd expected.

Professor Thistlequick danced aside as people slipped and slid past him on the frosty pavement, though he himself had no such problem. The shaft of his walking cane was filled with freshly boiled water, and the tiny heated spikes at its base melted away the frost at his feet.

He made an impressive dash through Regent's Park to Baker Street where he hailed a hansom cab. The driver wore a heavy hooded cloak and was wrapped in a nest of blankets and all the Professor could see of the man was his red bulbous nose.

"Crow Alley, please," Professor Thistlequick requested.

"Crow Alley. Are you sure?"

"Indeed."

"You won't find a soul foolhardy enough to take you anywhere near that God-forsaken place. I can get you as far as the Charing Cross Road but you'll have to walk the rest of the way," the driver warned.

The Professor nodded briskly as he climbed into the cab, glad for the respite from the cold wintry morning. The driver cracked his whip and drove onto the busy thoroughfare.

Soon, Jake's strange, disquieting story returned to him as he gazed up at the sky through the tiny windows, lost in his thoughts as the blurred city passed by.

HMS Watcher hovered over Hyde Park, its intense yellow searchlights sweeping over the rooftops like vigilant eyes. The Professor swallowed and dug his hands into his pockets. "You've nothing to hide," he muttered. "Nothing at all. You've done nothing wrong. Yet. It's a coincidence. It has to be."

Finally they stopped amongst a cluster of carriages in the theater district. Professor Thistlequick climbed out and paid the driver, adding a generous tip.

"That's very kind of you, sir," the driver said. "Look, I could probably find someone to run your errand in Crow Alley in your stead, if it suits you?"

"I'll be fine," Professor Thistlequick replied. "Thank you." He swung his walking cane and took a short cut down a shadowy passage.

The buildings became decidedly shabbier as he made his way out of Covent Garden. They were squat mean houses with soot-encrusted walls, their windows spider webs of broken glass.

People stood on street corners, and lurked in doorways, scrutinizing the Professor with cold, appraising eyes. He smiled at them, but his friendliness was not returned. Most of the street signs were defaced or missing from their posts, and soon he realized he had no idea where he was.

"Now, what would a gent like you be doing around here then?"

Professor Thistlequick glanced about, searching for the owner of the thin rasping voice.

"I asked you a civil question," the voice continued, "the least you could do is answer."

The Professor jumped as someone poked him in the side. He glanced down to find a tiny man in tattered clothes glaring back at him. "Ah, good day. I didn't-"

"See me down here," The man finished. "I know. You look like a man who's lost his way."

Professor Thistlequick wasn't sure how to respond.

"Literally," the tiny man continued. "Or perhaps figuratively too. What are you here for? Ladies? Gambling? Or something more surreptitious?"

"Would you happen to know the location of Crow Alley?"

"I would."

"Could you tell me where I might find it?" Professor Thistlequick dug into his pocket for a coin.

"I could!"

"How much would it cost for you to furnish me with such information?"

"Did I ask for money?"

"Not at all! I'm sorry it's just…"

"I look like a pauper."

"No." Professor Thistlequick felt his face reddening. "I'm sorry."

"You have the demeanor of a man who's spent his whole life apologizing. But that's by the by. So you're seeking Crow Alley are you?"

"Please."

"You're standing on it. Granted it's more of a street than an alley, but I didn't name it. Are you here for the world famous crow gallery? If so, I'd save your money, it's a shocking waste of time."

"Thank you, but I'm looking for The Tattered Crow."

"Really?" The man looked the Professor up and down, and then pointed ahead. "You'll find it down that way, toward the end of the alley. But I'll tell you this for nothing, you're not the usual kind of kipper who frequents that particular establishment. So you'd best be careful. Keep your airs and graces to yourself, and whatever you do, don't apologize."

"Right you are. Actually, I'm looking for a boy who works there. Jake Shillingsworth."

The little man rolled his eyes. "A journalist, eh? I'd have thought that tall tale was old news by now. Still, I don't get involved with newspapers, other than using them for insulation, and for cleaning my posterior." He led the Professor down the street. A few shops stood on either side, their windows dark and murky. Vendors stood before them, touting all sorts of exotic, dangerous looking wares.

"Well," the man said, as he nodded toward a tall, rickety building made of wood and stone. "There's your destination. And what a destination it is!"

A squeaky weather-beaten sign swung from a pole in the soot-encrusted wall. It showed the silhouette of a large, ruffled looking bird perched on a moonlit branch. Thick carved wooden letters read: 'The Tattered Crow'.

"Good luck, squire," the little man said. "And watch yourself in there. Should things go amiss, and I read about your murder in the newspaper, I'll wipe my rear with a different page."

"That's most generous." Professor Thistlequick took a deep breath and pulled the arched wooden door.

It wouldn't move.

"You might try pushing!" the little man said as he strolled off, shaking his head.

"Of course!" Professor Thistlequick shoved the door. It swung open and he stepped into a dim, smoky room. The air was thick and stank of stale sweat, sour wine, tobacco, vomit and what may have been horse manure.

Professor Thistlequick coughed into his handkerchief as he peered around. A knot of people stood around a fireplace while others hunched over tables, grimly clutching tankards, their faces lit by stumpy tallow candles.

"Would anyone-" Professor Thistlequick froze as something cold and metallic pressed against his throat.

He winced as the sharp edge nicked his skin. "Don't move a muscle," a low harsh voice growled in his ear.

CHAPTER TWENTY-EIGHT

Professor Thistlequick tried not to flinch as the blade bit into his skin. "I... erm... do you think you could stop? You're cutting my throat," he said to his unseen assailant. A few of the The Tattered Crow's patrons looked his way before turning back to their pints, as if this sort of thing was a common occurrence.

The knife pressed harder. "What do you want in here?" The Professor's assailant demanded. "Did the mutton shunters send you?"

Professor Thistlequick had precisely no idea what he was talking about and was about to protest his innocence when he noticed a grotesque looking man sidling towards them. Anger blazed in the man's large watery eyes as he reached out with a shaking fist. "You leave that patron h'alone, Spike. Can't you see he's a proper gentleman?"

"I found him first, Silas. He's mine." Spike growled causing a sour smell of whiskey to assail the Professor's nostrils. "Finders keepers."

Silas licked his lips, and gave the Professor a sickly grin.

"Listen here, Spike. You might be under the mistaken h'impression that the Crow is a lower class h'establishment and a place where anything goes, but you're wrong. The Tattered Crow is a candlelit solace where both ladies and gentlemen are most welcome. And there'll be no throat cutting, flim-flammery, or any other form of devilry under my roof! Now release this dear gentleman, or you'll find yourself out in the street. And seeings as you're banned from every other h'alehouse within the city walls; this will prove a fatal blow for you. Do you really want to find yourself reduced to a life grubbing around the streets without the reprieve of a foaming tankard of ale?"

The blade at the Professor's throat was quickly withdrawn and another blast of acrid breath soured the air as Spike muttered, "No harm meant." His tone suggested quite the opposite.

The Professor lowered his eyes as Spike crept into the shadows and smiled at his savior, trying not to focus too closely on the white flecks of spittle gathering in the corners of the man's lips. "Thank you."

"I'll hear nothing of it." Silas thrust a hand out for the Professor to shake. "Silas Grumble, here to serve you fine ales, culinary delights, as well as a place to rest your weary head. You won't find better h'accomodation outside of Buckingham Palace. A bold claim perhaps, but a truer one never spoken."

Someone in the gloom chuckled.

"I, ah, well very good, Mr. Grumble." Professor Thistlequick calmly extracted his hand from Grumble's damp grasp.

"It is my solemn duty to be as hospitable and h'obliging as I'm able. Especially in the company of a fellow gentleman. Now, how do you want to wet your whistle? I'd h'imagine ale isn't quite your cup of tea, if you'd pardon my pun. Perhaps sir prefers port, or a nice glass of wine?"

"Perhaps. But I'd sooner enjoy your hospitality after I've completed my errand." Professor Thistlequick smiled and did his best not to stare at the nest of grey hairs sprouting from Grumble's nose.

"And what errand might that be?"

"I'm looking for a boy by the name of Jake Shillingsworth. I believe this is where he lives?"

Silas Grumble frowned. "You're not a spreader of letters are you?"

"I-"

"A writer of gossip, and dare I say tattle? Have I mistaken a gentlemen for a fiend of ink?"

"A fiend of ink?"

"A journalist. A non-agricultural spreader of written muck, mire and effluence. An inventor of tall tales and fiendish falsehoods. Such individuals are most certainly unwelcome below this roof."

"Well I am an inventor, of sorts," the Professor admitted, "but not of words. My name's Professor Thistlequick, and I'm pleased to make your acquaintance. Now, perhaps I might have a quiet word with master Shillingsworth? It is a rather pressing matter."

"An h'appointment could be arranged. Although the child is currently locked away as punishment for last night's misdemeanors."

"Locked away?"

"Incarcerated, if you prefer. But only while I decide what to do with him. I caught him trying to break into my room, you see. He was after my sock."

"Jake was trying to steal your sock?" The conversation,

along with the heavy fumes of smoke and alcohol, was starting to make the Professor's head swim.

"Indeed. Naturally I wanted to exile him from this fine h'establishment forthwith, but he has his uses. I've employed countless other whippersnappers, but none cut the mustard like Jake Shillingsworth. Which leaves me with quite a conundrum and a half."

"I could see how losing one's sock might be jolly inconvenient, and I do sympathize. But would you be willing to allow me to visit the prisoner?"

Silas Grumble gave a sharp nod. "I'll grant you an audience, and after we'll discuss a financial settlement for my loss of time. Over lunch, if you please, as I cannot abide partaking in discussions of fiscal matters on an empty stomach. Do you know, you'll be the very first Professor I've ever broken bread with."

"I'm honored. Now, if we could-"

"Yes, yes. Come this way, I'll escort you to the monstrous turncoat." Silas Grumble led the Professor through the bar. "This may surprise you but I actually gave the boy his very own room, which is where he's currently idling. I know, I know, I'm far too generous and I very much doubt there's another innkeeper in the city who would grant their staff such goodwill. But generosity runs through my veins like blue blood runs through yours."

"I-"

"Up these stairs, if you will, sir." Silas Grumble climbed up a rickety staircase that looked like it could collapse at any moment. Black mould splotched the ragged wallpaper and spots of lichen grew on the railing. Professor Thistlequick thought about taking a sample, until Silas Grumble turned to regard him.

"The staff quarters are on the second floor, along with a bountiful selection of rooms. You may stay here whenever you visit, for I trust you'll become a regular in The Tattered Crow. God knows the place needs a touch of class. And class follows class, as sure as wasps follow... I don't know. Apples?"

"Maybe in autumn when-"

"Yes, yes. You shall have your very own h'exclusive room." Silas Grumble wheezed as he continued up the stairs. "Do you sleep much, Professor?"

"About eight hours a night, where possible."

"Of course. A bonafide gent would need eight hours at least, and not a moment less."

They entered a narrow hall, bare but for a crude painting of a wretched-looking sparrow mostly obscured by a layer of dust. Silas Grumble stopped before a door and rapped upon it. His face hardened as he wiped a line of drool from his lips. "You better be decent, sneak thief! You've a visitor. A gentleman no less!"

The muffled response that came through the door sounded like a particularly crude word.

"Did you just swear at me, boy? Could such a vulgarity come from lips so young?" Mr. Grumble barked, as he pulled a hammer from his pocket and used the claw to pry out the nails sealing the door shut. "Is that how I raised you?"

"Raised me?" Jake shouted, as the door swung open. "The only way you ever raised me was by my hair."

Mr. Grumble let forth a rancid sigh. "This is h'exactly the sort of gratitude I get from the whelk! Do you see what I have to put up with? And all without provocation. It makes me so angry, but I don't react on h'account of my spirituality! It runs through me like a mineral through rock."

"Does it indeed?" Professor Thistlequick felt a rare twinge of anger as he glanced at Jake's squalid room.

Silas swept his hand towards the threshold. "Enter, Professor. Speak with the boy, but bear in mind I shall have to lock you in to ensure the captive doesn't make good his escape. I'll return within the hour to release you, and then we can dine and settle our financial differences over a bottle of port. Like proper gentlemen." Mr. Grumble gave the Professor a peculiar self-invented salute, before ushering him into the room.

Professor Thistlequick jumped as the door slammed behind him. He peered around the room, which was little more than a box with a single grimy window.

Jake stood against a wall, a moth-eaten blanket clamped about his neck. "What do you want?"

"I've been thinking," Professor Thistlequick replied. "About your story."

"Have you now. That was big of you."

"Listen." Professor Thistlequick dropped his voice. "I believe you. Things are seriously amiss in London. Anyone can see that. I first noticed it when those scientists and scholars went missing."

"Along with a bunch of kids and people snatched off the streets. Not that anyone gives a stuff about them."

"I do," Professor Thistlequick said.

"You didn't care yesterday. You said you weren't interested. What changed your mind?"

"I never said I wasn't interested, I said I couldn't help. And I'm still uncertain I can, but I'll certainly try."

"How comes?"

"Mrs. Harker spoke to me after you left. She made me see sense, as she often does. I've been preoccupied of late, mostly with myself, I'm ashamed to admit. Sometimes I forget there's a world beyond my rooms and inventions. I apologize. Unreservedly. Now, I've no idea how I can help you face a flying craft and demons, but I'll give it my all. I promise."

Jake gave the Professor a strange look, before glancing away. "Did Grumble tell you why he locked me up?"

"He mentioned some sort of gibberish about you trying to steal his sock. Hardly the crime of the century!"

"The sock was full of money. Grumble's *savings* as he calls them. But they're mine, not his. He's never paid me a single penny since I worked here."

"Ah."

"Still want to help me?" Jake's face hardened.

"Of course, why wouldn't I? I'm sure you had your reasons, and I can see Mr. Grumble is a... difficult man."

"I always told myself I wasn't like those crooks down there." Jake waved his hand at the floorboards. "That I was better than that. But I'm not. I'm just like them. And I always will be."

"No, you're not. When I look at you I see a young man bursting with honor, persistence and loyalty. A lesser person would have fled when those beasts attacked their friends, but you didn't. Indeed, you showed far more bravery than I imagine I could have mustered."

The hard set of Jake's jaw softened. "Alright, so where do we start?"

"Well, escaping this room would be a good first step, I expect." Professor Thistlequick examined the nails sealing the window. He rifled through his coat and pulled out a pair of pliers.

"We're going out through the window? Can you climb?" Jake looked doubtful.

"Not really. But I'd sooner break my neck than suffer Mr. Grumble's rancid breath and lunacy again. Now, gather whatever you need and we'll go."

The trace of a smile lit Jake's face as he knelt and pulled up a floorboard.

Professor Thistlequick prised the nails out of the window frame and dropped them one by one to the bare floor. "Be quick, Jake. There are people to save and adventures to be had. Are you ready?"

"I suppose." Jake stood with a tangled knot of rags below his arm. "This is all I've got to take with me seeings as Grumble's got my money."

"Then out we go. And if I slip and break my neck, run as fast as you can. And never look back on this dreadful place."

CHAPTER TWENTY-NINE

Climbing down the side of The Tattered Crow took far longer than Jake was used to. The Professor was nimble enough but he kept pausing to examine the ancient bricks and moss, like they were the most fascinating thing in the world.

When they finally reached the ground, Jake led them through a series of alleys until they emerged on the Charing Cross Road. Professor Thistlequick flagged down a coach and driver, and helped Jake climb up the steps to the warm, comfortable interior.

Jake grinned as he gazed out the window. Usually he'd be clinging to the back of the cab, his hands freezing until they became numb. Now London passed by in a wintry haze, and soon the gentle warmth and trundle of the carriage caused him to fall asleep.

"HERE WE ARE," Professor Thistlequick said as they pulled up outside his house in Brightstar Terrace. He paid the driver and ushered Jake inside. "Now, we need to decide how best to solve your dilemma, but first, we should have some tea. You didn't seem overly enthusiastic with the nettle tea before, even though it matched your mood. So how about something else. Oolong perhaps, or Assam? Or perhaps a nice cup of Darjeeling?"

"Have you got anything... normal?" Jake stretched before the fire blazing in the hearth as its warmth spread through the holes in his shoes and trousers.

"I'll bring you a cup of the most normal tea I can find. And I was also considering a sausage and bacon sandwich with a healthy dash of mustard. What do you say?"

"That would be lovely. But, are *you*... making it?" Jake glanced at the scorch marks on the ceiling.

"Me? Are you mad? Fear not, I'll ask Mrs. Harker if she'll oblige." The Professor gazed wistfully into the fire. "T'was a black day for Primrose Hill the last time I attempted to fry a sausage."

As Jake finished the last of his sandwich, his eyes strayed to the letter displayed above the fireplace. "What's that?"

Professor Thistlequick ran a finger across the paper. "A reminder."

"Of what?"

"Of why we must never give up. A notion you seem perfectly aware of already, but it's something I need reminding of from time to time."

"What does it say?" The large writing ornately inscribed in dark blue ink seemed showy and larger than life. Jake wondered if it was the Professor's handwriting.

"That letter was delivered six weeks ago, and was sent to me by my uncle. Good old Claudius Thistlequick. It arrived by a pigeon, which must have taken a most roundabout journey. Sadly, those hastily written words were his last."

"Was he dying when he wrote it?"

"In a manner of speaking. He wrote that letter on the Edge of Dawn, a ship he'd chartered to explore the Norwegian Sea. He was searching for sea serpents, you see. It was his life's work. And I'm sure he would have found one eventually, had he not encountered an entirely different beast."

Jake had never been out to sea or even on a real boat, but he'd heard plenty of sailor's tales at the inn. Such journeys to far off places seemed unpredictable and perilous, and he often wondered why anyone would wish to attempt one. "What was it?"

"A giant squid, a behemoth large enough to swallow a man whole. The words you see there are Claudius' last. They describe, in nightmarish detail, how the beast wrapped its tentacles around the ship's prow and wrenched it in two. Most of the crew had been cast into the churning waters. They were lost, right there and then, but not my uncle. He grabbed pen and paper, and climbed to the crow's nest. That's where he penned his last words, and affixed them to a carrier pigeon in the hopes that I might know what he had to tell me..." A faint mist clouded the Professor's eyes, and he stood in silence for a moment.

"What did he say? If you don't mind me asking."

Professor Thistlequick smiled. "Never ever give up! Should adversity rear its ugly head, reach out and punch it on the nose. Uncle Claudius always had a flair for the dramatic and not even a giant squid could dampen his theatricality. But you don't need to bide by his words,

149

because you already know this. You never gave up on your friends, despite the insurmountable odds facing you, and neither will I," Professor Thistlequick vowed. He strode from the fire, and vanished behind the tower of books. "Come Jake. Follow me. I've a theory to put to the test, and I need your help."

Jake pulled his coat tight as they walked out into the back garden. They crossed a small patch of grass bordered with withered flowers, an apple tree and a large wooden shed. Something rested in the center of the grass, covered by a thick white sheet. "What's that?"

Professor Thistlequick pulled the sheet back with a flourish, revealing a huge brass telescope. He angled and adjusted it, before motioning for Jake to come closer. "You said you saw the craft hover over St. Paul's Cathedral, before shooting up into the sky." Professor Thistlequick took a map from his pocket and repositioned the telescope. "It's curious, because several dead bodies were found on the dome, just the other week. Smashed to a pulp." The Professor shivered. "I wonder if the two events are connected."

"I haven't got a clue," Jake said.

"Neither do I, but it's worth considering. And I wonder why the craft flew into the sky when HMS Watcher was in such close proximity? A strange decision, don't you think? Because if I were kidnapping people and consorting with demons, I'd stay low and fly as far away from the crime scene as possible. There must be a reason they made what appears to be such an illogical decision." He moved the telescope and adjusted a series of dials. "Now, look through this telescope. It's pointed towards the sky above the cathedral. Tell me if you see anything."

Jake squinted through the lens. "Clouds, clouds and more

clouds. But you don't need me to tell you that. You can see them for yourself."

"Perhaps. But I'm not certain I see everything you see."

"What do you mean?" Jake asked, as the Professor delved into his coat.

"Describe this to me." Professor Thistlequick produced a shiny blue-white egg from his pocket.

"It's a glowing egg."

"Interesting. Were I to ask most anyone else, they'd probably describe a delicately painted wooden egg. It's pretty for sure, but it holds no shine. And yet I'm reliably informed it once belonged to an ancient sorcerer."

"Really?"

"Really. Who knows what purpose it once held, but I suspect most of its magick is spent by now. I only purchased it because I liked its colors. But your description seems to prove my theory."

"Which is?"

"That you can see magick, Jake," Professor Thistlequick grinned. "Just like the Inspectors and spotters aboard HMS Watcher."

"If they're so good at spotting things, how comes they haven't spotted that giant brass flying fish? Its probably sailed all over the city by now."

The Professor's hand covered the egg. "Because something's blocking it, rendering it invisible to the authorities and general population. But the fact you saw it suggests your ability to see magick is infinitely more powerful than theirs."

"Powerful? I don't know about that. I just see weird colors. I started seeing them a few months back, but a lot more over the last few weeks. They don't last long. It's like when you peer up at the sun, and look away. And then you get those little squiggles over your eyes."

"How I wish I could see it for myself." The Professor gave the wooden egg a wistful look. "I've always wanted to see what magick looks like."

"I'd have thought a toff like you wouldn't want anything to do with magick, what with it being against the law."

Professor Thistlequick rolled his eyes. "It often feels like everything's illegal unless it's controlled and supplied by the hands of the few. Water, electricity, and no doubt the very air if they can manage it. But they can't halt and control every instance of magick, just as they can't tame the wind. Yet." He smiled. "I mean the powers that be can't even *see* magick without using its powers, which makes them the worst of hypocrites. But you can. You're a natural, Jake. Look through the telescope again, use your other eye this time."

Despite his misgivings, Jake did as the Professor asked.

"What do you see?"

"Nothing."

"Hmm." The Professor pulled a series of levels and turned a dial. "And now?"

"Okay, now I see something."

"What?"

"The same blue light I saw around that egg. It's faint, but it's definitely there. It's sparkling around that huge cloud."

"Point the telescope directly at it!"

Jake did as he asked and stood back as the Professor scribbled the settings in his notebook. He pulled a compass from his pocket and added further notes. "What are you writing?" Jake asked.

"Coordinates!"

"What are they?"

"A means for us to find that cloud."

"You can already see it. And you better make a sketch if you're that interested in it, because it won't be there for long," Jake said. "It's a cloud."

"I don't believe that's necessarily the case." The Professor checked the notes and gazed back to the sky. "Well, now we know exactly where to find it!"

"But we already know where it is!"

"Yes, but everything will appear quite different by the time we get up there."

"Up where?"

The Professor pointed to the sky. "Up there."

CHAPTER THIRTY

"What do you mean, up there?" Jake gazed at the sky. "Are you hiding an airship in your shed?"

"Clearly you believe I'm a man of far more means than I actually am. No, sadly there's no airship in my shed. But there is something I've been working on that may well serve to get us into the sky to continue our investigation."

"What?"

"A Penny Farthing." A gleam shone in the Professor's eyes as he led Jake to the shed. "And it truly is a mechanical wonder." He whistled cheerfully as he rattled his keys and unlocked four different padlocks.

"I must be hearing things, 'cause for a moment I thought you said we're going to use a bicycle to get into the sky."

"We are indeed!" The Professor vanished into the shed and a series of clatters and thumps came from inside. Finally, he emerged wheeling a Penny Farthing quite unlike any Jake had ever seen. Dozens of pipes and tubes ran along its frame and beneath its elongated seat rested a partially encased clockwork engine. The pedals were still recognizable but the handlebars were so loaded with levers and buttons that there was barely enough space left for steering. But by far the oddest modification was the pair of immense black leathery wings tucked back against its sides that made the contraption appear as if it had been swallowed by a gigantic bat. "What is it?" Jake asked.

"A flying bicycle, of course. I've been working on her for months. She was inspired by a very peculiar dream I had." Professor Thistlequick patted the bicycle's frame. "My hopes are that she'll become the first flying machine of her kind."

"And have you ever flown it?" Jake swallowed as he glanced up at the clouds.

"Yes. Over Primrose Hill just last week. We sailed over the Tower of London. It's truly stunning when viewed from above."

"We?"

"Happiness and I."

"You flew on that thing with your cat?"

"Oh yes. We went fairly high, although nowhere near as high as we're going to go today." Professor Thistlequick ducked back into his shed and emerged with a jar. He unscrewed the lid and removed a dollop of sticky black goo with a spoon. A revolting stench filled the air, even worse than Silas Grumble's bouts of indigestion.

"What's that?" Jake retched.

"Adhesive. It's for the stay-still-sticky-saddle." Professor Thistlequick glanced at Jake. "So I don't slide off... safety first... it's a long way down, you know!" Then he looked back at the spoon "Oh! Don't worry, the agent turns clear within a few moments of being exposed to the air. It won't stain your clothes."

"I don't care about that; my clothes are already beyond fixing. It stinks! What's it made of, cat vomit and pitch?"

"No, it's a mixture of seaweed, pine sap and... uh... spittle. But don't worry, it's not human spit."

"That's set me at ease," Jake said, barely hiding his sarcasm.

"Good." Professor Thistlequick screwed the jar shut, then tightened a few nuts and bolts. As he worked, he explained how he'd built the bicycle. Jake suppressed a yawn. "I don't understand half of what you're telling me. But what I think you're trying to say is you think this thing's safe enough to get us up to the clouds."

"I'd stake my life on it."

"You're staking both our lives on it." Jake glanced at the bicycle and shrugged. "But I don't suppose I have any other choice."

"Your enthusiasm's a tonic!" Professor Thistlequick winked. "Now, the air's going to be thinner up there so we'll need a means to breathe."

"That sounds like a good idea."

"Wait here, Jake, I'll be right back."

Professor Thistlequick fetched a wooden box from the shed and strapped it to Jake's back. The tubes at the bottom of the box dangled like copper snakes.

"Why's it so heavy?" Jake asked. "And how's it going to help me breathe?"

"It will pump air into your helmet."

"What helmet?"

The Professor ducked back into the shed and returned with a large brass diver's helmet. "This helmet."

Jake gazed at his reflection in the glass faceplate. He'd seen something similar last year when the police had dredged the Thames following a spate of riverside murders.

"Hold still." Professor Thistlequick placed the helmet over Jake's head and secured it with a rubber brace. It fit perfectly.

"Thankfully, I have a spare." The Professor's words were muffled through the thick glass. "They belonged to my uncle. It's funny; they're intended for exploring the sea, yet we'll be using them to explore the clouds. Although when you think about it, the sky often seems as vast and blue as the ocean. Now, all aboard." Professor Thistlequick pulled a step out from the side of the bicycle's frame. Jake climbed up onto the back of the seat.

The Professor pulled a latch on the side of the helmet, and the glass faceplate popped open, bringing a rush of cool air. Then he secured his own helmet, and climbed onto the saddle. Jake was about to ask how exactly they were going to get into the sky, when Mrs. Harker appeared.

"Off again, Professor?" A bemused look passed across her maudlin face as she glanced at the Penny Farthing. "Are you sure that thing is safe?"

"Fairly," Professor Thistlequick said. "But should we fail to return alive, please take care of Happiness. I've put money aside for her upkeep, as well as the rent. There should be enough to keep her in sardines for the rest of her life."

"As you wish, Professor." Mrs. Harker shivered as she made her way back to the house.

"What do you mean *should we fail to return alive?*" Jake tried to jump down from the saddle, but he was stuck firm.

"It was a joke. Of sorts. Now, hold on!" The bicycle wobbled as Professor Thistlequick unlatched a gate and pedaled out into the alley.

"I thought we were supposed to be flying!" Jake's words echoed inside the diver's helmet.

"We are, but taking flight is complex. First we need

somewhere to take off from. A place that will allow us to build up enough speed. I have a location in mind, but we'll need to get permission."

"Great. So we're going to parade ourselves across London first, are we?"

"What was that?" Professor Thistlequick called.

"Nothing. Just watch where you're going!" Jake called and scrunched down in his helmet, as the Penny Farthing shot from the alley and out into the street.

CHAPTER THIRTY-ONE

Heavy dark clouds filled the afternoon sky as the Professor pedaled down a street leading to the Embankment. Jake's cheeks still blazed with embarrassment from the crowds who had gawped their way as they'd passed through Trafalgar Square. It had felt like the whole world was laughing, jeering and shouting at them and he'd been glad for the steamed-up helmet hiding his face.

Professor Thistlequick cycled furiously, weaving in and out of the people walking along the narrow street. Then, he careered over the pavement, crossed the road and cut through a bushy gap leading into a park. With the flick of a lever they skidded to a stop before a tall, crooked building.

The Professor wobbled himself loose and climbed down. He removed the helmet from Jake's head, and took off his own.

"I can finally breathe," Jake said. "Now that you've taken off the helmet that was supposed to help me... breathe."

"You'll be thankful for it soon enough. Now, wobble to and fro and hop down. Yes, that's it."

Jake glanced at the building looming before them and the doorman standing before the set of tall arched doors. "What is this place?"

"Nanny Sompting's Tea Rooms."

"But we had tea just before we left."

"Tea's what makes our country function, Jake. You'd rue the day if we were to ever run out. Indeed the whole of our sceptered islands would grind to a crushing halt. Still, we're not here to imbibe, which is a shame because they serve a marvelous Earl Grey, and the Victoria sponge cake is exquisite. No, our business isn't with a tea pot; it's with a dear old friend. One who holds the key to getting our bicycle up into the air."

"Does he work here?" Jake asked, as they made their way to the building.

"No, but you can set your watch by the time she takes her afternoon tea!"

"Ouch!" Jake cried, as a barrage of hailstones suddenly fell like a torrent of hard white pebbles and spattered off the building's olive-green awning.

The doorman raised an eyebrow. "Good afternoon, Professor Thistlequick."

"Good afternoon, Giles. Would you be so kind as to watch over my bicycle."

"I would." Giles handed Jake and the Professor an umbrella from a stand beside the door. "Are you here to see Beatrix?"

"I am."

"Very good. Please, go inside before you catch your deaths in this icy monsoon."

Professor Thistlequick opened the umbrella, handed the doorman a tip and guided Jake through a set of gilded doors.

The room beyond was immense and a great sky-blue

mural spanned the walls. The image revealed sunbeams glistening on puffy white clouds while cherubs sipped from delicate china cups and sat on mounds of cushions shaped like sponge cakes.

A tall ancient oak tree stood in the center of the room. Its trunk rose up through a hole in the sloped glass ceiling and its curved branches arched out, over the roof top. Hail fell through gaps and cracks in the glass, bouncing off the sea of umbrellas set in stands below.

People sat around tables eating slices of cake and sipping from cups, with their pale little fingers held in the air. If they noticed the weather they paid it no mind as a low buzz of conversation competed with the crackle of hail.

"This way." Professor Thistlequick led Jake to a table on the far side of the hall. They approached a lady in a heavy tweed suit and her round glasses flashed as she looked up, her face wrinkling from below a thatch of white hair. "Afternoon, Professor." Her voice was low and deep, but held a hint of warmth.

"Good afternoon Beatrix. May I introduce my young friend, Jake Shillingsworth."

The lady gave Jake a curt nod. "Any friend of our clockwork magician is a friend of mine." She gazed back to the Professor. "So how can I help you, Aubrey?"

It took Jake a moment to realize she was talking to the Professor. *Aubrey!*

"I have a favor to ask, Bea. Do you think we might borrow the clock tower for a while? It shouldn't take more than an hour or so."

Beatrix glanced around before giving a slight nod. "Meet me there at four o'clock. Just try not to draw attention to yourself, as impossible as that probably is."

"Righto. Until four then." Professor Thistlequick steered Jake from the tea rooms.

"What was that all about?" Jake asked over the patter of hailstones.

"Elevation. We've just secured the best place in the whole of London to start our sky-bound adventures."

CHAPTER THIRTY-TWO

Jake shivered as an icy breeze swept along the Embankment, bringing a heavy scent of coal. Barges and fishing boats clogged the Thames, their smoke and steam writhing over the steel-grey waters like ghostly mist.

Big Ben loomed above the Gothic towers as they cycled towards the House of Lords, and the countless windows in the Palace of Westminster's ornate facade glittered in the yellow and red sunset.

"So what do we need to do now?" Jake's voice was muffled yet loud in the diver's helmet.

"Prepare for takeoff." Professor Thistlequick answered. "And from there we'll either soar into the sky or be dashed to our deaths on the cold hard ground." A muffled sound followed that may have been laughter.

If it was an attempt at humor, Jake thought it a poor one. He looked at the wings tucked away along the sides of the bicycle. Could they really hold them up in the sky?

He had no doubt the Professor was clever, but he was also

like a child, his rooms littered with half-finished projects and abandoned ideas. Was the Penny Farthing another of them? "I don't see anywhere to take off from," Jake said. "There's no hills round here and..."

"You don't see anything that might serve as a launching point?"

Jake glanced up as Big Ben struck four o' clock. Surely not... "You don't mean the clock tower, do you? Are you off your chump?"

"It's stunning isn't it? One of the highest points in London. Just wait till you see the view!"

Jake's stomach dropped as he spotted the boards and ladders jutting out from the side of the clock tower. Beads of sweat broke across his brow and he considered wrenching off the diver's helmet and leaping from the speeding bicycle. It was madness!

The Professor turned in his seat, as if reading Jake's thoughts, and grinned.

Jake sighed and held on tight. The Professor was deranged, totally insane. But... but at least he wanted to help. Maybe, he knew what he was doing. After all, he'd managed to get through life up until this point without killing himself. And besides, who else was there?

They cycled past the great statue of Boudicca in her chariot, careened across the road toward the Palace of Westminster and stopped at the gated wall that surrounded Big Ben. The Professor dismounted and helped Jake climb down. "I hope you're feeling fit," Professor Thistlequick said. "It's going to be a long climb." He swung the gate open and led Jake into a small, formal garden.

"And where do you think you're going?" A Policeman

appeared. He looked the Professor up and down, his brow furrowing as he glanced from Jake to the Penny Farthing.

"We're-" The Professor began.

"It's okay officer, they're here to see me." Beatrix rushed over as a small wooden door slammed shut at the base of the clock tower. She ushered Jake and the Professor back to the doorway. "So much for not drawing attention to yourselves," she muttered, gazing at the Penny Farthing. "You can leave that boneshaker out here."

"Actually," the Professor patted the handlebar, "we need to bring it with us. I'm hoping to cycle off the tower. By my calculations, the height should allow us to get enough speed and lift for a take-off."

Beatrix shook her head. "Are you jesting?"

Professor Thistlequick gave a toothy grin. "Not at all. The other day I observed the repairs being made above the clock. The scaffolding and planks stretching over the south side arch caught my attention, and that's when I first had my notion. You see, Primrose Hill was fine for a low flight over the city, but we'll need far more momentum for what I'm planning. Let me assure you, Bea, this isn't some hare-brained whim. This is serious business."

"Have you really thought this through, Aubrey?"

"Oh yes. I've done the calculations. That height is exactly what's required to get the lift that the Penny Farthing's wings will need for the ascent. And once the engine kicks in, we'll be well on our way."

"Well I hope your idea holds up." Beatrix's tone was doubtful. "For both your sakes. Though I've seldom known you to be wrong, Professor, at least in theory." She opened the stout wooden door and glanced over toward the Policeman. Thankfully, his back was turned. "My brain must be as pickled as yours. Come on." Beatrix nodded for them to enter the tower.

"Don't worry, Bea. It's not as if there's a law against cycling off Big Ben, is there?" Professor Thistlequick smiled.

"Not yet," Beatrix replied. "But that might well change within the next hour or so."

"They'll never know we were here. We'll be as quiet as mice." Professor Thistlequick said. "So no screaming, Jake. No matter how tempting it gets."

They wheeled the Penny Farthing through the doorway toward a narrow space at the foot of a staircase. Beatrix locked the door behind them. "Well, you better start climbing, gentlemen. I don't want to be here all night! Hand me those diving helmets, unless you'd rather wear them and drown in your own sweat."

Jake gawped when he looked up at the tall winding staircase. "How many steps are there?"

"Only three hundred and thirty four," Beatrix said. "But by the time you reach the top with that old boneshaker, it'll probably feel more like three thousand and thirty four".

"DID you imagine you'd ever see anything like this, Jake?" the Professor asked as the staircase wound past the four giant clock faces. The intricate stained glass glowed around Jake like a huge harvest moon, and the black silhouettes of the hands seemed as large as lampposts.

The Professor stopped and wiped his forehead with his handkerchief. "You'll have quite a tale to tell your friends when we find them."

"If I'm alive to tell it."

They continued to climb until they came to an arched opening where London's dusky panorama stretched before them through the plumes of smoke coiling into the late December afternoon.

"Now," Professor Thistlequick said, "we need a ramp to extend the surface when we cycle down the scaffolding. I don't suppose there's any tables up here, Bea?"

"There's some planks of wood in the maintenance room, and a few more boards." Beatrix gave the Professor a grim look as she caught her breath. "Are you certain about this?"

"I am," Professor Thistlequick said. "It's our best chance. Indeed it's our only chance. Now, would you be so good as to show me where I can find the maintenance room?"

Jake held the Penny Farthing and gazed down from the clock tower as Bea and the Professor vanished through a door. The large clouds looming above the dark buildings across the Thames seemed so high and impossibly distant.

I can't do this. Jake glanced at the stairs. *I could probably be halfway down them before the Professor even notices.* But then what? Return to The Tattered Crow? Scrub tables and be Grumble's whipping boy for the rest of his life? And what about Nancy and Adam?

An icy breeze blew through the archway and as Jake appraised the Penny Farthing, the machine suddenly seemed like something only a madman could invent. Certainly not something that stood a chance of reaching the clouds. But even if they did make it, would Nancy and Adam be there? And what about Kedgewick and that demon? Or the man who'd shot him?

H'exactly! Silas Grumble's voice whispered in Jake's ear. *Return to the Crow. Race away from this madness. Run, that's what you do, because you're not worth spit, boy, and you'll never h'amount to nothing."*

"Maybe not," Jake whispered. He clenched his fists. "But that won't stop me trying."

~

As HE WATCHED the Professor making a final check on the Penny Farthing's engine, panic fluttered through Jake's chest like a cloud of butterflies. He refused to feed it.

"Are you ready, Jake?" Professor Thistlequick asked as he steadied the Penny Farthing on the wooden ramp they'd laid before the window. "You look a little pale. Hardly surprising, I suppose, given you've never flown before. But I can assure you, it really is the most marvelous sensation."

"I'm fine."

Jake stared at the wall as the Professor secured the diving helmet to his head and attached the tubes to the box on Jake's back. "When you need oxygen, adjust this lever on the side of the helmet."

Jake nodded, causing the helmet to sway.

"Right." Professor Thistlequick climbed onto the saddle. Beatrix gripped the blocks securing the front wheel in place, shook her head and muttered something to herself.

Professor Thistlequick reached down and helped Jake up onto the saddle behind him. "This will work perfectly, Jake, I'm certain of it. But mistakes can happen, so before we set off, I need to know you're absolutely certain you want to go through with it."

"Let's just go if we're going."

"Right you are. Beatrix, remove the blocks if you will." Professor Thistlequick flipped a series of levers on the handlebar. The engine thrummed with life and the whole bicycle shook as its gears and cogs spun, producing a great cloud of steam.

"Wait. I-" Jake's words were snatched away as the Professor pushed down hard on the pedals and his scream caught in his throat as the Penny Farthing lurched through the open window and down a tiny slope, its wheels shuddering.

The end of the boards sped closer and closer, and then they shot over the edge.

For the briefest moment, it felt like they were hanging in the air.

Jake's heart thudded hard as he gazed down toward the distant streets of London.

And then they fell.

CHAPTER THIRTY-THREE

The ground rushed toward them in a hard, stony blur.

Jake's cries were lost in the shrieking air. The Professor seemed oblivious as he leaned over the handlebar and pulled a lever, his movements slow and deliberate. Like he had all the time in the world...

Jake could just make out the Professor's manic laugher echoing in his diver's helmet. "Do something!" he cried. It felt like his heart was about to burst.

Professor Thistlequick grasped a handle and tugged.

Whoosh!

The great leathery wings unfurled, causing the entire bicycle to shudder. The cobbled street rushed toward them and then they swept up, with inches to spare.

They soared into the air, passing the surrounding buildings, and ascending into the crimson and golden sunset painting the early evening sky. Far below, thick black smoke puffed from the stacks of barges and fishing boats sailing under Westminster Bridge. Jake could just make out the skiffs and dinghies following in the barges' wake, bobbing around in an endless stream of traffic.

The Penny Farthing flew higher, and Jake stared in wonder as a formation of geese flew towards them, the *wumph* of their wings impossibly loud.

"Marvelous, eh!" Professor Thistlequick grinned at Jake through the foggy glass "We're going to climb higher now, hang on!" He squeezed the handle and pushed a lever forward.

Jake held on tight as the bicycle hissed and released a huge cloud of steam. A large gear shifted into position and the wings rose high over Jake's head. When they reached their peak they thrust back down and the Penny Farthing began to climb.

With each flap the great wings took them higher and higher and soon the boats on the Thames were little more than specks, and the river a long, coiled silver-grey snake. In the distance, HMS Watcher seemed like a toy as it prowled over St. Paul's, and the Cathedral's immense white dome an upended tea cup amongst the sprawl of dark rooftops.

The wind whipped them to and fro, but the Professor pulled another lever and slowly the bicycle steadied. "All we need to do is find a decent air current and-" The Penny Farthing shot forward, as if led by a team of invisible horses. "Ah, there we go!"

They rose higher and now the city looked like a jam stain upon a vast green checkered tablecloth.

The Professor threw back his head and roared with laughter. "It worked! It's marvelous!" He pointed ahead. "Look, over there."

A vast gray and blue expanse stretched out far to the South. "Is that-"

"Yes! The sea," Professor Thistlequick replied. "Or the English Channel, to be more precise."

Jake stared in disbelief. He'd always wanted to see it with his own eyes and often daydreamed of sneaking onto a train with Nancy, and going down to Brighton. Dreamed of the pair of them strolling on the famous pier as the waves glinted in the twinkling sunshine.

"We'll be rising above the clouds soon," Professor Thistlequick shouted. "The air's already gotten thinner. Make sure you turn this." He pointed to a small lever on the side of his diving helmet. "And breathe deeply. I'm going to circle around until we locate our destination" He leaned over and checked a gauge, before nodding. "We should be able to sustain flight for at least another hour or so."

The wings slowed and they wheeled around back toward London. The temperature fell as the sun vanished below the horizon and the undersides of the clouds glowed with one final burst of purple and orange light.

The Professor pulled a handle and the Penny Farthing slowed further. He removed a journal from his pocket and squinted as the pages flapped in the wind. "That strange cloud you spotted should be about here..." He glanced around. "Can you see anything?"

"Nothing."

"In that case we should go higher in case its been obscured by the others. Hopefully we'll spot it from above."

They swept up into the clouds and it felt like being enveloped by a thick soft, wet fog. Jake snatched at it and his hand came away soaking wet and freezing cold. Everything was silent, except for the whir of clockwork, the sputter of the engine, and the slow beat of the wings. Jake realized he'd never felt such peace before. He felt free, profoundly happy and calm. A solitary tear blurred his eye. He let it fall.

When they broke through the cloud, they emerged beneath a canopy of stars that twinkled snowy-white upon the night sky. The moon hung brilliant and full, casting a silvery gleam upon the carpet of clouds. Jake narrowed his eyes against its glare. It seemed almost as bright as a midday sun. "It's beautiful!" he cried.

The Professor nodded. "Indeed! I've never... oh!" He pointed ahead. "Look!"

Jake followed his finger.

Lightning flashed in the distance. Jake waited for the sound of thunder, but none came. As the flash came again, Jake realized it wasn't lightning.

It was a beacon.

CHAPTER THIRTY-FOUR

J ake watched as the light flashed and vanished again.

"It's a pattern," Professor Thistlequick said. "It flashes every four point two seconds. So either someone has immaculate timing, or it's automated. I wonder what its purpose is?"

"We should go back to London," Jake said. The beacon unnerved him and the sense of wonder he'd felt as they'd first cycled through the clouds was gone. He shivered as an icy blast of wind rattled the Penny Farthing and the engine sputtered and spat. How long would it hold out for?

"I find it best to aim forwards in life, rather than backwards," Professor Thistlequick called. "So onwards!" He released a lever and the bicycle produced another burst of steam before thrusting down and soaring towards the light. "It's the most delightful conundrum, eh! A mysterious light in the dark... and coming from a cloud no less! But why? What's its purpose?"

Jake felt sick. Somewhere far below was London, and he felt a terrible craving to be back there tramping its streets in his ragged shoes. Better that than messing around in a place intended for birds, and stars. Not people.

The light flashed again, close and bright above a misty swirl of cloud. Jake grabbed the seat as a dark looming shape appeared before them. It was a giant stone tower and they were heading right for it!

"What the blazes!" Professor Thistlequick twisted the handlebar and grabbed a lever. The Penny Farthing tilted and turned, sweeping past the tower with a groaning squeak as the tip of a wing scraped the stone.

Jake looked back. Below the tower was a huge building, and all of its upper windows were dark, except one. Were Nancy and Adam trapped inside? Was this strange place on the cloud where they'd been taken?

The bicycle shook as they wheeled back, dipping back down into the cloud.

Thud!

"Ow!" Jake cried. They'd struck something solid and as the shudder ran through the bicycle's frame, he suddenly understood why it was called a bone shaker. They continued to jitter and bump along the cloud until finally the Professor braked hard and brought them to a halt.

"This is all quite impossible of course!" Professor Thistlequick flipped a switch and the clockwork engine began to slow. The wings hissed and vanished in a burst of steam as they tucked themselves away. "And yet, here we are." He wobbled from the saddle and leaped down. The lighthouse flashed once more, illuminating his manic grin. "How splendid!" He clapped his hands. "Come, Jake. Step out upon the cloud with me!"

Jake shook his head and gripped the saddle. "This isn't right. Get back on the bicycle!"

"It's neither right nor wrong. It is what it is. Trust me, the ground, if you can describe it as such, is perfectly firm." Professor Thistlequick glanced up at the building. "Now, we should give that place a closer look." He rummaged through his saddlebag and produced a lantern. Its soft yellow light illuminated the rising tendrils of cloud.

"Have you got a gun?"

Professor Thistlequick gave Jake a puzzled look. "No. Why would I?"

"Don't you remember when I told you about the demon and the giant in the brass armor, and that weird old cove who shot me?"

"Yes, but… I don't own weapons, Jake. I'm a creator, not a destroyer."

"That's all very admirable, but what are we going to do if they attack us?"

Professor Thistlequick gave a rueful smile. "To be honest, I hadn't thought that far ahead. But something will spring to mind, it usually does." He rapped his knuckles upon the cloud causing a dull clang to ring out below them. "This cloud, for want of a better word, is partially hollow. Although why, I have no idea. Interesting. Now come, let's investigate that curious building."

Jake fought the urge to curse as he wobbled from the saddle, landed with a deep thud, and gazed down at the cloud below his feet.

"Wonderful, isn't it?" Professor Thistlequick gave him another lopsided grin. "Take a closer look."

Jake reached down through the swirls of vapor. The surface felt like cold, smooth glass, and there through the mist he could see a faint nimbus of blue light. Magick. "What is this thing?"

"I don't know. Yet. But whatever it is, it's ingenious! Someone made it!"

"Why?"

"That's what we need to find out." Professor Thistlequick stroked his beard as he began to stroll toward the tower.

Jake glanced back at the cloud. He could just about see through it, as if it was made of ice. The city lights twinkled dimly below. London. His home, for better or worse. From this distance he could just about grasp the city's sheer vastness and it made him feel smaller than ever. Insignificant, his life in the streets of St. Giles a sliver of straw in a haystack.

"Jake?" The Professor's voice was ghostly as it came upon the breeze. Jake pulled his coat tight and strode across the cloud, the moon shining down like a great cosmic lamp as he headed for the dark, ominous building.

CHAPTER THIRTY-FIVE

Such was Jake's disorientation, that he barely heard the Professor as they walked across the cloud and he had to force himself to pay him attention.

"...which of course means," the Professor continued, "that the cloud almost certainly contains a compound of Heliumosis Aether. Which is most exciting, to say the least! I mean it's purely a theory, and a mad one, because of course it should be fundamentally impossible. And yet here we are!" The Professor chuckled and slapped Jake on the back. "But the real question we must ask is how on earth this artificial cloud maintains stability at such an altitude. And-"

He shrieked and vanished from sight.

Jake dropped to his knees before the gaping dark hole stretched before him. "Professor!" He peered over the chasm half expecting to find the Professor falling through the sky, but then he spotted his gloved fingers clinging to the edge of the hole.

"Umph!" Professor Thistlequick's face was pale through

the diving helmet's steamed-up glass. "I don't like to create melodrama, Jake. But my fingers are slipping."

"Hang on!" Jake reached down and they grasped each other's wrists.

"That would be entirely sensible given the circumstances! I'm trying not to panic, Jake. Panic's counterproductive in most situations, including hanging off fake clouds. But could you hurry?"

"I'm trying, help me!" Jake gritted his teeth and pulled.

Thankfully, Professor Thistlequick was not much heavier than the barrels of beer Grumble made Jake haul up from the cellar. He wrenched him up as high as he could until the Professor got his elbow over the edge and hoisted a foot onto the cloud. Then, he writhed up through the hole and rolled onto his back, his breath labored as he sprawled out.

"I thought you were a goner." Jake nursed his aching shoulders.

"Thank heavens you were with me. You saved my life!"

"I have my uses. Including saving posh old sods from falling through clouds and..." Jake's words faded as he spotted the figure rearing up behind the Professor and the flapping wings stretching from its back.

"What is it, Jake?" Professor Thistlequick asked.

"There's an angel behind you. An angel carrying a bloody huge gun!" Jake scrambled back as the light from the building passed over them and the winged figure became a dark blur.

"Angels don't carry guns," Professor Thistlequick said. And then he followed Jake's gaze. "Except for this one." He flinched as the barrel of the rifle clanked against the base of his diving helmet. "Would you mind pointing that somewhere else?"

Jake squinted at the bizarre figure.

It was a man with a pinched, heavily bearded face and

beady eyes. A pair of silver goggles rested on his forehead, holding back a wild fall of platinum hair that hung to his muscular shoulders. His lips drew back in a feral snarl as his long filthy white gown and wings rustled in the breeze.

"Good evening," Professor Thistlequick said, as if everything was perfectly normal.

"Are you with *them*?" the man asked. An edge of panic laced his deep, well-spoken voice.

"Perhaps." Professor Thistlequick gave Jake a slight shake of the head.

"What business do you have here?" The man's voice became an almost sing-song tone. "Who are you? And what function does this one have?" He pointed his gun at Jake.

"That's Jake," Professor Thistlequick said. "And he doesn't have a function, so to speak. Other than-"

"No function? Then what are you doing here? He didn't tell me to expect visitors!" The man gave Jake a look of distaste, before turning back to the Professor.

"Didn't he?" the Professor asked, as if he knew who the man was referring to. Jake decided to play along if it came to it. "He must have forgotten. I take it he's not here presently?" He kept his tone light and calm, but Jake saw him glance back to the Penny Farthing.

"Take off those ridiculous helmets. I can barely hear you." The man brought up his rifle again. Professor Thistlequick reached over and removed Jake's helmet, and then his own.

"There," The Professor said. "Now, where did you say he is right now?"

"I don't know. He has many refuges, and this one's clearly fallen out of favor. He was here earlier, fiddling in the engine room, and when he left he wouldn't meet my eyes. I took that to be a bad omen."

"He was here earlier you say?" Professor Thistlequick smiled. "Well it's a shame we missed him. Now, I'm sorry to say he didn't mention your name..."

"I'm the keeper of the cloud, and of the hall and the light. And you are?"

"Late," Professor Thistlequick said. "And we should be on our way."

The man grasped the Professor's wrist and yanked him to his feet. "No. You'll come with me, and you'll wait until I decide what must be done." He waved his rifle from Jake to the Professor. "Hurry."

"Alright," Professor Thistlequick said. "But may I ask if we might expect to find any more holes in this cloud?"

"No, I only made the one."

"I see. Can I ask to what purpose?"

"You may not."

Professor Thistlequick glanced at Jake. "Right you are. Then we'll be extremely careful." His eyes flitted to the Penny Farthing and he gave Jake a slight nod.

The man hastened them along toward the building, which loomed before them like a great black crypt. Jake threw his hand over his eyes as the light from the tower flashed again.

"It seems an unusual place to find a lighthouse," Professor Thistlequick said.

"It's a signal for lost souls." The man's voice held a tone of melancholy as he opened the doors. Through them was a huge hall filled with warm, bright lights. "Lost souls like you two, for what else can you be?" the man asked. "Now, go inside." A nasty gleam flashed in his eyes as he glanced at Jake and added, "You and your odious servant."

CHAPTER THIRTY-SIX

The man's gaze remained fixed on Jake, his eyes vicious and cruel. "Do not look at your betters, boy. Servants should know their place."

"Servant?" Professor Thistlequick looked baffled. "Oh, you mean Jake? He's not my servant, he's my companion."

The man's face darkened. "I already suspected the very fabric of society was coming apart, which was why I chose to help with the creation of this place. I shudder to think how debauched the world below has become by now." He glanced at Jake. "Magick plays around you like a cloud. What are you? A lesser demon?"

"I'm not a demon," Jake blurted.

"No, he is not," Professor Thistlequick chimed in.

"That's exactly what a demon and its bedazzled servant would say." The man shook his head. "What is the city coming to? Where will it end? In chaos, ash and dust. Unless we bring about salvation."

"We?" Professor Thistlequick asked.

The man ignored him as he continued to appraise Jake. "Enter, and do not speak again unless spoken to." He raised his rifle and shoved Jake through the door into a wide bright hall.

A blazing fire in a grand hearth threw a warm orange golden glow over a long stone floor. Paintings covered the high, ox-blood red walls. Most of the scenes were of rural places, and pale, sour looking people. Jake looked from them to the row of polished brass pipes running beneath the ceiling, just below the crown molding. They vanished into the darkness looming above a grand staircase, and as they clanked and rasped he wondered what they carried.

"What a beautiful place." Professor Thistlequick said. He smiled but his eyes flitted to the rifle crooked in the man's arm.

"It's not mine," the man said as he slammed the door shut. "It was conceived and brought to the heavens by a man more exceptional than I could ever dream of being. It's my honor to be his agent on the few occasions he grants me the gift of serving him." As he stepped into the room the firelight revealed the wings on his back in finer detail. And then Jake saw that they weren't wings, but thick sheets of paper covered in strange blue symbols with quills at their ends, their nibs stained with dried ink.

Professor Thistlequick examined the wings closely. "Am I right in thinking those musical notations are from Mozart's Requiem in D Minor?"

The man shrugged. "Indeed. So you are educated, except for when it comes to the question of keeping better company." He sighed. "However, no matter the boy's standing, you're both passing through this place on your own roads, whether they lead to heaven or hell. I should not pass judgment; I have no divine wisdom, merely faith and a gun. But come, let us dine and then you may pay respect to the founder before proceeding along your chosen paths."

He led them to a small chamber with an oaken table at its center. Nine chairs surrounded it and all but one was covered in a thin layer of dust. A tall portrait in a gilded frame dominated the wall. It portrayed a man standing before a raging bonfire on an empty grey moor. He wore a black coat and top hat, and something about his posture made Jake glad he couldn't see the man's face. Dark storm clouds gathered in the background and a great black bird was perched upon a church spire, while the church itself was little more than a charred ruin.

"A most striking picture," Professor Thistlequick forced a lightness to his tone, but Jake heard his underlying alarm. They had to get out off the cloud, and fast. Just as soon as they found Nancy and Adam.

"That's the founder." The man waved his hand in the air, causing his wings to tremble. "This place is his inspiration."

"Who is he, if you don't mind me asking?" Professor Thistlequick asked.

The man gave him a long, hard look. "You said you knew him. You implied that he called you here. Are you a liar as well as a fool?"

Professor Thistlequick extended his hands. "Come, let's trade names rather than insults. I'm Professor Thistlequick and this is my friend Jake Shillingsworth. And you are?"

"My earthly name was Hieronymus Lear."

The Professor coughed. "A most... unusual name, Mr. Lear. What an honor it is to meet you. So tell us, how did you come to reside in such a magnificent place? And, when will we have the honor of meeting the other residents?"

"There are no others. I live alone on this cornerstone."

"Cornerstone?"

"The cornerstone of what was to be New London Above the Clouds. The foundation of a bright new future. A haven for the keenest of minds, and the purest of souls." Mr. Lear gave Jake another withering look. "A respite from filth, vermin and squalor!"

"How fascinating," Professor Thistlequick said. "I see there's a few chairs set around the table. Tell me, what happened to the others who lived here?"

"They returned to London soon after the founder left us."

"And why did your founder leave?" Professor Thistlequick asked.

"He has a most restless mind. It's a keg of gunpowder and fireworks. As remorseless as it is bright. He grew tired of this place, of its quietude and distance. After he left I had... differences of opinions with the others. So they had to leave too. And now, only I remain as a humble servant of the great lady, and a guide for the newly departed."

"The great lady..." The Professor said, like he was hoping to prompt Lear to say more, but he remained silent. "And who might the departed be?"

"The dead waiting to ascend." Mr. Lear's eyes wandered to Jake. "Or descend."

"I see," Professor Thistlequick said. "But how do you survive up here? I imagine there's enough moisture on the cloud to provide water, but food crops must be almost impossible to maintain. Does someone bring supplies?"

"I have no need for fruit or grain. Miraghus is my sustenance."

"Miraghus?"

"You'll soon learn of its wonder and miraculous taste. That is, if you still have the faculties to savor it."

"I'm not sure I follow?"

Mr. Lear smiled. "It's a simple matter really." He glanced from Professor Thistlequick to Jake. "If you're here it means you're dead. Or soon to be."

CHAPTER THIRTY-SEVEN

Cold dread passed through Jake as Lear glanced from him to the Professor.

It had been plain there was something wrong with the man from the moment they'd encountered him, but he seemed to have grown even more insane since then. Jake gazed at Lear's rifle and wondered if he'd have time to snatch it before Lear could use it.

"I hadn't realized we were dying, or dead even." Professor Thistlequick kept his tone light.

"Of course you hadn't," Lear said, as he gestured for them to follow him through the chamber. "Fear and denial are powerful forces."

"How are we going to get out of here?" Jake whispered.

"We need to wait for our moment," Professor Thistlequick replied. "It will come."

"What are you whispering about?" Lear demanded.

"We were just marveling at the decor. It's truly stunning." Professor Thistlequick pointed to the paintings, but Lear ignored him as he opened a door and gestured with his rifle for them to go through.

Jake scuttled past him into a large study filled with desks, chairs and easels. The towering bookcases lining the walls were mostly empty, their books scattered across the floor, while wooden boards covered in charts and diagrams lay collapsed in the corner.

As he scrutinized the room, Jake's thoughts returned to the people who had lived here. And again, he wondered what had happened to them. He flinched as Lear's eyes bored into his and a nasty sneer tugged at the man's lips.

"What a wonderful study!" Professor Thistlequick paused by a large terrarium, its glass fogged with condensation. "What's this, may I ask?"

Lear opened the top of the cabinet, revealing a cluster of fleshy mushrooms. Their skin was dark purple with mottled yellow spots and the caps were cone shaped, just like witch's hats. Lear broke off a piece of mushroom and held it up as if it were gold. Then he bit it, and chewed slowly and deliberately. "Sustenance. And enlightenment. A salve for the hungry of stomach and mind. A bite's worth will leave you sated for hours and by the time you return for more, you'll find the mushrooms have re-grown. Eat, Professor. I guarantee you'll find it utterly delectable." He reached into the terrarium and handed a mushroom to the Professor.

Professor Thistlequick pulled a magnifying glass from his coat pocket. "Most curious. Clearly a fungus, and yet unlike any I've ever seen."

Lear stroked the edges of his beard. "Not only did the founder create the cloud we stand upon, he also invented sustenance so we could be self sufficient. As I said, the man's a genius. Now, eat."

Professor Thistlequick held up his hand. "I'd love to, but Jake and I dined just before we arrived. Might I take a sample though? For later?"

"Eat now. Both of you." Lear said. "It will be your last supper before you retire."

"Why not then?" Professor Thistlequick broke off a sliver of mushroom and handed it to Jake, with an almost imperceptible shake of his head. He then took a piece for himself and popped it into his mouth. "Ah! It tastes exactly like Mrs. Harker's roast potatoes. How extraordinary!"

"The fungus has the ability to trigger memories of your favorite flavors." Lear's eyes narrowed as they focused on Jake. "What will you taste boy? No doubt something crass and unrefined. Drippings? Turnips? Tripe?"

Jake rolled the mushroom's soft sticky flesh between his fingers. It felt revolting and made him think of the balls of wax Silas Grumble often farmed from his ears.

"Don't play with it. Eat it!" Lear barked. Professor Thistlequick glanced quickly at Jake and lifted his tongue. The mushroom sat below it. As soon as Lear turned, he fished it out and dropped it into his pocket.

Jake took a bite and pretended to chew. He almost flinched as a remarkable flavor filled his mouth. It was the exact taste of the drinking chocolate he and Nancy had shared one distant Christmas past. His mouth watered, and the taste was so flavorful, he almost swallowed it. "Delicious! Could I have some more?"

"You may not," Lear said. "Miraghus is a meal for those with restraint, not for the gluttonous. Too much and you'll start to see-"

"My, my!" Professor Thistlequick pointed at the walls.

"Look at those birds! I've never seen plumage so... the colors! And... and those eyes... they're almost human."

"There are no birds." Lear said, with a knowing smile. Slowly, he closed the terrarium. "They're merely phantoms of your mind. The Miraghus can do that. Now enough talking, I've duties to attend to. Come, I'll escort you to a room where you'll rest and wait."

"Do the dead need rest?" Professor Thistlequick asked.

Lear jabbed his finger into the Professor's chest. "You're still corporeal, but it's only a matter of time before you fade and begin your journey to the other side. That's why you've arrived at this way station between worlds. It's merely an interval until your time is up. Everything will become clear once I've consulted with the lady."

"The lady?" Professor Thistlequick looked around. "You mentioned her before. I wonder, are we going to have the honor of-"

"You will do as you're told, and nothing more." Lear raised his rifle. "Perhaps it is I who is meant to hasten your journey. Perhaps that's why you're here."

"No!" Professor Thistlequick exclaimed. "It's not. Now, please, show us to our rooms while we wait to begin our final voyages."

"Follow me." Lear led them into a short corridor and up a flight of stairs. Darkness yawned before them, broken by the waxy yellow flicker of candelabras. They walked along a hallway until Lear hesitated before a door, before opening it and glancing inside. "Not a good idea..."

"Tell me, who else lived here?" Professor Thistlequick asked. "We're looking for a boy and girl-"

Lear slammed the door. "That room belonged to the

architect, but we won't speak of him. He passed on. Now follow me, and don't tarry."

"We've got to get out of here!" Jake whispered. The Professor gave a sharp nod but recoiled as Lear wheeled around to face them.

"Whisper whisper." Lear smiled. "You're like a pair of muttering mice."

Horror crept through Jake as he stared at the wall behind Lear. Someone had scratched words he couldn't read across it in red paint. Or blood...

"The lady knows," Professor Thistlequick whispered, as he nodded to the scrawled words. "She sees everything."

"She does." Lear stared hard at him. "Everything." He unlocked a sturdy wooden door "These quarters will suffice. There's a bed for you and a chair for the boy."

"You're too kind," Jake said.

Lear glowered at him. "What did you say?"

"He was just thanking you for your kindness," Professor Thistlequick added. "You've been most gracious, Mr. Lear. A light in the darkness. Literally."

"I was merely answering my calling. Now come." Lear pushed the door open and lit a lamp. The light threw ghostly shadows across the floral wallpaper as he led them into the room. "You'll rest here while awaiting judgment."

"Thank you." Professor Thistlequick clasped his hands together. "The room is well appointed... a dresser and bookshelf and a bed. We couldn't have asked for more." He removed his long coat and hung it on a stand as he yawned. "My my, I hadn't realized how tired I was."

Lear gave a short nod and left the room, locking the door behind him. Professor Thistlequick raised a finger to his lips as he inclined his head towards the door. Jake shuddered as he pictured Lear lurking silently outside.

"What a thoroughly pleasant chap," Professor Thistlequick said loudly, winking at Jake. "Who would have thought we'd meet such a kindly soul all the way up here?" He shook the sheet on the bed and lay down. "I trust you'll be comfortable on the chair, Jake."

"I'm sure, Professor. Our host is most gracious." Jake sat. The chair creaked and moaned. He imagined Lear's delight at his discomfort.

"I think I'll rest now." Professor Thistlequick said. "And await whatever judgment the lady deigns for us." He dowsed the lamp, plunging the room into darkness.

A few moments later, the floorboards in the hallway creaked and they heard the sound of receding footsteps.

Silence fell over the room until the Professor struck a match, his face eerie as he relit the lamp. "We'll leave," he whispered. "But not before we've searched for your friends. There's answers here Jake, I'm certain of it. Now here's my proposal. You find Lear, and keep an eye on him and I'll look for your friends, or anyone else left in this God-forsaken place. Once we've found them, or the clues I'm sure are here, we'll make our escape. What do you say?"

"Lear hates me even more than he hates you. If he sees me-"

"He'll shoot you. Agreed." Professor Thistlequick smiled. "So don't let him see you. Be the ghost he thinks you are."

Jake was about to protest, but hesitated. The plan made sense. He was lighter on his feet than the Professor, thanks, no doubt, to a lifetime of sneaking around The Tattered Crow trying to avoid Grumble's black moods. "I'll do it. But if he kills me, you'll have my blood on your hands."

"Only until I find soap and water." Professor Thistlequick slid off the bed and pulled his coat on. His brow furrowed as he delved into his pockets, and then he grinned. "Aha!" He produced a thin, pointed device and fed it into the door's keyhole. After a moment of fiddling there was a faint click. "Who needs keys, eh?"

"You know how to pick locks?" Jake whispered. While lock picking wasn't an uncommon skill in his world, he'd never expected someone like the Professor to know about such things.

"I'm forever locking myself out of the house," Professor Thistlequick said. "And Mrs. Harker isn't overly fond of taking the stairs." He opened the door and peered outside. "All clear. Now remember, we need to creep like cats in extra creepy slippers. Find Lear, but don't let him find you."

"And what if he does?"

"Run. As fast as you can."

"Where? We're stuck on a bloody cloud!"

"True," Professor Thistlequick conceded. "So you better make sure he doesn't see you. Now, I'll lock the door in case he returns. If you need to get back inside can you…"

"Yes," Jake felt his face redden with irritation. "I know how to pick a lock. Not that I've got any means of doing it."

Professor Thistlequick handed him the pick. "Take this." He gave Jake a serious look. "Did you see how much Miraghus Lear stuffed into his pocket? I'm certain it's the mushroom that's sent him completely cuckoo. It only took one bite to addle my head and I didn't even swallow it. I believe it has made Lear's mind a simmering pot of water, which is about to boil over. And we need to be as far away from here as possible when it does." Professor Thistlequick pulled a pocket watch from his waistcoat. "Do you have a watch?"

Jake nodded.

"Good. Then meet me back here in thirty minutes. Yes?"

"Fine. I'll go and find the lunatic, and you go and enjoy yourself exploring."

"Good man." Professor Thistlequick gave Jake one last grin, before turning and padding to the end of the corridor. He waved one final time, and then he was gone.

Jake turned and tip-toed down the hall towards the candelabra's flickering light and the thick, shifting, unquiet shadows.

CHAPTER THIRTY-EIGHT

The end of the hallway was lost to gloom.

Jake paused and listened for any sign of Lear. The very thought of the man filled him dread, but he kept going. And then a muffled voice came from the corridor ahead and a door opened, spilling golden light out into the hall.

Lear's silhouette stretched across the hall and onto the wall and ceiling, his wings even more sinister in shadow form.

"But I had to be certain of their intentions." Lear's voice was high and agitated as he moved from the light, taking his shadow with him. Jake strained to hear who he was talking to.

A din of machinery rang out and the floor began to shake with such force that Jake lost his balance and slammed into the wall.

"The end is almost upon us. At last!" Lear cried out. "Thank you lady, thank you!"

The noise subsided into a low heavy thrum as Jake crept across the shaking floor, his heart matching the droning beat that seemed to issue from the very cloud itself.

~

"Ah." Professor Thistlequick said. "This door's the only one they've bothered to lock, which should mean there's something good behind it." He reached for his pick, but then recalled he'd already given it to Jake. "Fiddlesticks! What else can I use?"

A cursory rummage through his pockets revealed a stale cheese and cress sandwich, and below it, a pouch of emerald green marbles and an extendable magnifying glass. He delved further until he found the comb his father had given him for his seventh birthday.

Professor Thistlequick glanced heavenwards and gave a silent apology as he snapped one of the longer tines off. Next, he pulled a pencil from his waistcoat pocket and pressed the tine into the unsharpened end.

As he slid the makeshift pick into the lock, he closed his eyes and concentrated. It didn't take long to analyze the mechanism. "Here we are." Professor Thistlequick twisted the tine. The lock clicked.

He glanced down the hall to make sure he was alone, before plucking a candle from a sconce in the hall and slipping into the room. The Professor lit a kerosene lamp by the door and stepped further inside, his shoes sinking into the deep, plush carpet.

A large ebony desk sat in a commanding position on the far side of the room, with an ornate oil painting on the wall behind it. It was a portrait of the same man from the painting downstairs, his head turned away once more, a crow perched on his shoulder. The city of London burned in the background as the man looked on.

Professor Thistlequick narrowed his eyes as he detected a

pattern within the blazing inferno; a dim outline of a huge fiery red and black phoenix.

"Curious. The great fire was in 1666, yet this man's wearing modern attire..." The Professor was about to examine the signature at the bottom of the painting, when the room shook.

"An earthquake? But we're in the sky... a cloud quake? Are such things possible?" Books tumbled from the cases and scattered across the floor. "Not good," Professor Thistlequick muttered as he grasped the edge of the desk, and prayed to whoever the goddess of calm and stability might be.

Jake edged closer to the room at the end of the hall but paused as Lear called out. "I should have told you. I know!"

No one replied.

"Great!" Jake whispered as he crept to the doorway and peeked around the corner. A colossal round window filled an entire wall and it was lit by the moon. She was full and bright and her glow deepened Lear's shadow as his paper wings rustled in an icy breeze.

"Yes, yes, I know. I cannot apologize enough, my lady." Lear looked crestfallen as he stooped and gazed through the huge telescope in the center of the room. The instrument was pointed directly ahead and now Jake realized who Lear was talking to.

The moon.

The pot of water the Professor had said was Lear's mind had finally boiled over.

"The man's clever," Lear continued. "He inferred Spires sent him here when they first arrived, but I didn't believe him for a single moment." Lear cupped his ear, as if listening. "Yes, the boy's a rat-child vagrant, full of dark sorcery and malice." Lear shook his head. "No, neither will leave. Not alive at least." He grinned. "The boy's bound for Sinner's Drop, and a bullet will suffice for the other. He at least deserves a more refined death than plummeting to earth."

Lear stepped away from the telescope and bowed. "Of course my lady. It must be dreadful for you suffering their presences so close to your majesty. But I shall fix that right away." Lear danced across the room and seized his rifle. He slowed as the building shook once more, and swayed towards the door.

Jake turned and ran down the hall. When he glanced back he cried out as he found Lear watching him.

"There you are!" Lear shouted as he brought up his rifle, took aim and fired.

CHAPTER THIRTY-NINE

Professor Thistlequick grasped the desk tighter while he waited for the shaking to subside. As the quake slowed, a distant thrum rang through the cloud.

"Clearly we're going somewhere," he whispered as he gazed at the compass, and a list of coordinates scribbled on a notepad. He had no idea what they meant.

Pushing them aside he found a diagram of the cloud. Beside it were a list of times, numbers and calculations and an illustration of a complex network of cables and pipes running beneath the structure.

Several of the pipes had been circled and he traced his finger along the lines linking them to the notations. "Those two compounds should never be mixed together... that's not good. Not good at all! But why? Why destroy it?"

The Professor grabbed the desk as the cloud shook again. He checked the drawers as he steadied himself.

Empty.

He stooped to rifle through the small bin beside the desk. Inside was a printed tide table for the Thames. "Curious." He folded it and placed it in his pocket. "It all has to mean something..."

Professor Thistlequick crawled to the fireplace in the corner. Papers lay curled and charred upon dim glowing coals. He used his comb to sort through them. Most were burnt, but one small crumpled receipt had drifted off to the side of the grate. He pulled it free.

It was an invoice from a book shop on the Charing Cross Road for an order sent to an address in North London. "Interesting." Professor Thistlequick glanced up at the man in the painting above the desk. "Who are you? And what is this game you're playing?"

He stooped and searched through the books scattered across the floor. "Subjection of Elemental Forces. Erasing Magical Footprints. Of Daemons and their masters...." He glanced back at the painting. Was it his imagination, or had the man turned a little?

"Preposterous. It's just a picture. Although it wouldn't be the first time I've had a problem with a painting not being what it seems." Professor Thistlequick glanced at the pair of black shoes in the corner. They were caked with dried mud that was a light, curious shade of amber. He'd seen it before. "But where?"

The answer was almost upon him when a shriek rang out, followed by a loud bang. Professor Thistlequick's arms turned to gooseflesh.

The shriek was Jake's, and the din had sounded exactly like gunfire.

He jumped to his feet, his heart thumping hard.

~

JAKE RAN as Lear's savage cries followed him down the hallway.

Another blast of gunfire rang out and a bullet whizzed past his ear. Jake ducked as the wall beside him exploded with powder and dust.

"Keep still you little worm!" Lear bellowed. "I'm trying to murder you!"

Jake glanced back as Lear charged after him, his goggles over his eyes, his hair wild. "Years ago I hunted pheasants," Lear called out. "Now I hunt peasants. And I have to say it makes for a far more interesting sport."

Jake was almost at the end of the hall when he heard the rifle being cocked. He feigned a right, but dodged left as a bullet tore into the wall.

He fled down the shadowy corridor, glancing back, half-expecting to find Lear right behind him, but the hallway was empty. Jake stopped to catch his breath, closed his eyes, and tried to listen through the blood thumping in his ears.

He could hear nothing beyond his pulse and the distant muffled thrum and shake of the cloud.

An eerie stillness fell over the building.

Jake forced himself to continue down the corridor until a flight of stairs opened up before him. He paused as he peered down into the darkness below.

Where was Lear? Had he somehow gotten ahead? Was he waiting below, lurking like a wolf in the gloom?

"No!" Jake cried as the skin on the nape of his neck shivered. He spun around to find Lear right behind him, his eyes glinting madly as he seized Jake by the throat.

"Got you!"

CHAPTER FORTY

J ake pulled at the fingers clamped around his throat.

"Not so clever now, are we?" Lear crowed.

"Get off!"

Lear's grip loosened just enough for Jake to breathe. "Is that better? I wouldn't want you to die, not like this. No, you're going to go the same way as the others."

"Others?" Jake tried to dig his heels into the carpet but Lear pulled him down the stairs.

"The so called thinkers, artists and scientists who lived here. The *high minds* our founder gathered to build a new future. High minds my foot! They're not so high now, are they? With their bones all twisted and ground to dust."

"I don't understand." Jake said. He wanted Lear to continue talking, for each time he did his grip on Jake's throat loosened a little more.

"Everything will soon be as clear as glass to you, boy."

"Please let me go!" Jake cried out. He hoped the Professor could hear him, but even if he did, what could he do?

"Stop shouting." Lear scoffed, and squeezed Jake's throat so tight he could barely breathe. "Make your peace and repent with the little time you have left. Seek forgiveness for being a blight upon our green and pleasant land. Ask absolution from the lady who has had to shine her light upon your loathsome form." Lear dragged Jake through a set of doors.

Cold wind howled around them. It was still dark, but a distant patch of dawn lit the clouds stretching to the east.

"The lady's retiring to sleep," Lear said, and scowled at the red glow of sunshine lighting a fleet of clouds as if they were stormy waves crashing upon a shore.

"The lady?" Jake asked. "Do you mean the moon?"

"Of course I mean the moon. There's only one true lady." Lear shoved Jake sprawling to his knees and a low, hollow sound rang out below him.

"It's time for your tumble, boy." Lear brought up his rifle. "And if the terror doesn't still your heart, gravity will."

Jake scoured around for the Penny Farthing.

It was gone.

"Your friend won't help you," Lear said. "He's cleverer than you are. He's gone already."

"No!" But it seemed Lear was telling the truth, the cloud was empty. Jake flinched as Lear kicked him towards the same hole in the cloud the Professor had almost fallen through only hours before.

"I call it Sinner's Drop," Lear said. "It's where I let the others go after the founder deserted us." He opened his rifle, checked the barrel and snapped it shut.

"Why did you kill them?" Jake asked, trying to buy himself time as he gazed through the hole.

They'd long since drifted from London and all he could

see was a distant grey patchwork of fields and trees. The cloud juddered again and when he looked up, he found himself facing the end of the rifle.

"The founder made me the keeper of the light and watcher of the skies. He knew how deep my commitment to the cause was, but after he left, the others began to question my authority. I warned them to hold their tongues and they did, for a while at least. But I soon heard their conniving whispers. They plotted to overthrow me, but their so called intellects were paper tigers when faced with a rifle. I marched them out here, one by one, and let them drop. They fell like screaming babies, all the way back down to London's filth and pestilence."

A light shiver ran across Jake's shoulder as he recalled the story in the newspaper, of the corpses found on the dome of St. Paul's Cathedral mere weeks ago. It had irritated Silas Grumble, as he'd ranted about how it was supposed to rain cats and dogs, not people.

"It's your turn now." Lear prodded Jake with the cold end of the rifle.

Jake's legs were heavy and numb. He couldn't move.

"Stand!" Lear smacked the rifle's barrel against the side of Jake's head. Jake howled and clamped a hand over his head as he glanced woozily to the hole in the cloud.

He tried to climb to his feet, but fell.

"I told you to stand!" Lear pulled Jake up and he teetered, the tips of his tattered shoes hanging over the edge of the gaping hole. Icy cold air screamed up through the opening, battering his coat and whistling past his ears.

Jake glanced around one final time, hoping to see the Professor in his last moment.

There was no sign of him.
He gazed from the rifle to the hole below.
There were two options.
Dying quickly or dying slowly.

CHAPTER FORTY-ONE

Surely I'll die from fear before I hit the ground, Jake thought.

He pulled his head back as the wind shrieked through the hole, and glanced to the stars. They twinkled and gleamed, the only audience to witness his final moments. He recalled the nights he and Nancy had tried to count them and wiped a tear from his eye. He'd let her down. Adam too. He'd never see either of them again.

"It's no good crying, boy. No one will mourn your passing. The world's piled high with vermin and detritus. You won't be missed. Now jump and be gone."

"No." Jake's voice broke. "I... I can't."

"You can and you will." Lear pressed the rifle against Jake's back. "Do it now."

Terror spread through Jake like a fever as Lear shoved him.

The howling wind whipped Jake's hair into his eyes. He tried to crawl away but Lear's foot pressed into the small of his back.

"Stop!" someone shouted.

Jake looked up.

"Who goes there?" Lear demanded.

A bright, vivid light like a tiny moon appeared in the gloom by the side of the building. Lear threw his hand over his eyes against the glare.

"Step away from the hole, boy," the voice boomed.

"Who are you?" Lear demanded as he peered between his fingers.

"Someone you should treat with respect. I bring a message from the silver lady. Release the boy; he's not ready to pass from this world."

"He is!" Lear insisted. "The sinner must drop!"

"No Hieronymus, you're mistaken." The light bobbed and stopped so close before them that it seemed Jake could reach out and touch it. "The boy's no sinner. He's a servant of the lady, just as you are."

There was someone standing behind the light, a dark, indistinct shape.

"Are you suggesting the boy serves the silver queen?" Uncertainty filled Lear's voice.

"Indeed," the voice replied. "And the queen demands you release him at once."

"The white and silver queen in the stars?" Lear asked.

"The very same. Now put down your weapon before you incur her wrath."

Jake scrambled back from the hole as Lear lowered his rifle.

An uneasy silence fell until a mechanical click came from behind the light that very much sounded like clockwork.

"If you're the queen's messenger then reveal yourself," Lear called. "Before I blow your head off!"

The light bobbed, arced and swept towards them. Lear shrieked and his rifle went off with two monstrous cracks of thunder as a lantern with a magnifying glass attached to it struck him in the head.

Professor Thistlequick dropped the rolled cone of papers he'd been speaking through. "Look away, Jake."

"You!" Lear cried as he rubbed his head and began to stand.

A blinding light flashed before them and an acrid chemical tang filled the air.

"Hurry, Jake!"

Jake staggered in what he hoped was the right direction.

His foot hovered over thin air. "No!"

A hand grabbed his wrist and pulled him up. A moment later Jake slumped into the saddle behind the Professor but before he could settle, he heard the sound of Lear's rifle snapping into place behind them.

The Professor positioned his feet on the pedals and grabbed a lever on the Penny Farthing's handlebars. The folded wings burst open, catching the wind as the bicycle sped across the cloud.

Gunfire roared behind them and a bullet whined over Jake's head.

"Damn you to hell!" Lear roared.

Jake glanced back to see Lear feeding bullets into the rifle's chamber. The insanity was gone from his face and in its place was rapt concentration. He strode after them like a hunter and brought his rifle up slowly and methodically.

"He's going to shoot!" Jake cried.

"I know!" Professor Thistlequick pulled a lever and a cloud of steam billowed from the Penny Farthing. The wheels rattled as they surged toward the edge of the cloud.

Jake glanced back.

Lear knelt, one eye closed, the other gazing along the barrel of his rifle. A flash of light lit his face and his rifle cracked like a whip.

The Penny Farthing shook and a terrible screech filled the air as it shuddered and bucked.

Jake threw his arms around the Professor's waist as they sailed over the cloud. The wings fluttered in the open air and Jake cried out with elation as they swept down through the sky.

But his relief was short-lived as the engine clicked, sputtered and wheezed.

And then it stopped altogether.

CHAPTER FORTY-TWO

The wind shrieked.

Jake fought to catch his breath as the icy air whipped around him. *I'm going to die.* The thought whirled through his mind as the Penny Farthing hurtled down, its wings frozen in place.

They plunged through wisps of amber clouds, falling faster and faster.

Jake clung to the Professor as tight as he could, for all the good it would do. The Professor seemed oblivious as he leaned over the handlebar and fiddled with a lever.

"Lear... shot... the... engine!" Jake's words were snatched from his mouth. A terrible numbness spread through his limbs as he gulped air into his lungs.

"Aha," The Professor said, as if he'd just found a penny he'd dropped in the street. "I... need... to ...inspect... the... workings. Let... go... of... me."

Jake had to fight his instincts, which were telling him to do the very opposite, as he let go of the Professor. He grabbed the edge of the seat and watched dumbstruck with horror as the Professor slowly leaned out over the Penny Farthing.

The Professor muttered and nodded, as if working on a crossword puzzle, seemingly unaware of the grassy hills rushing up towards them.

Jake's heart pounded. They were moments from smashing into the hard green and chalky-white ground. "Do something!"

"Do you have any string?"

"No!"

"Fiddlesticks!" The Professor delved into his pockets and leaned back over the bicycle.

Jake stared transfixed as the ground hurtled toward them in a blur of brown, white and green. They were so close now he could see the morning light glinting on the hard flint stones churned in the freshly plowed field below them.

They'd be the last thing he'd see.

Jake dug his fingers into the saddle's edge, closed his eyes, and waited for the end.

CHAPTER FORTY-THREE

"Balloon!"

Jake opened his eyes as the Professor pulled a deflated balloon from his pocket.

"Please!" Jake screamed.

Professor Thistlequick leaned over the bicycle, then rose back up onto the seat and pulled a lever.

With a rumble, the engine sputtered to life and the wings began to flap.

"Here we go!" The Professor yanked the handlebars and the bicycle swept up and over the hills. "Lean with me!" he called over his shoulder. Jake shifted to the side and the Penny Farthing soared over a grove of bare winter trees. "We've got to land!" Jake cried. "The wind's taking us back up!"

"Hold tight! And please stop shouting, it's most distracting!"

"You're madder than Lear!"

"I'll take that as a compliment. I tend to find sane people perfectly tedious."

They rose through the air, gliding over villages and woods.

Jake searched the sky for Lear's cloud, but there were so many it was impossible to pick it out. Weary relief washed over him and the hypnotic beat of the bicycle's leathery wings caused him to close his eyes. He fell asleep huddled against the Professor's back, the special seat keeping him in place.

JAKE WOKE to find them sweeping towards Primrose Hill, the ground gleaming with frost, as if dusted with millions of tiny diamonds.

The Professor pulled a pair of levers and within moments they descended toward a long smooth footpath. Jake held his breath as he waited for the wheels to hit the ground.

The bicycle hissed and issued a cloud of steam as they jolted and lurched down the hill.

Professor Thistlequick flicked a switch and the wings hissed and tucked themselves away. "Well that was certainly quite an adventure!" Professor Thistlequick said as he braked and brought them to a gentle stop. He dismounted, reached up, and helped Jake down.

"I thought we were going to die. Over and over again." Jake gulped in the morning air, and released it in great white puffs.

"But we didn't, we survived." The Professor's eyes twinkled as their childlike gleam returned. "And you might like to know I found some clues that should help us find your friends. But its been a long, harrowing night. We need rest, and a nice hot cup of sugary tea to sharpen our wits. Come, to Brightstar Terrace. Bacon and Happiness await these intrepid adventurers."

Jake followed the Professor, and even though his heart wanted to try and find Nancy and Adam right away, he knew he needed to rest and settle his nerves. He allowed himself a grateful smile as he gazed at the early morning frost glittering in the trees.

He'd never felt so alive.

MRS. HARKER APPEARED AS SOON as they arrived in front of the house on Brightstar Terrace. She waved her hands, her expression caught between anguish and relief.

"You're alive!" She grinned at Jake. "Thank the heavens. I was just on my way to purchase a newspaper. I said to myself, if anything's happened to them, it will be in the newspaper. Providing their corpses were found of course."

"I'm most grateful for your concern," Professor Thistlequick said. "It's certainly been quite a night. We've been all over the place and I'm more than a little frayed."

"I'll put on a pot of tea for you. Just this once."

"Would a pair of bacon sandwiches be in the offing too?" Professor Thistlequick asked.

"I suppose." Mrs. Harker shook her head, but smiled fondly at Jake before vanishing into the house.

JAKE SET his empty plate on the armrest of the chair and warmed his hands before the crackling fire while Professor Thistlequick patted Happiness on the head and fed her a scrap of bacon.

"Now." The Professor said, as he dug into his coat pocket and held up a glass vial before his eyes. "Where have I seen you before?"

"Seen what?" Jake forced back a yawn. The comfort of his full belly and the warmth of the fire was making him drowsy.

"I found some muddy shoes while you were distracting the utterly insane Mr. Lear. But they couldn't have been his; they were far too small. I suspect, by the mud's freshness, that they came from someone who visited the cloud recently. Perhaps the mysterious founder, Lear mentioned. The dirt's a very curious color. I know I've seen it before…"

"I don't know how you can tell the difference. Dirt's dirt, isn't it?"

"Not at all. There are many subtle variations to consider; silt, minerals and… ah." Professor Thistlequick rifled through a cabinet and produced a strange pair of spectacles fitted with several sets of odd looking hinged lenses. He fitted the strap around his head and when he pulled them down over his face his eyes grew to twice their normal size.

"You look ridiculous." Jake yawned. He wanted to snooze, and the Professor's seemingly endless energy was beginning to grate upon his nerves.

"You're too kind." Professor Thistlequick replied as he examined the glass vial.

Jake flinched as Happiness leaped onto his knee, turned in a circle, and settled down to sleep.

"You're in her chair." Professor Thistlequick chuckled. "Which means you've now become her chair. A chair within a chair if you will. Happiness is set in her ways, and this house is her palace. We're merely her minions."

"How long have you lived here?" Jake forced back another yawn.

"Seven years, five months and thirteen days. I count myself incredibly fortunate to have found Brightstar Terrace, and Mrs. Harker, of course. She's absolutely delightful."

"Delightful I'm sure," Jake said in a faux posh voice. "But I'd have thought a toff like you would live in a mansion."

Professor Thistlequick's magnified eyes seemed almost insect-like as he glanced at Jake. "Again, I fail to understand why you think I'm so affluent. My parents left me with more debt than money, and sadly, I'm a similarly poor judge when it comes to finances. As for business skills, I can assure you I have none. So no, I'm not a gilded lord. I earn just about enough to pay for my rooms, my materials, and to feed Happiness of course."

"It's still better than being stuck under the same roof as Silas Grumble."

"I'm sorry you had to live like that, Jake."

"I just got unlucky, I suppose. You're either born to something or to nothing in this world. And if you've got nothing, then that's all you'll ever have." Jake gazed at the clutter filled room. "So why don't you sell your inventions if you've got no money?"

"I did. I sold something that took me the best part of five years to create. I say *sold*, but I was never paid. Not really. But the swine who purchased my blueprints is making the most tidy profit from them. Enough to hire one of London's most ruthless solicitors to hound me into silence."

"That's wrong! You should stand up for yourself. You're too soft."

"I agree. So perhaps I should start standing up for myself with you, Jake. Stop judging me and assuming everyone else's life is easier than your own. That belief only serves to make everything even harder for you, because what we believe," Professor Thistlequick tapped his head, "either ensnares or frees us. Besides, you know nothing about me." He lowered his voice and gave a half smile. "But I hope that will change and that we can become better friends once this whole mess is over. For I believe I could learn a great deal from you, Jake Shillingsworth."

"I doubt it."

"I know you do. Listen to me; you have a great fire within you, and it can be used for all sorts of good. Just don't allow it to burn those who try to help you."

Jake placed Happiness on the arm of the chair, stood, and offered his hand to the Professor. "I'm sorry. I'm tired."

Professor Thistlequick nodded swiftly as he shook his hand. "Apology accepted. But if you call me a toff one more time, I'll strap you to the Penny Farthing and set it to fly into the Thames..." He paused and a slow smile played across his lips. "The Thames! That's where I saw the mud!"

"This might be news, but the Thames is pretty long and there's plenty of mud along its banks."

"But I know exactly where I've seen this silt, it settles along the banks near the docklands. I had to clean it from my shoes after I went to see my uncle set sail on The Edge of Dawn." Professor Thistlequick tapped his fingernails on the vial. "So our adversary has visited the docks and recently. Now, we need to find out why." Professor Thistlequick pulled a crumpled piece of paper from his pocket. "Maybe we should start by visiting his earthly house."

"What's that?" Jake asked.

"An invoice with an address in North London. I found it on the cloud. We should pass it on."

"To who?"

"To the police! We need help. We're no match against such diabolical forces."

"It's a waste of time, they won't listen."

"Perhaps, perhaps not. But we won't know unless we try."

CHAPTER FORTY-FOUR

"We're not flying the Penny Farthing again, are we?" Jake asked nervously as Professor Thistlequick handed him a paisley scarf at least three sizes too large for him.

"Wrap up well, and no, we're not taking the Penny Farthing. Not until I can repair the engine with something more durable than a balloon." Professor Thistlequick said as he buckled the strap of his top hat under his chin. "Fare well, Mrs. Harker," he called as he opened the door and they set off.

Jake took care on the icy pavement as they strode into the street. HMS Watcher hung in the crisp blue morning sky over West London, its searchlights shining down like beams of sunlight. "They're looking the wrong way. They should be checking the sky," Jake said.

"True. But perhaps once we've told them about our sky-bound adventures, they'll reconsider. Although who knows where Lear is by now. The cloud was moving south at a fair clip and I found evidence that indicated it might not be long for this world." Professor Thistlequick held up his hand, flagged down a horse and carriage and ushered Jake inside.

"Where to?" The driver called.

"Snow Hill police station, please. We have a serious crime to report."

"Right you are," the driver murmured as he cracked his whips.

JAKE GAZED at the blue lamps framing the stout imposing doors as he stood outside the stark grey police station. "I don't know what we're doing here. They'll never believe us."

"Perhaps, perhaps not," Professor Thistlequick said as he held the door open for Jake.

A portly desk sergeant glanced up, his eyes droopy as they entered the station. He looked like he'd just woken, or was about to fall asleep. His thick wiry eyebrows rose as he looked from the Professor to Jake. "Right, let's be having it."

"Having what?" Professor Thistlequick asked.

"Your story," the man said. "And it better be a good one."

"Right. Where to start..."

"The beginning's usually a good place, sir."

THE SERGEANT GAZED COOLLY at the Professor. "Just to clarify. You're contending that there's an invisible flying craft terrorizing London and kidnapping children?"

"And adults," Professor Thistlequick added.

"And adults." The desk sergeant scrawled on his notepad. "And these villains... are they the same ones mentioned in that poppycock story I read in the newspaper last week? As *witnessed* by a boy with queerly colored eyes." He gave Jake a severe glance.

"Exactly," Professor Thistlequick said.

"I see," desk sergeant said, even though it sounded like he really didn't. "And since that story, which included a demon from the depths of hell itself and a brass giant who uses an umbrella-like apparatus to fly over the chimneys, you've discovered their abandoned lighthouse stronghold on a cloud. Which is inhabited by a man who thinks he's an angel. Is that correct?"

"Well," Professor Thistlequick said, "when you put it that way, it does sound a touch fantastical."

"A touch fantastical is a masterful understatement, sir" the desk sergeant said. "I'd describe it more as the ravings of an addled lunatic. And this here boy," he glanced at Jake, "is your sole witness to these diabolical events?"

"Well technically, I'm *his* witness," Professor Thistlequick said. "It was Jake who brought this terrible business to my attention."

"Did he now?" The desk sergeant's nose twitched and he gave Jake an unpleasant look. "Have our paths crossed before?"

"No!" Jake thrust his hands into his pockets.

"Might I suggest," the Professor rapped his knuckles upon the desk, "that instead of harassing my friend, whose standing I can happily vouch for, you deal with the matter at hand. You need to send your colleagues on HMS Watcher to apprehend the cloud. Time is of the essence!"

"And who exactly are you to command Her Majesty's Royal Constabulary?" the desk sergeant asked.

"My name is Professor Aubrey Thistlequick."

"I've never heard of you."

"And I'd never heard of you until I entered this station. And now I wish I'd taken Master Shillingsworth's advice and hadn't bothered."

"Get out!" The tips of the sergeant's ears turned red. "Before I have you both arrested!"

"For what crime?" Professor Thistlequick enquired.

"Wasting police time and general uncouthness!"

"Well, in that case you might consider arresting yourself. Good day!" Professor Thistlequick steered Jake through the doors and out into the street. "You were right, they're not going to help us. If we mean to find your friends and stop these odious crimes, then it seems we must do so ourselves."

"Exactly," Jake said, glad that the Professor was finally seeing things his way.

A cold wind blew as they hurried along the street. Ahead, a newspaper boy held up a paper and the Professor slowed to read its headline.

"Oi!" the newspaper boy growled. "These papers are for selling, not browsing."

"Right you are," Professor Thistlequick dropped two pennies into the boy's hand and took a paper. His eyebrows lowered as he scanned the front page.

"What does it say?" Jake asked.

"That there was a loud explosion near Hastings this morning. It was described as a great thunder clap that boomed across the sea. The authorities are speculating there's been an airship disaster, but they've found nothing to support their claims so far."

"Do you think it was Lear?"

"I've no doubt. But whether or not Lear destroyed the cloud himself, remains to be seen. Well, there goes the only evidence we had. By now it will be at the bottom of the sea, and Lear with it I shouldn't wonder." Professor Thistlequick pulled the invoice from his pocket. "Which just leaves us the address in North London and a handful of mud. It seems our foe, whoever he may be, is most fastidious in tying up loose ends. Come Jake, let's hope our luck will change."

CHAPTER FORTY-FIVE

The house on Hobart Street was set back from the road and half hidden behind a pair of tall wooden gates and a high wall. Strands of ivy covered the red brick facade and partially obscured several shuttered windows. Jake stood keeping watch as the Professor gingerly tried the gate.

It opened with a creak.

"Well that was easier than anticipated." Professor Thistlequick stepped through the opening, but stopped in his tracks. Two uniformed men with low brimmed hats and long dark coats stood under the portico arching over the front door. They wore hard expressions as they stared ahead but showed no sign of noticing either the Professor or Jake,.

"They don't look right," Jake whispered.

"No, they don't." Professor Thistlequick closed the gate. "I think we can agree I'm better equipped to get us inside that house and that you're fleeter of foot. Yes?"

"Probably. Why?"

"Because I'll need someone to distract those two living

statues guarding the door if we're to have a hope of getting inside. And that someone's probably going to have to be you."

"How?"

"I don't know, but I'm sure you'll think of something. Lure them away, I'll slip inside the house and find a window around the back to let you in."

"Just like on the cloud then."

"The cloud?" Professor Thistlequick looked puzzled.

"You know, when I put my life in serious danger while you crept around?"

"Yes, that's a most accurate comparison."

"Right." Jake opened the gate and strolled along the stony path. A wall stood on one side, a formal well tended garden on the other, leaving nowhere to hide should everything go wrong. The men gazed at Jake, their eyes lifeless and he began to wonder if they were blind, until one inclined his head toward him.

"Get out," the taller guard bellowed. He lifted a gloved hand and pointed to the gate.

Jake held out the palms of his hands. "Do you know the way to-"

"Leave!" the other demanded. His voice was stilted and he stared at Jake with unblinking eyes.

"Make me." Jake swallowed.

The taller man pulled a long blade from his coat and lumbered towards Jake, the other close behind. Jake backed away, goading them to follow. Within seconds their stumbles turned to strides.

Jake ducked through the gate and ran across the empty street towards an alley cutting between two townhouses. He glanced back to find the men standing before the gate, watching intently.

"Come on!" Jake shouted.

They remained motionless.

Jake bent down, scooped up a rounded clump of what he hoped was mud, and threw it.

As the dirt struck the taller guard on the side of his face his eyes flashed and he thundered towards Jake, his blade gleaming.

PROFESSOR THISTLEQUICK TWISTED the pick and lifted the pins until, finally, the lock clicked. He glanced over his shoulder to ensure there were no witnesses before slipping inside and softly closing the door behind him. "Stealth is of the essence," he whispered to himself. "And... argh!" He screamed.

A great brown bear towered over him, its eyes almost as ferocious as its gaping maw. It took a moment for the Professor to realize the bear was stuffed, just like the blackbirds, magpies and rooks staring at him from around the room. "Good morning," he whispered to his glassy eyed audience.

The house seemed empty, but he knew appearances could be deceptive. He listened carefully near the banister of the carpeted stairs leading to the next floor, then slipped down a narrow hall leading to the back of the house. The door at the end opened to a sizable room, furnished with a grand piano and an ebony stool.

Paintings decorated the walls. Most were too dark for the Professor to discern, but the one situated behind the piano was a large abstract and its canvas filled the entire wall with textured ridges of heavy black and purple paint. "Cheery stuff," Professor Thistlequick muttered, and he was about to open the window at the back of the room, when something slithered through the door.

He froze.

Was it a snake?

No... it was a shadow, seemingly cast from thin air.

JAKE RACED for the alley as the two thugs ran in pursuit. They were faster than he'd expected.

He turned a corner and came face-to-face with a high brick wall. Cold sweat bathed him as his pursuers' pounding footsteps echoed off the walls.

He ran back toward the alley, and spotted a sharp turn he'd missed. Jake dodged down a brick lined passage and weaved through its twists and turns straight into another dead end.

The wall was too high to scale...

Jake spun around as the men closed in on him. They walked slowly, their faces emotionless as they shuffled closer.

He looked frantically around, searching for a way out.

A wooden door stood halfway between him and the men. He ran, leaped and grabbed the top edge. Splinters dug into his fingers as he pulled himself up. He was almost over when the one of the men seized his coat. The man grinned, his mouth filled with blackened stumps of teeth.

"Get off!" Jake yanked at his coat. It tore free and he scrambled over the door and fell, landing hard. Tiny stones bit into his chin and palms.

The door shook violently as the men pounded upon it. Jake sprang up, ran through a back garden and leaped across a frosty ornamental fish pond. He was almost at the house when the door behind him shattered to pieces.

Jake reached the back door and wrenched the handle. It opened! He ran through into a spacious kitchen.

Muffled voices filled the house. Jake threw a door open and staggered into a large room filled with well-dressed men, women and children. They stood before a towering bushy Christmas tree, hanging baubles upon its fragrant green branches.

"What is the meaning of this?" a tall, bespectacled man blurted.

"Sorry," Jake dodged past the man's outstretched hands. "Merry Christmas," he called, as he ducked through another door. A clatter of dishes smashed in the kitchen and moments later, a chorus of screams rang out.

Jake wrenched the front door open and slammed it behind him.

His lungs felt like they were on fire as he skittered out into the street and ran hard down the road. He glanced back, relieved to find no sign of his pursuers as he turned onto Hobart Street and darted through number 23's high wooden gate.

The ivy wreathed house loomed, just as empty and dark as it had seemed before. Jake ran around the building, checking the windows as he went, hoping the Professor had made it inside. One was ajar. Jake pulled it up, and was about to climb through when a deep, sinister sound boomed from within.

CHAPTER FORTY-SIX

J ake shuddered as the heavy tone rang out again.

A large piano sat in the corner of the room beyond the window and for some reason the Professor was crouched behind it. As he pulled himself up, the Professor struck several more keys, producing another loud sinister din. He glanced over at Jake, held up a hand, and nodded to the floor.

Jake followed his gaze to the long thin shadow coiled upon the polished floorboards like a snake. Slowly it unfurled, and weaved its way toward the piano.

Professor Thistlequick rifled through his pockets and backed towards the wall. He pulled out a small silver hand mirror and clenched it in his hand.

The shadow slowed and rose up like a cobra. As it hissed, filaments of deep sapphire light crackled through its form.

"Um-" Professor Thistlequick began.

As the shadow lunged, he thrust the mirror towards it.

A burst of sizzling blue sparks filled the air as the shadow snake smashed into the glass. With a long feral hiss it swelled, reared up and struck the glass again.

The mirror shattered and rained down in a shower of twinkling blue embers as the snake wavered and recoiled. Then it toppled to the floorboards, its form diminishing as it weaved across the room and vanished through the door.

"Come in," Professor Thistlequick said.

Jake climbed through the window. "What the hell was that?"

"I'm not sure, but I think it was some kind of hex. Not that I've ever seen anything like it before." Professor Thistlequick smiled. "It's good news though when you think about it. It almost certainly means we're in the right place."

"I'm glad to hear it seeing as I nearly got clobbered by those maniacs guarding the front door."

"Nearly, but not quite. We should be safe now, it seems the hex lost some of its vitality when it struck the glass. And-"

He paused as a crunching sound came from the gravel path outside.

"Someone's coming!" Jake whispered.

Professor Thistlequick pulled the window shut and slipped the clasp in place. He grabbed Jake, rushed across the room and ducked behind the door.

"Can you see anything?" the Professor whispered.

Jake groaned and peeked around the corner. "Yeah, one of those spooky men."

"What's he doing?"

"Looking in through the window."

"Is he still there?" the Professor asked after a long pause.

"Yeah. He's still there, staring like a creepy statue."

There was a faint whistle near the front of the house and

Jake watched as the guard turned his head and slowly walked away.

"Great! He's not at the window anymore but it sounds like the other one's come back."

They slipped out of the room and walked down the hallway.

The interior was nothing like Jake had imagined. Everything was perfectly clean without a trace of dust anywhere, and perfume from an elegant crystal vase of lilies filled the air. Jake was about to comment as they entered the foyer, until he spotted the countless beady little eyes staring back.

"They're all stuffed," the Professor whispered. "Not that I realized that at first. The bear nearly scared me to death. It's pretty impressive, eh?"

"That's one word for it. So what are we going to do now?"

"We need to split up and look for anything that can tell us where your friends were taken, and who our foe is. Beyond this," Professor Thistlequick waved to the taxidermy, "which clearly indicates an obsession with both death and fastidiousness. A curious combination. Anyway, you check this floor, and I'll peek upstairs. Be as quiet as possible; we don't want to alert our friends outside."

Jake agreed, even though the last thing he wanted was to be on his own in this horrid dark place. He watched as the Professor tiptoed up the stairs, one by one, and disappeared. Then he turned, snuck down the hall and slipped through a large swinging door, checking every shadow as he went.

A wide bowl filled with apples sat upon a large smooth wooden table, but other than that, the kitchen and larder were bare. Jake slipped an apple into his pocket and crept to the window to peek through a crack in the curtains. The men were back at their post, guarding the front door.

Jake scurried from the room and was about to check upstairs when he spotted a small door beneath the stairs. A cold draught blew across his face as he pulled it open, bringing a heavy scent of must.

Dread shivered through him as he peered at the rickety cellar steps leading into pitch darkness. He found a small box of matches on a candle stand near the door and struck one. Its light was meager and turned his shadow into a sinister looking apparition.

Jake swallowed as he regarded the stairs. There wasn't a single part of him that wanted to descend them to whatever lay below.

"Don't be such a meater," he muttered to himself. He *had* to go down there. He'd promised to search for clues, and finding Nancy and Adam could very well depend on it.

The stairs rasped and creaked and the smell of damp grew stronger. Mice squeaked in distant corners. Huge black spiders lurked in thick white webs and skittered across silken threads, throwing writhing shadows across the pockmarked walls.

"Ouch!" Jake scowled as the match singed his finger. It fell dull and red, before being swallowed by the darkness.

Something scratched in the murk.

Jake scrambled to open the box and light another match. His fingers throbbed and felt like they were three times their size. As the match sparked to life, its light revealed an old wooden writing desk and three stumpy candles. Jake lit them and examined the cellar.

There were a few old crates stacked near a bed in the corner. Dust covered the blankets and pillows as if they'd been frosted from a heavy fall of snow. Curled yellowing posters hung on the walls; old advertisements for boxing matches with etched illustrations of the opponents.

Jake's heart skipped as he looked at one of the fighters. He was a tall, swarthy man with strong defiant eyes, and coal-black hair.

Kedgewick.

But he was younger, and without his brass suit. He looked normal, and alive. So different to how he'd appeared when Jake had first encountered him.

He returned to the desk and carefully moved the broken, wooden chair blocking the top drawer. As it slid open, an empty rum bottle clattered around between a sheaf of newspaper clippings and a large daguerreotype.

Jake reached for the picture. Its dark frame was cold and heavy as he pulled it from the drawer. It revealed an image of Kedgewick tenderly holding the hand of a thin frail woman as they sat on a settee. Between them was a boy who couldn't have been much older than Jake. His head had lolled to one side and he appeared to sleep as the woman and Kedgewick stared lifelessly ahead.

"This isn't right," Jake whispered as he ran his finger over the black velvet mourning ribbon stretched over the top corner of the image. It felt wrong looking at the picture; the pain of other people's lives and deaths frozen in time, even if one of them was a man he'd gladly see hang.

As he returned the frame to the drawer, a cabinet card fell from the back and landed at Jake's feet. He carefully picked it up. Another photograph, clearly from an earlier time; the family standing before a house, smiling, their eyes gleaming with life.

He was about to check the rest of the drawers, when something scratched in the darkness.

"The hex," Jake whispered, imagining it slithering from the shadows.

He slipped the picture into his pocket, grabbed one of the candles, and raced up the stairs. The darkness shifted around him as the candle flickered and a loud hard *thump* landed on the step behind him.

~

"FIDDLESTICKS" Professor Thistlequick muttered as he approached the final door on the landing.

So far, he'd found nothing but a bathroom, bedroom and guest room. He placed his head against the wood panel and listened carefully. Nothing stirred as he slowly tried to turn the knob. The door was locked and it took longer than most to pick, but finally it clicked open.

The room inside was spacious and gloomy, with a large cold stone fireplace at the far end. Heavy grey drapes covered the windows and tall wooden bookcases lined one wall.

It was eerily similar to the room he'd discovered on the cloud.

As he slipped around the door, he was surprised to find a thick sturdy armchair facing a large paneled wall, which was pinned from floor to ceiling with hundreds of slips of paper, most of them handwritten notes.

The Professor lit a hurricane lamp upon the floor and quickly checked the corners of the room for unquiet shadows. As he passed the books on the shelves, he noticed they were in keeping with the ones he'd seen on the cloud. Tomes on London history, the Government, and the Royal Family.

Stacks of monographs that charted the Thames, its tributaries and local waterways as well as books on military weapons, overseas conflicts and ancient wars.

Then his eyes strayed to a set of dark volumes adorned with esoteric titles and symbols, nestled beside a fat leather grimoire and a book on demonology.

A bird cawed and pecked at the window, reminding Professor Thistlequick of the outside world and the two guards lurking below.

He turned back to the wall of notes and spotted several pages detailing various strains of fungus and bacteria. "Interesting!" It seemed to be research for the Miraghus, and someone had scrawled notes about its dangerous side effects, although clearly counteracting them had been a low priority.

There were also notes and designs on the manmade cloud, as well as what looked like arrows making trajectories below it. "As if something's going to be dropped onto London..."

Professor Thistlequick shivered. Then his gaze fell to a neatly clipped section of a map depicting the county of Devon. Scratchy arrows pointed to the perimeter of Dartmoor and a crude drawing of a door. "What is it?" Professor Thistlequick checked the next note for any correlation to the others. It appeared to be a page torn from an old book with a detailed sketch of a pyramid and something scrawled in a language he didn't recognize.

He looked closer at the first part of a word that appeared to be a variation of Mort. "Death." Professor Thistlequick pulled his scarf tighter around his neck to ward off a sudden chill. "How does this all connect?" he muttered as he backed away from the board and collided with the armchair. A single piece of paper rested upon the seat. He scooped it up.

It was the deed for a warehouse on the docks. The

Professor quickly noted the address and returned the paper, positioning it exactly as he'd found it. "What does it mean?" he whispered. "And how-"

The hairs on the nape of his neck prickled and his heart raced as he turned to the door and saw the shadowy hex slithering across the carpet, right toward him.

Professor Thistlequick cast around for something to repel it, but there was nothing to hand. He backed away, but it was too late as the shadow lunged and struck his foot. And then it reared up and began to shriek.

"Shhh! No! Stop it!" Professor Thistlequick clamped his shaking hands over his ears as he ran.

Jake appeared on the stairs, his face ashen as the hex's screams grew ever louder. "What-"

"No time. Run!"

They pounded down the stairs and as they reached the bottom, the front door flew open.

CHAPTER FORTY-SEVEN

J ake rounded the banister just as one of the guards appeared in the doorway.

"The piano room, Jake" the Professor cried.

Jake sprinted with him down the hall.

The guards took off after them, their footsteps hard and heavy. Jake slid into the piano room, grabbed the edge of the door and slammed it shut. There was a loud thump and a muffled curse as he twisted the lock.

The door rattled in its hinges as the Professor fumbled with the window.

"Go!" Jake cried as he raced over and helped him shove it open.

"After you!" Professor Thistlequick replied.

The kicking and pounding grew louder and the door bounced in its frame. Jake scrambled out onto the icy sill and jumped down to the garden.

The Professor's top hat caught the top of the window frame as he clambered through. Seconds later the men burst into the room behind him.

"Run!" Professor Thistlequick cried as he fell to the ground.

They took off on the frosty path, ducking around the side of the house, out through the gate and down the street.

Jake glanced back, but there was no sign of their pursuers.

They bolted down several roads and alleyways, and finally stopped running. Professor Thistlequick leaned on a garden wall, his cheeks blazing red. "I haven't run like that for years!"

Jake checked the street to make sure they'd given their pursuers the slip. It seemed they had. He told the Professor about what he'd found in the cellar, and showed him the photograph he'd taken.

"So Kedgewick was a boxer when he lived. And that was his son, or so I'd imagine. They have the same eyes." The Professor handed the photograph back to Jake. "Hold on to it for now, it might prove useful later."

"Did you find anything?" Jake asked, as he double-checked the street once more. His nerves were still jittery.

"Yes, but nothing that made sense. Our foe is planning something foul, clearly. But what it is, I couldn't say. The lair on the cloud, the kidnappings... The demon and the dead man... I wish I knew his purpose. However, I did find an address at the docks. We should investigate it, but this time, we'll ensure we have help on our side."

"But the police don't want to know."

"I was thinking of help of a more... esoteric nature. Perhaps it's time to fight fire with fire."

"How?"

Professor Thistlequick gave Jake a lop-sided grin. "I happen to know a demon."

"What, in London?"

"Yes."

"Where does it live? In a plague pit? The tunnels? A crypt?"

"Above a shop, actually."

"Oh." Jake felt strangely disappointed.

"Yes. Although saying that, I have no idea where the shop is right now."

"What do you mean?"

"Well I could tell you where the shop *was*, but not where it is. It moves, sometimes up to three or four times a day." Professor Thistlequick pulled the newspaper he'd purchased earlier from his coat pocket and frowned as he leafed through its pages. "Giant crab seen in Lambeth," he muttered. "Polite but angry protest in the British Library. Albino tiger spotted in Mincing Lane. No, no, no."

"What are you looking for?"

The Professor flipped the pages impatiently, before stopping. "Ah, here we go; Lost on the mountains of the moon, a tale of doomed treasures, curious particulars and devilishly hot mustard! Doors open from eleven till dusk on Strawberry Lane. That's not too far from here." Professor Thistlequick folded the newspaper and set off down the street.

"So the shop's on Strawberry Lane?" Jake called, as he struggled to keep up.

"No. That's just the location of the first clue."

"What?"

"You'll see!" Professor Thistlequick's eyes glinted as he turned and tipped his hat. "Yes, you'll see alright, Jake Shillingsworth!"

CHAPTER FORTY-EIGHT

"This is Strawberry Lane, isn't it?" Jake said as they stopped before a dilapidated grocer's shop. "I think Grumble sent me here once before. So what are we looking for?"

"Finding London Particulars is like setting out on a great treasure hunt." The Professor lifted a flyblown theater poster revealing a cluster of symbols chalked upon the wall. "Very good!" He spun on his heels, waited for a break in the bustling traffic and led Jake across the street. They turned down a long alleyway and stopped before a broken window.

The Professor reached through the empty window frame and removed a piece of canvas marked with charcoal symbols. "It used to be easier to find the shop, but they've been raided enough times to exercise extreme caution." He placed the canvas back inside the window. "In fact, it happened the last time I was there, which was terribly unsettling."

They continued down a maze of increasingly derelict streets until Jake had no idea where they were. "This doesn't look like a good place to be out in," Jake said. "At least in St. Giles I'm on nodding terms with most of the cutthroats."

"If this was a nice place, there'd be more people about, which would defeat London Particulars' objective."

"I thought you said it was a shop. What sort of shopkeeper puts a shop in a dodgy place no one wants to go to?"

"The sort of shopkeeper who sells things that are... Ah, here we go!" Professor Thistlequick darted toward a tall woman leaning against a wall near the corner of the street. Her long ragged coat brushed the pavement and she had a scar running from her forehead to her chin. A hazy blue cloud of pipe smoke bellowed from her lips as she glanced at Jake.

"Good day." Professor Thistlequick said.

The lady turned, stared ahead, and puffed deeply on her pipe. "How many cards does my master keep in his pocket?"

"Seventy eight," Professor Thistlequick said. "Next!"

"Why does the first have no number?"

"Because he's a fool."

The lady gave a sharp nod. "Take the alley on the left. Walk to the end. Across the street is a house with a red door."

"Wonderful." Professor Thistlequick dropped a coin into her pocket and hurried on.

They crossed the road and strode by a cluster of children loitering near the alley. The Professor tossed a palmful of pennies down as they hurried by and the children descended like pigeons on scattered bread. The houses along the street were squat, dingy and streaked with soot.

"So this is where the demon lives?" Jake's heartbeat quickened as he gazed at the dark windows.

"Shhh." Professor Thistlequick cast a nervous glance behind them as he hurried across the road to a house with a red door. He knocked seven times and delivered two stout kicks to the warped wood. A hidden panel slid open and a pair of chestnut-brown eyes appraised them.

"Good day, Mr. Crane!" the Professor called. "Might we come in?"

The door swung open and a handsome man with a long grey ponytail and an immaculately clipped mustache appeared. His eyes twinkled in his lined, dusky face as he gave a bow. "Professor Thistlequick, what an honor! Come in my friend, quickly if you please!"

Jake shaded his eyes as he followed the Professor inside. Bright almost blinding blue light permeated the shop, glimmering like a mountain of jewels. Jake's nose twitched at the profusion of scents filling the warm air: perfumes, spices, incense, and all manner of exotic fragrances. Clockwork ticked and tocked amid thumps, bangs, bird song and a low, persistent growl.

As the magical glow waned from his eyes, Jake found himself inside a tall open wood-paneled room, not unlike the hull of a ship, and it was much larger than it had appeared from outside. Long rows of oak shelves laden with incredible wares towered around him and vanished back into the darkest depths of the shop.

Bright, colored lights twinkled on the ceiling above and their lights reflected in the hundreds of ornate glass apothecary jars and the smooth polished stone floor. Customers flitted down the aisles, their heads bowed as they kept to the shadows. Some wore hoods or low-brimmed hats, and their furtive glances reminded Jake of the people who shopped in Crow Alley. "What is this place?" he asked.

"London Particulars!" Mr. Crane replied. "The one place you'll find anything you're particular to. In London, at least, or wherever we may happen to move to." He grasped Jake's hand with a firm, friendly shake. "Jeremiah Crane. At least that's my name for now. Pleased to make your acquaintance. And you are?"

"Jake Shillingsworth." Jake found himself warming to Mr. Crane.

"You must be chilled to the bone. Come, I'll fetch you a nice cup of tea." Mr. Crane led them through the shop to a beautiful carved stone fireplace where a crackling fire burned merrily in the hearth. "Please, take the weight off your feet." He gestured to a heap of cushions.

"Would it be possible," Professor Thistlequick lowered his voice, "to speak somewhere more private."

"Of course." Mr. Crane glanced at Jake, who had already settled on a mound of pastel colored cushions with his hands held towards the fire.

"Don't worry about me," Jake said. "I'll be fine here."

Professor Thistlequick and Mr. Crane walked further into the shop and disappeared into its murk. Jake yawned. He hadn't realized how tired he was. The fire was as warm as a lazy summer's day and he closed his eyes, lay back, and within moments fell asleep.

JAKE WOKE to a sound of rattling china, and glanced up as a tall, elegant lady appeared carrying a wide silver tray laden with the most delicious looking cream tea he'd ever seen. An ornate silver teapot glimmered in the firelight next to a delicate china cup. Golden scones teetered in a towering pyramid with pots of clotted cream and a jewel-like crystal bowl filled with jam the color of amethysts.

The woman's long fiery auburn hair seemed to blaze as she set the tray down on a short round table. Jake struggled to get a glimpse of her face, for every time he thought he'd seen one of her features, it seemed to change. So he fixed his gaze upon the beauty spot on her cheek, and his reflection in her purple round eye-glasses. Jake swallowed. "I'm Jake."

"Llysandria." The lady sat beside him and offered her hand. Jake didn't know whether to kiss or shake it, so he plumped for the latter. Her hand was soft, but surprisingly strong.

"Jake. Jake Shillingsworth!" He wrinkled his nose and shook his head as he realized he'd already told her that!

She gave a wide, generous smile. "So... do you like the shop?"

"I do." Jake gazed into the fire as he tried to place her accent. It was odd, certainly not from London, or England for that matter. He wanted to ask her where she was from, but it felt as if his tongue had been tied in knots.

Llysandria filled a cup with tea and held it out. "The tea is delicious, but the jam is even better. The Professor introduced it to us. I believe his landlady, Mrs. Harker, makes it. Have you tried it before?"

Jake could almost feel the warmth of her eyes from behind her dark lenses. "No, but I've met Mrs. Harker. Weird old lady with funny hair." He smiled sheepishly. "So how do you know the Professor? Is he a regular here?"

"Yes. Although he's what Jeremiah calls an irregular type of regular, which is our favorite kind. The first time I met him, he saved my life. He's a good man."

"Yeah, I suppose he is."

Llysandria passed Jake a scone with a lavish dollop of jam and cream. Jake bit into it and his mouth almost exploded with the taste of sweet tart blackberries and thick silky cream.

"You don't sound too sure of the Professor," Llysandria said.

"I only just met him really."

"Well, I can vouch for him, Jake. Though it's wise to reserve judgment sometimes." She reached up and removed her spectacles. "Sometimes people have more than one face."

Jake gasped and dropped the scone as he looked into her gleaming emerald green eyes. They were round and snakelike, with thin black lines running down the centers, and as he peered into them, the whole world seemed to fall away.

CHAPTER FORTY-NINE

"I ..." Jake's words faded as he tried, and failed, to tear his gaze from Llysandria's eyes.

Her laughter was light and friendly and the sound of it broke the spell. "I assume you've never met a demon before?" she asked.

"I have, actually," Jake said. "He tried to kill me. But he didn't look like you. Not at all."

"My eyes are all that remain of my natural form. I took the Professor's advice and changed my appearance soon after I arrived here. And I'm glad I did, because he was quite right when he advised me demons aren't particularly popular in London these days." She put her spectacles back on. "I'm sorry I alarmed you, Jake. I thought you'd be used to things of a more unusual nature, what with you being a friend of the Professor's. Now, would you like a fresh scone to replace the one you dropped?" She refilled Jake's cup and passed him another scone. Jake was glad for the sugary tea, it helped settle his nerves.

They both glanced up as footsteps pressed the floorboards.

Professor Thistlequick strode towards them accompanied by Mr. Crane, who gave Llysandria a troubled look as he said, "Our friend has a favor to ask of you, Llysandria. Quite a hefty one, to say the least."

Llysandria smiled. "I'm in your debt, Professor. Ask what you will, I'll always help you if I can."

"My request is a most dangerous one." Professor Thistlequick's voice was heavy as he added, "Perhaps mortally so."

"I vowed to serve you however I can," Llysandria said. "And my vow is unbreakable. Tell me what you need."

"There's a… fellow demon roaming London. And he doesn't share your values."

Llysandria nodded. "I've sensed him of late. There's so few of us here it's almost impossible not to detect each other. Was he the one who attacked Jake? I found his scent the other night. It came on the breeze, ferocious and bloody. He's dangerous. Do you need me to dispose of him?"

"Yes." Professor Thistlequick looked even more uncomfortable as he added, "As painlessly as possible. I can't condone the shedding of blood. Even his."

"That I cannot promise," Llysandria said, "but I'll try. There was chaos and wildness in his scent. I'll use them for his undoing if I can."

"Thank you," Professor Thistlequick said. "I'd never ask if was avoidable."

"Let me gather what I need," Llysandria said, and stepped into the shadows.

Jake was about to stand and stretch when there was a bustle of movement and someone yelled, "Hurry!" Jake sat up as a curious sound filled the shop. It was part fog horn, part crow caw, and it seemed to come from everywhere at once.

Llysandria appeared, wrapped in a long black winter cloak with a hood covering her fiery red hair. She offered her hand and pulled Jake to his feet. "What's that noise?" he asked, as a deep rumble passed through the shop.

"An alarm," Llysandria replied. "HMS Watcher is overhead, and that's definitely not a good thing."

"Attention, ladies and gentleman!" Mr. Crane shouted, as he ran down the main aisle. "Grab hold of whatever you can. London Particulars is moving and its going to be a rough ride!"

The floor rumbled again and Jake clutched a shelf as customers darted from the aisles. They dropped all manner of strange objects as they grabbed pillars, table legs, and even each other. Several ran for the door at the far end of the shop.

"You can't get out," Mr. Crane shouted. "The door will have locked itself by now. Grab a hold, and get ready." He leaped over the desk and landed with the grace of a cat before a giant brass wheel mounted to the wall. As he gave it a spin great belches of steam poured from the vents along the wall. Jake clamped his shirt over his nose and mouth as the steam grew thicker.

"Good, good!" Mr. Crane scrambled to an obsidian plinth. Long wires ran from it to the vines of a tall bushy plant in the corner, and deep waves of blue-white color pulsed from the plant's leaves.

Bright yellow light flashed through the window at the back of the shop. It was HMS Watcher's beam, and like most people in the city, Jake had witnessed it on similar raids before. Within moments fully armed officers and Inspectors would descend in their steam-powered crafts and swoop down on the place.

Jake listened for the thrum of their engines and grabbed a book shelf as the entire shop shook again.

"If we're going to have to move, then we should use it to our advantage. Where did you say you needed to go, Professor?" Mr. Crane called over the din.

"As close to St. Katherine's docks as you can get," Professor Thistlequick called from the opposite aisle to Jake's.

Dust drifted from the ceiling and a blindingly bright light spilled into the shop.

Mr. Crane ran to his desk, rifled through the drawer and pulled out a heavy knot of rope. He placed it on the obsidian plinth and glanced up as the tall bushy plant shuddered, its tendrils whipping the air as another thin cloud of steam gushed from the walls.

"This is perhaps the finest marriage of science and magick, I've ever seen." The Professor told Jake.

A deafening hum filled the room as the airship swept over the shop. Searchlights flickered in the window and an Inspector peered through the glass. A blue glow crackled across his goggles as he glared at Jake, then he raised the butt of his rifle and smashed at the window.

Jake jumped as someone pounded on the front door behind them. Muffled voices screamed orders he couldn't hear as the gas lights flickered, and Mr. Crane spun the huge brass wheel.

The lights dimmed, plunging the room into darkness and the shop shook, sending Jake sprawling into the bookcase. He clung to it and prayed it wouldn't fall and squash him flat. Then, Mr. Crane released the wheel and yanked a great silver lever. Jake's breath caught in his throat and for a moment it felt as if he was deep under water.

The shop shuddered and fell silent.

Suddenly, the din of HMS Watcher vanished and the steam pouring from the vents began to thin. Jake glanced at the window.

The bright lights and rifle-wielding Inspector were gone. All he could see through the shattered glass was a red brick wall that definitely hadn't been there before. "What happened?" he asked.

"We moved." Llysandria handed Jake one of the sugar cubes scattered upon the tea tray clutched in her hands. "Eat it. It will help quell the shock."

Jake popped it in his mouth and looked around the shop. It was almost exactly as it had been, except larger, and now its shelves barely met the walls. Customers queued before the till and quietly waited to pay for their goods, as if nothing remarkable had taken place.

"Where are we?" Jake asked.

Llysandria raised her head and sniffed deeply. "Coal, fish, and an excess of vulgar words. I'd say we're no more than a minute or two from the docks."

"How?"

Professor Thistlequick smiled. "Jeremiah Crane comes from a long line of magicians. His father was a great explorer and his mother was a mystical sorceress who used her powers, in part, to decipher some of the mysteries of the great pyramids." Professor Thistlequick lowered his voice. "Few people know this, but there are secret chambers within the pyramids where it's possible to hop from one pyramid to the next without ever having to take a single step. Fascinating stuff!"

"Right," Jake said. It was fascinating, and just as crazy as everything else that had happened since he'd met the Professor.

"Jeremiah uses similar principles to move London Particulars," Professor Thistlequick continued. "Usually twice a day at dusk and dawn so he can stay one step ahead of the authorities."

Jake watched as Mr. Crane served the customers and apologized for the inconvenience of the move. Then, once he'd shown the last of them from the shop he gave Llysandria a grave look and returned to the desk.

"Don't fret, Jeremiah," she said. "It will be fine. I'll be back before dawn."

Mr. Crane nodded. "I hope so." He smiled at Jake. "And I hope you find your friends unscathed. This is a terrible business. I'd help if-"

"No," Professor Thistlequick said. "I won't bring anyone else into this. And were it possible, I wouldn't have asked Llysandria either. But there's the matter of the demon and his hexes. Or *demons*, if you count the man pulling the strings." He glanced at Jake. "But we will prevail. Never, ever give up, eh. And, we're going well armed. With Llysandria's help, and Jake's implacable bravery." He shook Mr. Crane's hand. "We'll see you soon. Wherever London Particulars happens to be."

Jake thanked Mr. Crane, and followed the Professor and Llysandria out into the cold dark night.

CHAPTER FIFTY

T he street outside the shop was narrow and desolate, and a curtain of fog billowed around them. Jake glanced up for any sign of HMS Watcher, but the sky was grey and silent.

A sulfurous earthy smell rose from the river and the low eerie sound of fog horns echoed off the crumbling buildings as they strode down the center of the cobbled street.

Llysandria's long cloak fluttered in the mist as she walked between Jake and the Professor. Her face was unreadable, her eyes hidden behind her dark glasses and the deep shadow of her hood. Professor Thistlequick gazed ahead, his face grave and when he glanced at Jake he smiled, but it didn't last long.

Is he as frightened as I am? Jake wondered. The man had shown very little fear so far on their adventures, but perhaps he was just good at hiding it.

They walked through one dank street after another, until Jake spotted a row of warehouses behind a long, tall iron fence. Was that where Nancy and Adam were? It was a desolate place, and usually Jake would expect to see lights and hear the bustle of dockers, but it seemed empty. Where was everyone?

Slow creeping dread seeped through him, and gnawed at his spirits like a dog with a bloody scrap of bone. "Ouch!" Jake cried as his fingers brushed the fence's iron railings. They were freezing cold.

Beyond the rails, warehouses loomed in the fog but there were no sounds of industry from the dockyard. No sparks, no clangs, no cries. The place seemed abandoned.

Jake pulled his scarf over his mouth as smoke drifted from the nearby factories across the river, bringing a heavy smell of coal and soot. There were no such scents from the dockyard. "Are you sure this is the right place?"

Professor Thistlequick pointed to a brass plaque attached to the nearby gates. "That's the address I found in Hobart Street."

"This is it," Llysandria said. "It reeks of the demon. He's close."

"Come, let's find a less conspicuous way inside." Professor Thistlequick led them along the railings, and stopped behind a heap of crates piled in the yard along the fence. "Perfect cover!" He rapped his fingers upon the railing and nodded. "Cast iron. This should be fun."

"How are we going to get over?" Jake asked as he glanced at the cruel spikes gleaming along the top.

"We're not going over," Professor Thistlequick said, "We're going through." He delved into his pocket. "A sock, half a potato, a spoon. No, I need something more... ah!"

Llysandria moved him aside, took off her gloves and glasses and placed them in her pocket. And then she grasped the heavy iron bars. She whispered strange, harsh words as she pulled and slowly her hands transformed, turning from pale and delicate to thick, dark and leathery. As she gripped the bars tighter, they sizzled and burned, the iron blazing bright orange as it bubbled and blistered.

A bitter scent filled the air as she worked her way along the barrier. "Move back." Llysandria pulled the rails apart. They snapped, and she removed them one by one before setting them upon the ground. "After you," she said, gesturing to the gap in the fence.

Jake stepped through, followed by the Professor. The ground crunched as they walked along the dock, and coal glistened amongst the frosty gravel. Slowly, cautiously, they made their way toward a huge warehouse, its tall wooden doors giant and heavy.

"Stop!" Llysandria grabbed Jake and pulled him behind her.

He followed her gaze to the single figure perched upon the warehouse roof. Its silhouette was framed by grey silken fog and it watched them with eyes like blistering red embers. A pair of wings snapped open as it sprang from the roof and rose into the air.

Llysandria tore her cloak off. Bright eerie light enveloped her, making her glimmer like a star.

Jake threw his hands over his eyes, and when he looked again, Llysandria was gone and in her place was a tall, agile creature covered with black iridescent scales. Long inky blue hair framed her face, and her eyes glowed emerald green. She flexed her long clawed fingers and grinned at Jake, revealing jagged fangs. "Still your thrashing heart."

If her words were meant to comfort Jake, they failed.

CHAPTER FIFTY-ONE

Jake glanced up as the other demon hovered above them. It was the same creature who had attacked him in The Tattered Crow. His bright red eyes blazed as he swept down, his savage howl echoing off the buildings and out across the Thames.

"Move." Llysandria shoved Jake to the ground and stood in his place.

The other demon beat his wings and wheeled away with a rush of wind that stirred the dust and ruffled Jake's hair. He watched as the creature swept low across the ground before rising and treading the air like it was water.

All traces of Llysandria's humanity were gone and her eyes shone with feral excitement as she addressed the demon. "You know who I am. And you fear me, just as you should." Two barbed wings snapped from her back as she kicked off from the ground and soared up into the night.

Jake watched as she hung in the air, challenging the demon to approach her. The beat of their wings seemed impossibly loud and their eyes blazed like lanterns. Llysandria spoke to the creature, but her words were too low for Jake to hear. The demon snarled, and with a savage growl, he spat at her.

She continued to speak, her claws flexing.

"We should go," Professor Thistlequick said. "Llysandria's buying us time. Let's use it and-" He stopped as the demon raced toward her, sweeping his clawed hand at her throat. She parried it, but his other hand was filled with a ball of bright blue fire. Llysandria tried to dodge but the fireball exploded around her and as she held her hands over her eyes, the demon turned and plunged towards Jake.

Fear rooted Jake to the spot.

"Jake!" Professor Thistlequick tried to reach him, but he was too late.

The demon crashed down and grabbed Jake with claws like red hot knives before lifting him and carrying him into the air.

Jake glanced down numbly to the Professor far below, his upturned face stricken with horror.

Together, they swooped over the warehouse climbing higher and higher. The docks receded and the river became a grey serpent slithering through a sea of twinkling red and yellow lights. Jake's heart raced as the growling rasp of the demon's breath filled his ears. "Please!" he begged.

The demon gave a guttural laugh and shifted his beating wings. "I could let go if you'd like?" He smiled and loosened his grip on Jake.

Jake fell and the air screamed past him until he was yanked back as the demon grabbed him by the scruff of his neck. The demon's eyes blazed as he growled, "How many are there?"

"How many what?" Jake felt sick as the city swayed beneath

him. And then he looked past the demon, towards the orb of light racing towards them. It was like a shooting star returning to the heavens. Whatever it was, the demon hadn't seen it.

"How many have crossed over from my world? Or is the traitor alone?"

Jake could just make out Llysandria's lithe form below the incoming orb. "Go to hell!" He cried as he wriggled free and dropped.

The demon caught him by the tips of his claws, but his snarl of victory was cut short as the orb of light smashed into his face. He gave an agonized scream, and a thick stench of burning flesh filled the air. As he reached up toward his blazing face, he let Jake go.

Jake fell like a stone. He reached out but there was nothing to grasp but air.

The dock rushed up in a dizzying blur.

Jake screwed his eyes shut, waiting for the impact until suddenly he found himself shooting sideways.

"I've got you!" Llysandria beat her wings as they pirouetted toward the yard. Jake's legs gave way as she set him down and he slumped to the ground.

"Are you alright?" Professor Thistlequick asked as he helped Jake to his feet and led him toward the warehouse. "We need to find cover. Fast."

Jake glanced back to the sky. "Llysandria!" he cried, as he saw the demon speeding towards her. She turned, but it was too late. The demon slammed into her and together they tumbled across the ground in a whirl of wings and claws, hacking and slashing at each other.

Llysandria roared as the demon's nails sought purchase between her scales, and then he released her and staggered back, his face half charred and still smoking from where her fireball had hit him.

Llysandria raised her hand, conjured another orb of ice-blue fire and slung it at the beast.

The demon sidestepped and the orb hit the ground, shattering like glass.

Llysandria glanced at Jake as she climbed into the air, ascending with the grace of a swallow. The other pursued her as she led him off towards the river.

A crack of gunfire roared across the docks.

"Where did that come from?" Jake looked around.

"I don't know," Professor Thistlequick said, as he rushed Jake towards the warehouse. "Help me get these doors open!" He pulled at the handles and Jake joined him as the demons swept away over the warehouse roof.

"Careful," Professor Thistlequick said, as the doors slid open with a thunderous rumble and they entered the great black darkness beyond.

THE FIRST BULLET whizzed past Llysandria, but the next hit her square in the back, shattering her scales. They fell like silver glitter. She gritted her teeth and wheeled around as the demon sped towards her. Llysandria lunged away and he shot past her, his claws raking the side of her face.

The crack of another bullet split the air and tore through her wing. She followed its trajectory back to the sniper.

A man hovered over the warehouse. Moonlight gleamed on his brass armor and the two umbrellas spinning above his head. Her senses told her the man was dead, and yet that didn't stop him raising his rifle and taking aim once more.

Llysandria summoned an orb of fire and slung it. It blistered through the fog and caught the man square in the chest, igniting him in a ball of roaring blue flames. He clattered to the roof and fell over its side before striking the dock below. His rifle landed beside him and discharged a single round into the sky.

Where was the other? Llysandria glanced back as the demon slammed into her.

The air rushed from her lungs and she flinched as claws sliced at her throat. She let herself drop, taking the demon with her. Their wings tangled as they fell and Llysandria flipped over and over, using the demon to break her fall.

His head smashed into the icy ground with a satisfying thud, and his eyes rolled in their sockets. She backed away from him, searching for a way to banish him from this world and send him to another.

And then she found what she was looking for.

A frozen puddle reflected the moonlight shining through the thinning fog. Llysandria crouched before it and chanted soft, ancient words. Words that had probably never been uttered in this city before, words older than the moon.

The puddle's surface glimmered as spidery black beams of light passed across it like a dark web. Llysandria hurried her chant, willing the puddle to transform. The ice twinkled and shattered and its surface liquefied, revealing stars glowing below it. Stars from another world.

As the other's footsteps approached, Llysandria gripped the puddle's edge and prised it away, leaving a yawning hole in the ground. Smoke hissed up and merged with the fog as the other crept closer.

She could hear his nails flexing, nails that were moments

away from being thrust into her neck. Llysandria jumped into the hole and cast a spell to slowly close it behind her.

The other followed, his eyes filled with savage intent.

As the hole above them collapsed, sealing the portal, Llysandria flew into that other night sky, desperately searching for a way to lose her murderous opponent.

CHAPTER FIFTY-TWO

The warehouse was so vast its ceiling was lost to the darkness. Long towering racks stretched into the gloom and each of the wide plank shelves was stacked with trunks, barrels and oblong metal boxes that reminded Jake of coffins. He wrinkled his nose at the bitter smell wafting through the air.

"Gunpowder," Professor Thistlequick whispered. "Lots and lots of gunpowder." He placed a hand on Jake's shoulder. "Stay alert, there's bound to be guards." He pulled a brass tube from his pocket, and with a twist and flick, a tiny wick encased in glass burst to life.

The Professor used the light to examine one of the racks, before snapping a case open. Inside was a pile of neatly stacked rifles. He gestured to the racks around them. "There must be enough weapons stockpiled here to start a war, right in the middle of London. Interesting, and troubling. Can you see any traces of magick?"

Jake scoured the darkness. "No, nothing."

"Hmm," Professor Thistlequick dowsed his light and gestured for Jake to follow him.

They made their way towards the center of the warehouse, but ducked behind a large crate as a man appeared carrying several lanterns. He stopped ahead of them and set the lamps down upon a large crate.

Other men appeared. They carried cases and stacked them one by one into a pile upon the floor. All of them had the same expressionless demeanor as the guards at the house on Hobart Street.

Jake flinched as a door slammed near the rear of the warehouse and clomping footsteps rang out. He recognized the metallic sound at once. "Kedgewick," he whispered.

They watched as the brass man lumbered into view, his armor scorched and battered in the glow of the lamplight. Jake almost retched as his gaze fell upon the glass porthole in the giant man's chest and the malformed heart within. And then he saw the small boy walking behind the giant, his face lost to shadows.

"Listen," Kedgewick barked. The men looked up at him. "We have trespassers. Find them, deal with them, and toss their corpses into the Thames."

The men pulled long knives from their coats, their blades flashing in the lantern's glow. Slowly, they spread out and began a methodical search of the warehouse.

"We should get-" Jake stopped as he squinted at the boy beside Kedgewick. Even though his features were hard to make out, there was something familiar about him. Kedgewick muttered something and the boy scurried to a shelf, and as he returned carrying a bulky case, he passed within the radius of a lantern and its glow lit the side of his face.

"It's Adam!" Jake whispered. Yes, it was Adam alright, but there was something wrong with him because his expression was still and blank, his eyes glassy. Kedgewick growled something and they vanished into the shadows.

"We've got to go after them!" Jake was about to set off when the Professor grabbed his wrist and pulled him back.

And then Jake heard it; the sound of footsteps drawing toward them.

CHAPTER FIFTY-THREE

Llysandria dove through the other world's sky. The land below was as black as midnight on a moonless night, its terrain filled with distant scarlet and gold glowing lines. They seemed to spread like veins across the dark earth, and it took Llysandria a moment to realize they were streams of lava. She could feel their warmth on her scaled flesh, even from where she flew.

Wooosh!

She heard the fireball before she saw it.

Llysandria danced nimbly aside as it shot by, crackling and fizzing with blue flames.

The other demon hung in the air above her, his leathery black wings framing him, his scarlet eyes staring down. He remained there for a moment, before plunging and shooting toward her like a black spear of malice.

Llysandria folded her wings and dropped, holding her arms and hands taut against her body to allow herself to fly faster.

She could hear him close behind, the rasp of his breath, the snap of his teeth.

The air shrieked as she headed down, plummeting fast. A canyon loomed below, the river of golden lava running through it blisteringly hot even at her altitude.

She glanced back as the demon followed. He was fast, but his fury made him ungainly and slow as he held his arms out before him, his claws poised to tear and shred.

Llysandria slowed as she spotted a tunnel in the canyon's side. She could hide in its darkness. She stopped and hovered over the roiling heat, waiting for her foe to reach her. He shot toward her, his jagged teeth clenched, and as his claws were almost at her face, she sidestepped.

The demon plunged past, but not before she raked her claws through one of his wings, shredding the spongy skin and causing him to howl in fury. He ground to a halt below and spun around, his hand summoning a ball of blue flames.

The fireball roared toward her but his anger had marred his aim and it shot by, its flames warming the side of her face. He summoned another, and another, throwing them hard and fast.

Llysandria dodged them, but one hit its mark, striking her in the leg and causing her to scream in agony. The pain was more intense than anything she'd known, and its bite spread from her leg to her hands as she batted it out.

Her foe laughed as he summoned another ball of flames.

Llysandria hung woozily in the air, watching the flight of each crackling blue ball of fire, dancing aside as they came at her. The demon was slowly running out of magick and the effort of raising the flames was draining him.

She waited until fatigue furrowed his brow, and

summoned her own fireball. Llysandria sent it racing down. It struck him square in the chest, knocking him down to the river of lava below.

Fury contorted his face as he wheeled and slowed, patting out the flames as best he could. He was off balance, his one shredded wing only half as efficient as his other.

Llysandria gazed at the tunnel in the rock wall beside her again and hoped it went as deep as it appeared to. As the demon raised another fireball, his eyes narrowed, and she could see he was tempering his anger into concentration as he prepared to throw it.

She dove, shooting toward the passage and as she passed into its darkness, the fireball flew past her and set the stone ceiling ablaze with blue flames.

The tunnel before her was long and filled with smoky black air. Soon, she heard her enemy behind once more; his ragged breath, the savage beating of his wings. Llysandria glanced back to find his eyes like pinpricks of scarlet as he closed in behind her.

"I'll tear you apart!" His threats echoed down the passage.

Llysandria flew on, but as she turned a bend the tunnel's end loomed before her.

She was trapped...

She swallowed. She'd have to fight hand-to-hand, claw-to-claw, and Llysandria had no doubt her opponent's viciousness would win.

He slowed as he passed the bend, as if sensing her fear and apprehension.

A terrible heat rose from below her, and as she looked down, she saw what appeared to be tiny golden worms in the dark rock below her. They spread over the passage and lined the wall behind her. It was lava, revealed through the cracks in the stone tunnel.

The walls were thin…

Llysandria summoned a ball of fire and cradled it between her cupped hands. It was weak compared to the ones the other demon had conjured, and her energy was ebbing fast.

"Is that all you have?" The demon halted before her. "It won't hold me off."

"Finish me then," Llysandria said.

He flexed his muscles, revealing his strength.

She smiled. She'd need that strength, every ounce of it.

The demon came at her, his wings beating hard, his hands outstretched. Before he could reach her, Llysandria tossed the fireball into the air and closed her eyes as it flashed and exploded.

She dropped to the tunnel's floor and felt him shoot overhead, half blinded by her fireball.

Boom!

He struck the cavern wall.

She glanced back as the passage wall gave way to molten lava and his spindly form turned from black to liquid gold as the fire consumed him. Mercifully, the echo of his final scream was short lived, but it felt like she'd hear it for the rest of her days.

Llysandria wavered. The unbearable heat from the exposed lava was almost too much to bear. She flew back down the tunnel, her limbs aching, her wings heavy as the last of her energy melted away.

She wanted to find somewhere to rest, to close her eyes and recover what was left of her energy.

But there was no time; she had to find a portal back to the

city and quickly. Jake and the Professor were in mortal danger, she'd seen that surely enough. And there was every chance one or both would be gone before dawn rose over London.

CHAPTER FIFTY-FOUR

A figure appeared in the murk before Jake. It was one of the Kedgewick's men and he was heading right for them.

"Fiddlesticks!" Professor Thistlequick muttered as he dug through his pockets.

"Do something!" Jake whispered as the man drew nearer.

"I am!" Professor Thistlequick carefully produced what looked like a small clockwork duck with a key sticking out of its back from his coat.

"What..." Jake's hope of escaping alive plummeted. The man was seconds from seeing them, and then Jake spotted the length of rusty pipe clutched in thug's hand. "What are you doing?" he whispered frantically, as the Professor leaned down, wound the duck up and set it on the floor.

The duck flapped its wings and waddled across the flagstones, its ticking gears and springs raising a din. As the man turned toward it, the clockwork duck sped up and toddled between his outstretched feet.

"This way," Professor Thistlequick led Jake off in the opposite direction, "One," he whispered, "two, three!"

The duck gave out a series of angry quacks, each growing louder and louder. Soon the warehouse rang with a din of footsteps pounding through the darkness. The Professor and Jake scurried down a warren of aisles to a sliding door and wrenched it open wide enough to slip through.

"There!" Jake pointed across the dockyard to where Kedgewick and Adam were entering a huge brick building beside the dock. Tendrils of grey fog rose like writhing tentacles from the Thames and licked across the side of the building. They dashed across the dockyard, their shoes crunching the coal dust.

The brick building was dark and foreboding and its barred, blackened windows were set too high to see through. Jake was almost at the door when a desolate scream rang out.

It was a child's scream, and a fountain of blazing orange and red sparks filled a window as another cry rang out. "What are they doing?" Jake shivered with horror, and then anger as he pulled at the door handle.

It was locked.

"I don't know," Professor Thistlequick said. "Let's find another way." They strode around the building, pausing as another glow of sparks illuminated the windows and the cries rang out again.

Jake glanced back the way they'd come. London's lights were dim through the rising fog and it seemed like the city was a world away from this nightmarish place. He wished he could go somewhere else, somewhere safe. But first he had to find his friends, and if Adam was there, there was a strong chance they'd find Nancy too.

Professor Thistlequick strode ahead and peeked around the corner of the building before motioning for Jake to follow.

Finally, they found another door set into the sooty red brick wall and this time the door handle turned.

Jake was about to enter when the Professor barred his way. "Are you sure you want to go in there?" Professor Thistlequick asked. "I can search the place on my own if you'd prefer?" His weak smile did little to dispel the fear in his eyes.

"I'm coming with you," Jake said. "Adam's in there, maybe Nancy too. I have to help them."

"Right," Professor Thistlequick said. "But stick with me."

The door gave an almost hungry creak as it swung open.

A large, spacious room filled with bulky work benches stretched before them. Rusted knives, trowels and long spiked forks were laid upon the benches, and a heavy odor hung in the cold dank air, reminding Jake of mulched leaves. Candles flickered upon upturned barrels and their weak waxy light danced upon the walls.

At first glance, Jake thought the closest wall had been sloppily coated in dark purple paint, but then he heard something softly unfurling upon the brick surface.

Professor Thistlequick examined it carefully. "It's Miraghus," he said.

The mention of the strange name reminded Jake of chewing the fungus on the cloud, and brought back the recollection of drinking chocolate with Nancy on a Christmas many years ago. But as the fungus rippled and stirred on the walls, he also recalled the madness in Lear's eyes and shivered.

"This way..." Professor Thistlequick peered through a door in the corner of the room, before beckoning Jake to follow.

A murky corridor stretched before them and they stuck to

its shadows, just beyond the reach of the gas lamps lining the walls. Shafts of light punctuated the darkness from the open doors set into the hallway.

As they crept past the first, Jake caught a glimpse of blazing firelight and a heavy scent of freshly dug roots and tar billowed out into the corridor. Inside was a group of emaciated, dead-eyed people stirring huge iron pots filled with black bubbling liquid, with baskets of Miraghus mushrooms resting beside them. Jake hurried past them as a shout came from a room further down the hall.

The Professor's brow furrowed as he peered inside. Jake glanced past the doorframe to find a room lit with gas lamps. It was a small chamber and its back wall was lined with shelves holding dozens of glass jars and bottles. Jake recoiled as he looked closer. Each jar held a twisted, withered form floating in amber liquid. Whatever the specimens were, they made him think of hairless rats crossed with hunched, crooked birds.

He shuddered as his gaze fell to the figure watching from the corner of the room. At first he thought it was a girl until he saw her porcelain face and those dead black eyes. It was a doll, and he glanced around, half expecting to find Mrs. Wraythe lurking in the shadows.

"This is an evil place," the Professor whispered. "Come, let's search for your friends and leave as soon as we find them."

They crept through the door at the end of the corridor into another.

Light spilled from an open doorway ahead, and Jake almost screamed as a crazed looking woman jumped out and seized the Professor's arm. "They're coming," she said, her eyes bright and wild. "They're coming! When the gate opens and the ravens fall. When the black birds are down."

"Thank you for letting me know. Now rest," the Professor said as he gently patted her hand and unpicked her fingers from his wrist. The woman laughed and grasped for Jake, but the manacles chaining her feet snapped taut, stopping her from reaching him.

Inside the next room a boy sat at a table, his head inclined to the ceiling. Beside him, a tethered ragged teddy bear levitated in the air over an iron brazier filled with smoldering coals.

"How is he-" Jake fell silent as the boy glanced at him. Suddenly the bear fell onto the fire, and the child cried as it burst into flames.

"It's okay!" the Professor told the boy as he ran inside, snatched the bear from the fire and stamped out the flames.

The boy regarded them in silence as the Professor rifled through his pockets and tried every instrument he carried to undo the child's manacles, but they were locked tight. "We'll get you out of here," Professor Thistlequick promised, but as he met Jake's eyes, his face grew grave. "Come," he whispered. "Time's of the essence."

As they passed the next room, Jake froze. Inside a man sat strapped to a high-backed chair and spirals of royal blue smoke spilled from his mouth, and writhed about his bald head like serpents. But that wasn't what arrested Jake's attention; it was the figure looming before him. He wore a long black winter coat and a top hat rested imperiously upon his head. And even though his back was to Jake, Jake could see enough of his mask-like face to know who he was.

It was the man who had shot and left him for dead on the

rooftop. The man with the eyes that had seemed to stare from some impossibly deep, damned underworld.

"Jake!" Professor Thistlequick whispered, and motioned for him to hurry on.

It took every last ounce of Jake's will to force himself to move before the man heard or saw him. "It was him," Jake whispered as they reached the end of the corridor and a final closed door. "The man who shot me."

Professor Thistlequick nodded. "I saw his likeness in a painting on the cloud. This place, the cloud, Lear, it all seems to be his doing. Come, let's find your friends and leave while we can." It seemed he had more to say, but instead he tried the handle of the stout door at the end of the hall.

It was locked. The Professor's fingers trembled as he took out his pick. Moments later, the lock clicked. He peered through the keyhole, turned the handle and slipped inside.

The room was long and wide and its windows were covered in heavy dark curtains. Children sat around a circular table filled with flickering candles. They stared at their hands, their faces slack and emotionless.

"Nancy!" Jake whispered as he spotted her sitting between a pair of twin girls. Streaks of soot covered her face and her hair fell in long thick tangles as she stared down, perfectly still. Jake hurried toward her but the Professor grabbed his wrist.

"Wait!"

"Why? No!" Jake tried to squirm free. "I need to get her out of here."

"We need help, Jake. And we have to get them *all* out, we can't just take Nancy. I won't leave a single soul behind. But I don't want our enemy to be alerted until I find help. We'll

284

need a distraction, something to draw the city's eyes to this terrible place. Something to attract HMS Watcher's attention."

"What?"

The Professor stared into the shadows, and slowly, a thin smile crept over his face. "I have an idea. But I need you to wait with your friend. It will be safer." He glanced at the door. "If I'm not back within twenty minutes, run. Run like the very devil is here, and he may well be for all I know. Do you understand?"

Jake nodded. He understood perfectly.

CHAPTER FIFTY-FIVE

J ake waited for the Professor to lock the door before he returned to the table. The children continued to sit in silence, as if playing a game of statues.

"Can you hear me?" Jake whispered. Nancy continued to stare into nothingness. Jake placed his hand on her arm. She showed no comprehension, not even a flicker. He searched the room for another way out in case they needed it.

A heavy scent of mildew rose from the drapes obscuring the windows and they were damp to the touch. Jake pulled one back to reveal thick iron bars covering the murky windows. "Which means the only way out is the corridor..."

The flickering candles cast eerie shadows beneath the children's faces as he returned to the table. "Nancy," he whispered again. "Please wake up. You've got to be ready when we need to go, and-" He stopped.

Had her finger moved? Or was it a trick of the light?

He held her hand, willing his warmth to spread to her and for her to give him a sign she was okay. She didn't move, and slowly his concern turned to blazing anger. "The man outside did this to you, didn't he? I wish he'd drop dead. I looked everywhere looking for you, Nance. Above the clouds, in the streets, and now here. Me and the Professor... He'll be back soon, and then he'll make you better. I know he will." As Jake leaned over to brush Nancy's hair from her eyes, his elbow nudged the girl next to her and her head lolled down. A tremor ran through her body, and then her hands began to twitch upon the table producing a loud, thumping sound.

"Stop!" Jake whispered. But the girl's fit worsened and her whole body began to jitter as her fingers beat upon the wood.

"Please!" Jake begged.

Her crazed, panicked eyes flitted from Jake to the ceiling and her shoes struck the table. *Thud!*

"Please, stop!" Jake placed what he hoped was a calming hand upon her shoulder. She was as cold as the grave.

Suddenly, the girl let forth a terrible, blood-curdling scream.

Jake clamped his hand over her mouth but it was too late. A thump came from outside the room and the door handle began to rattle.

Ice-cold dread shivered over the back of Jake's neck as he heard the unmistakable sound of a key turning in the lock.

CHAPTER FIFTY-SIX

The Professor stepped briskly across the gleaming coal-encrusted ground that stretched before the warehouse like a void. As he marched toward the building, the terrible horrors he'd just witnessed in that devil's laboratory played through his mind. It felt like the darkness he'd seen was seeping into his very soul, and he had to force himself to smile. "I'll put a stop to it," he vowed. "I'll brighten this hellish place up."

Professor Thistlequick ducked into the warehouse and listened for the guards. It seemed he was alone, but he continued slowly through the labyrinthine place to ensure it had indeed been evacuated. The place was bigger than it had seemed before, and as he wound through the towering, darkened aisles he realized it was a little like shopping at London Particulars, only infinitely more dangerous.

THE WATCHMAN, who had long since been locked in a curious, half waking dream, tensed as he heard faint clomping footsteps in the murk. He clutched his knife and hunched down as a dark figure approached.

It was a man in a top hat and coat and he instantly reminded him of the master, only this man was different. He didn't inspire even the briefest flicker of fear in the watchman as he stopped in the middle of the aisle and muttered, "Fiddlesticks!"

So, if it wasn't the master, the watchman dimly thought, and it wasn't the demon, or Kedgewick, it had to be the intruder...

The watchman lumbered towards the man but as soon as he made his move the other ran and slipped around the corner of the aisle. "Intruder!" the watchman yelled.

Within moments he heard the others running into the building, drawn by his cry of alarm. He rounded the corner, expecting to find the interloper right before him...

Nothing.

The trespasser had vanished.

"Out here!" a voice called, and then the watchman heard someone clapping their hands in applause. He slipped out through the warehouse doors toward the dock.

The man was stood before him, a burning match glowing in his gloved hand. The watchman started towards him as he heard the other guards approaching.

"Would you like to see some fireworks?" the man asked. His words made little sense to the watchman, but they didn't need to. The watchman had had his orders, and that was all he needed.

Intruders, Kedgewick had commanded, needed to be tossed in the Thames. It was as simple as that.

"Watch!" the man in the top hat said as he dropped the burning match onto the ground. A trail of sparks ignited and sped along the glistening black earth. They shot right between the watchman's feet and he followed their path as the sizzling fire zigzagged towards the warehouse.

He had no idea what the purpose of the fire was, but he knew, in his cloudy mind, that it was something bad. Something that would enrage the master.

"I…" he began as the line of fire swept through the gap in the warehouse doors.

"One… two… three… boom!" the man in the top hat cried.

Flashes of light roared through the warehouse, producing an almost blinding white glare. The watchman threw his fingers over his eyes as an explosion sent shockwaves through the surrounding air.

The ensuing tide of heat hit him hard in the chest, lifting him, and throwing him down to the ground. Explosion after explosion boomed across the dock as flames licked the warehouse windows.

"You…" the watchman said, as he climbed to his feet and scoured the dockyard seeking the man who had caused the explosion.

But he was gone. Like he'd never been there.

CHAPTER FIFTY-SEVEN

J ake searched for something to block the door with as the handle began to turn, slowly, cautiously. There was nothing to bar the door with so he ran toward the drapes to hide, but it was too late.

The twitching girl's screams faded as the door creaked open.

"Silence," the man said as he stepped into the room. It was the same devil who had been experimenting on the people outside the room. The devil who had shot Jake on the rooftop.

Gooseflesh ran along Jake's arms as their eyes met.

The man inclined his head. "It's you," he said. "We've met before. I thought I'd killed you, so why, pray tell, aren't you dead?" He took a slow, cautious step toward Jake. "What kind of dark magick do you wield?"

Jake was about to answer, when a huge explosion boomed outside and rattled the grimy glass in its frames as a fiery glow lit the windows through the drapes.

The man didn't even flinch as he continued to stare at Jake. "I suppose that din is your handiwork?"

Jake winced as another explosion roared outside.

"I asked you a question, child," the man continued.

"I'm not a child." Jake forced himself to stand as tall as possible. And as he glanced to Nancy and the other children, his anger burned so intensely it seemed to match the great fire outside. "What have you done to my friend?"

The man shrugged. "I merely tried to measure her mettle. She was strong actually, but she has no talent for magick." Slowly, casually, he removed a revolver from his coat. "A mutual acquaintance of ours assured me that you had great gifts, Jake Shillingsworth. Yes, I know who you are. But," he nodded to the window, "it seems my plans and research are about to go on a hiatus for now. I assume the wanton destruction of my stockpile is your handiwork?"

"Not mine." Jake forced a smile. "But I'm pretty sure I know who did it. And I definitely know who took your demon away."

The man aimed his revolver squarely at Jake's chest. "Good for you. Yet this..." He swept a hand around the room. "Is merely a prologue to my plans. But you won't live to see the story's end."

"Put the gun down!" a voice commanded from beyond the door.

"Llysandria?" Jake glanced past the man to the corridor beyond the room.

The gaslights burst with light as Llysandria stormed past them. The glow of firelight played upon her hair and the dark round lenses of her spectacles as she approached the room. She was human once more, at least in appearance, and she smiled at Jake, but he saw her limp, and her barely concealed grimace of pain.

"If you harm my friend," she said to the man as she stepped into the room, "I'll-"

The man shrugged, turned, and fired at her. The sound was thunderous and a high whine rang in Jake's ears as he staggered away from the cloud of gun smoke.

Llysandria clutched her hand to her chest. For a brief moment, her form shifted, changing from woman to demon, and then back to woman again. Both faces were filled with agony.

"No!" Jake cried.

"Ah," the man said. A cruel smile tugged his lips as he looked Llysandria up and down. "A demon. I assume it was you who challenged Mortaphir and removed him from my command." He fired again.

Llysandria staggered back, growling, her hands clenched, her nails turning to claws.

Then the man swept his arm around and aimed at Jake.

Jake waited for the roar of the bullet, but the hammer clicked on an empty chamber.

The man reached into his pockets, producing a handful of bullets. But before he could load his gun, Llysandria lunged at him. He ducked away, and fled through the door, slamming it behind him. Llysandria wavered, clearly torn between pursuing him and coming to Jake's side. She chose the latter. "Are you alright?" she asked, her face human once more.

"I think so."

Llysandria clasped Jake's hands in hers. Her eyes were wracked with pain but she didn't seem to pay it any mind as she appraised the shocked children huddled in the room. "Poor mites," she said. "We need to-"

The door flew open and the Professor blundered in, peering around, nodding and muttering to himself. He glanced from Llysandria to Jake. "Good, good, good. Everyone's in one piece, including both of you."

"They need help," Jake said as he gazed at the watching children. "Something's wrong with them."

"Indeed. And they'll have help," Professor Thistlequick said. "Trust me. But first we need to leave this infernal place. My little diversion caused quite a stir. HMS Watcher's soaring across the city toward us, as well as half of London's Inspectors I don't doubt. Which means it's time for us to make our escape."

CHAPTER FIFTY-EIGHT

Jake and Llysandria helped the children up from the table and they moved sluggishly as Professor Thistlequick led them from the room.

"What can you do for them?" Jake asked, his gaze straying to Nancy, who still seemed to be in heavy shock.

"We should leave them in the protection of the police," Professor Thistlequick said. "Their doctors should be able to free them from this wretched, torpid trance."

They moved through the building as the inhabitants screamed and shouted, their voices loud and shrill. "Don't worry," the Professor assured Jake, "everyone will be rescued shortly."

Jake braced himself for the cold wintry air, but as he stepped outside it was as warm as a May evening. The warehouse burned bright, lighting the overhead sky in a blaze of orange and red. Explosions continued to boom inside, sending sparks and embers dancing into the air.

"They're here!" Llysandria said, her face grim as she pointed to the two blinding searchlights sweeping over the docks as HMS Watcher descended. A smaller police craft followed behind the floating leviathan and flew down and landed upon the ground. An Inspector emerged, his goggles flashing as he surveyed the scene.

"You should go," Professor Thistlequick said to Llysandria. She nodded and flitted into the shadows. "Follow her, Jake. Flee while there's still time."

Jake gazed at Nancy as she stood beside him staring lifelessly at her feet. "I'm not leaving her. She can't look after herself."

"She'll be fine, the police will attend to her." Professor Thistlequick placed a hand on Jake's shoulder. "But they'll have questions for us, and I'd rather not answer them for now."

Jake was about to disagree, when he saw the police swarming from their craft. The Professor was right. They'd take care of this business better than he ever could, and there was no benefit in being arrested. "You'll be alright, Nance." Jake smoothed her hair from her face. "I'll come and see you as soon as I can." She continued to stare down, as motionless as a statue.

"Come on." Professor Thistlequick led Jake around the building toward the river. As they ran, Jake caught a gleam of brass from the corner of his eye and he stopped to regard the small group of figures scurrying away down the dock. Moonlight gleamed on the huge, towering figure guiding them.

It was Kedgewick, leading a group of children from the dock. Was Adam there? It was impossible to see their features in the murk.

"Jake?" the Professor called.

Jake ignored him as Kedgewick stopped along the dock,

and pointed down toward the river. The figures fell to their knees at once and began to descend from view.

"There must be a ladder there," the Professor said. "Maybe there's a boat waiting to carry them away."

Together, they ran to the edge of the dock, and as Jake reached it, he had to throw his hand over his eyes.

Vivid blue-white light filled a patch of water, and it was so intense he could barely see anything. Slowly, his eyes adjusted and he saw the huge fish-like craft resting in the water. It was the airship that had flown over the city on the night Nancy and Adam had been taken.

"I don't see anything..." the Professor's words tailed off as a low rumble came from the river. "But I hear it."

Crackles of magick lit the gloom as the craft rose up, its spines glistening in the moonlight. Its engine roared and churned, and the sludgy river bubbled into white froth while dead fish rose around it.

"What is it?" the Professor asked.

"It's their ship!" Jake called over the din. He looked back to see if the Inspectors on the dock had noticed the craft, but they were huddled around the building instead. "We've got to stop them!" Jake said, and began to run.

"Wait!" Professor Thistlequick called, but Jake wasn't waiting for anything. They'd saved Nancy, now it was Adam's turn.

Jake slowed as he reached the craft. The entire thing rumbled and shook as it prepared to take off. The Professor joined him, scouring the water and totally missing the huge airship before them as its invisibility cloak confounded his eyes.

"We should-"

Jake ignored the Professor and jumped, landing hard on

the top of the ship with a deep, metallic clang. He grasped the hatch mounted before the spines and pulled with all his might, coughing and spluttering as thick acrid steam poured through the air.

Thud!

The Professor landed beside Jake, glanced down, and shook his head in bewilderment. "It's like I'm standing on thin air! I can't see a thing!"

"There's a hatch here," Jake pointed down. "Help me get it open!"

The Professor reached out until his fingers were on the edge of the hatch. "I can feel it," He called. And then he joined Jake, pulling with all his might, until finally the hatch began to lift.

Together, they dropped through it, landing nimbly in the belly of the beast.

CHAPTER FIFTY-NINE

"I can see it now!" the Professor cried, as he glanced around them. Jake followed his gaze along the short corridor, its brass riveted walls and floor shining under mounted gas lamps. It was hot inside the craft, and the air was thick with the scent of burning coal.

"We should close the hatch!" the Professor said, and climbed the ladder beside them, reached up, and pulled the hatch down. Jake was about to set off looking for Adam, when the entire ship shook and rumbled.

"Stoke the furnace. Faster!" The cold clipped voice seemed to come from everywhere around them at once.

"There!" The Professor pointed to a long pipe running below the metallic ceiling, and then to another on the opposite side of the aisle. "The voice is coming from the pipes. They're using it to communicate throughout the entire ship. Clever!"

"It's him," Jake said. "The man who took Nancy and Adam."

The Professor gave a solemn nod, but then his gaze alighted on the walls and he ran his fingers over the rivets before gazing out through a porthole. "This vessel really is a triumph of craftsmanship. It's far larger than I'd anticipated…"

"We've got to find Adam, and-" Jake stopped as heavy footsteps approached them.

"Quick." Professor Thistlequick hurried to the end of the corridor and climbed down a ladder to a lower deck. Jake followed as the measured footsteps clanged closer.

They ran down another short passage and turned a bend to where it ended in a row of long interlocked brass spikes. It took Jake a moment to realize they were the mechanical fish's teeth.

The craft shook again and Jake had to grasp a spike to steady himself.

"We need to find the device he's using to cloak the ship," Professor Thistlequick whispered. "If we can switch it off, the ship should become visible to HMS Watcher." He ran to a nearby door and spun a wheel before glancing inside. "Nothing of interest. But where…"

A desolate cry rang out from below them. Professor Thistlequick hurried down the corridor and lifted another hatch. "Quick, we need to find the children before this thing takes off."

Sweltering heat engulfed them as they climbed down a ladder. Before Jake could look around, the Professor pulled him behind a huge hopper overflowing with coal. "Careful," he whispered as Jake peeked over the mound.

The firelight cast an orange glow on Kedgewick's armor as he stood before two children, supervising them as they shoveled coal from a barrow into the great furnace before them.

"It's Adam!" Jake whispered, pointing to his friend.

"Quicker!" Kedgewick slapped the gangly boy next to Adam. He stooped faster, his arms shaking as he worked.

"We've got to do something." Jake said, suppressing his anger and forcing himself to whisper.

"We are." Professor Thistlequick replied. "As soon as we find the cloaking device we can attend to the children. We have to alert the craft to the authorities, we can't win this battle on our own. Come on." He waited until Kedgewick's back was turned, and climbed back up the ladder.

The ship shook violently as Jake followed him, stumbling from the hatch, and crashing into the wall. He grasped a porthole to steady himself as churning water splashed against the window and clouds of steam billowed around them while the craft rose higher over the surface of the river.

"It's too late to stop it!" Professor Thistlequick cried as the ship sputtered and dipped back down. Roiling water filled the porthole. "They're building up power to make the craft airborne!" Professor Thistlequick grabbed a pipe. "Hang on!" he cried as the craft surged forward and shot through the water.

The din of straining machinery was almost deafening. Jake fought to stay upright as the craft burst ahead, cleared the river, and rose into the air. They shot up at what felt like an impossible speed as the docks and HMS Watcher descended below them.

"We don't have much time," Professor Thistlequick said. "If they get too far from the city the authorities will never see them. We have to uncloak them, now!"

They ran along the corridor and the Professor spun a wheel at the end and pulled at a heavy steel door. It led to a small chamber with an iron bench and manacles tethered to the floor.

"This must be the brig." Professor Thistlequick strode to a high shelf and picked up a strange glass vial. He sniffed the black powder inside and grimaced. "I think this is how they've been controlling their workers and guards. It's some kind of mind control agent, probably a derivative of the Miraghus." He slipped the vial into his pocket and led Jake back out to the corridor.

Several more empty cells stood between them and the final door. Professor Thistlequick stopped before it and turned to Jake. "This has to lead to the cockpit. Find a place to hide. Let me deal with this on my own."

"No," Jake said, "I'm coming with you. Two are stronger than one." He forced a tone of bravery into his voice that he didn't feel as the Professor nodded, spun the wheel, and yanked the door open.

CHAPTER SIXTY

Cold dread filled Jake as he spotted the man in the winter coat sitting ahead of them in a tall leather chair. He was busy tending the ship's wheel, which was set into a long control panel loaded with buttons and levers. The two immense round windows in the wall before him were the eyes of the great ship, and far below them the rugged countryside rushed by in a dark blur.

"Why have you left the engine room unattended, Kedgewick? I specifically-" The man stopped speaking as he turned towards them. A slight furrow troubled his brow as he gazed at Jake. "You again. You've caused me no end of problems, boy." And then he glared at the Professor. "And I see you've brought a friend." His gaze darted to a revolver on the table behind Jake. The Professor lunged forward and snatched it up.

"It seems this night has no end of surprises," the man said as he pulled two levers, taking the craft soaring up. "Tell me, sir, will you show more nerve than the boy did when he last aimed my gun at me? I must say, your posture lacks conviction."

Professor Thistlequick snapped the revolver open, emptied the chamber, and dropped the bullets into his coat pocket.

"What did you do that for?" Jake demanded.

"He's quite right in his assessment; I wouldn't be able to shoot even if I wanted to." The Professor smiled at the man. "Professor Thistlequick. And you are?"

"You may call me, Mr. Spires. And I've heard of you. Thistlequick. The so called Clockwork Magician."

"Indeed I am. Is Mr. Spires your real name?" Professor Thistlequick asked.

"What do you think?" Spires' voice was filled with scorn.

"Probably not." Professor Thistlequick inched forward as Mr. Spires pulled another lever. "Now, I shall have to request that you steer us back to London right away."

Spires rolled his eyes. "I'd put an end to your prattle this very instant if I wasn't preoccupied with the ship. Were it able to fly itself…"

"Actually, I could probably invent such a device to fulfill your wishes," Professor Thistlequick offered. His voice was light, but his gaze was serious as it darted around the cockpit and settled on the small glass pyramid beside Mr. Spires's chair. The red smoke swirling hypnotically inside it drew Jake's attention, and whatever it was, it seemed to be of importance.

"You're going to die," Spires said. "Both of you. You've crossed me twice tonight, destroyed my investments and breached my craft. You will pay dearly."

"Perhaps. Or better yet," Professor Thistlequick said, "you could just take us back to the city and release the children."

Spires gave a dry chuckle as he gazed through the window, but his hooded eyes flitted over Jake in the glass reflection.

"You know," the Professor said, inching forward again, "I've seen plenty of your handiwork over these last few days and I must say, I'm impressed. Really impressed! This craft is a work of beauty and as for your cloud...well that was simply ingenious. As was the Miraghus, or at least its potential, for I'm sure you'll agree it's less than ideal in its current iteration. I believe it almost certainly led to your friend Lear's insanity-"

"I can assure you Lear was never of sound mind in the first place," Spires said.

"Perhaps not. But the Miraghus clearly didn't help. And those poor people thrown to their deaths from your cloud-"

"That *was* regrettable," Spires said. "But Lear paid the price for it once he became as defunct as the cloud. So you and the boy went there did you?"

"We did," Professor Thistlequick said. "And from there we found your house, and then the warehouse. Tell me, what on earth were all those guns for?"

"What do you think, man. Guns are for war."

"What war?" Professor Thistlequick asked. He inched forward again ever so slightly toward the tiny glass pyramid.

"The war between-" Spires twisted in his chair and scowled. "If you take another step closer I'll gut you."

Professor Thistlequick held out his hands. "I'd sooner you didn't." He smiled. "But I have the feeling you'll try and harm us no matter what I want. But before you do, could I ask what any of this is for? The cloud, the demon, the dead man walking... the weapons... everything!"

"It's for the death of London," Mr. Spires said, "and its subsequent rebirth."

"Ah. So after you've demolished the city, you intend to

rebuild it. Following whatever visions you have for it, no doubt." The Professor smiled, but there was no humor in it.

"Exactly." Spires gazed hard at the Professor Thistlequick, as if trying to work out what exactly he was. Jake was relieved the man's attention was diverted from him.

"Tell me, Mr. Spires, has it ever crossed your mind how your inventions and discoveries could advance mankind? The Miraghus alone, if developed and made stable, could feed the entire world."

"And why would I want to do that?"

Professor Thistlequick shrugged. "To be nice?"

"You really are a most foolish individual." Spires reached inside his coat and withdrew a long blade. "Clearly you thought engaging me in your banalities would buy you time to edge forward, ever so slowly, in order to attempt to destroy the cloaking device." His gaze flitted to the glass pyramid. "Am I correct?"

"I'm afraid you are," Professor Thistlequick said.

Spires gave a slight, false laugh, then flicked a switch on the control and spoke into a long thin pipe. "To the cockpit, Kedgewick." He turned back to the Professor and Jake. "I'll have him throw you from the craft."

"I'm sure you will," Professor Thistlequick said. "But before we die, humor me. What is your vision for London, after its been absolutely demolished?"

"I'll allow it to lie fallow. The old order strangles innovation and creativity. They're weeds choking the blossoms of potential. All they seek is to further their own shortsighted ambitions. They control magick as if it were a commodity, but I will set it free. I'll set everything free."

"They say the road to hell is paved with good intentions,"

Professor Thistlequick said as he took another step toward the pyramid.

Spires spun around. "Step back or I'll cut you to ribbons."

"I have no doubt that you will." Professor Thistlequick delved into his pocket. "And I can assure you, Mr. Spires, I have no intention of going anywhere near you. For it would be like approaching a serpent, or a malevolent spider." An almost absent smile played over his lips as he removed a catapult from his coat.

Spires gave a thin, dry laugh. "A formidable weapon, Professor."

"It's not a weapon, actually." Professor Thistlequick placed a marble in the sling.

Jake flinched as the door behind them exploded open and Kedgewick thundered into the room.

"Finally," Mr. Spires muttered.

Kedgewick lunged at the Professor but he leaped aside, pulled back the catapult's sling and let the marble fly. It whistled past Spires' head and smashed into the glass pyramid.

"Idiot!" Spires threw a hand over the ruptured glass, but it was too late.

Wisps of red smoke spilled out, filling the room with a scent like burnt almonds. The craft flashed and a blue lightning-like charge rippled across its exterior, before vanishing.

Jake ran to the window and scoured the skies for HMS Watcher but the lights of London were far away and there was nothing but darkness below them.

They were alone.

CHAPTER SIXTY-ONE

J ake tried to duck away as Kedgewick seized him in his cold brass arms. "Get off!" he cried.

"Let him go!" Professor Thistlequick demanded.

Jake could hear the clockwork ticking inside the giant's armor, and the thump of his bloody pulp of heart. A stench of decay pricked his nostrils, causing him to retch.

Spires clutched at the hole in the glass pyramid as the last wisps of red vapor poured between his fingers. Finally, he let go. "Kill them, Kedgewick. Kill them both!" Spires pulled a series of levers, causing the floor to hiss as a trapdoor opened beneath them. Steam and freezing air billowed into the cockpit. "Throw them out."

Kedgewick dragged Jake to the trapdoor. The Professor tried to block his path but Kedgewick backhanded him across the face, sending him sprawling to the floor. The Professor raised his head for a moment, and then collapsed out cold.

Jake gazed in horror at the inky black darkness below the craft. "Please!" he begged as Kedgewick grabbed him around the neck and held him over the opening. The giant muttered something, but Jake couldn't hear him over the shrieking wind.

"Let me go!" Jake fought to pull himself free, but Kedgewick's grip didn't waver. It was like being encased in iron.

Jake's gaze strayed to the roaring darkness below and he thought of the cloud, Lear, and Sinners Drop.

But this time the Professor wasn't going to save him, for he was lying unconscious on the floor.

I'm going to die, he thought as he glanced down at the distant treetops. *But at least Nancy's free...*

And as he thought of Nancy and the children in that dark, squalid room, a memory flitted through this mind. Of the boy in the photograph he'd taken from Kedgewick's cellar lair. He still had it. Perhaps it could buy him time...

"Say your last words and be at peace," Kedgewick said.

"Like him?" Jake thrust the photograph before Kedgewick's dark eyes. "Did you kill him too? Did-"

Jake's words were snatched away as Kedgewick dropped him beside the trapdoor and swiped the photograph from his hand. Cold fury glowered in his eyes as they flitted over the crumpled image. "Where did you get this?" Fury wracked his voice, and then sorrow. "Where?"

"Never mind that," Spires called. "Throw the child out and then Thistlequick. Now!"

"My boy," Kedgewick muttered, his eyes locked on the photograph. "My poor, poor boy."

"I said now!" Spires growled.

"No." Kedgewick smoothed the crumpled photograph in his huge fingers. "I've seen enough death already."

"Don't defy me, Kedgewick. Remember who gave you your life," Spires said, his voice as hard as ice.

Kedgewick gave a bitter laugh. "Did I ask you to bring me back to this?" He held up the photograph. "To be apart from my boy? To live this half life? " Tears glistened in his eyes. "I want to be with my child. I want to be at peace. Take us back to London, I've served enough of my borrowed time. I want to be with my loved ones. That's where I belong."

"They're dead, Kedgewick," Spires said as he gripped the wheel and watched them in the window's reflection. "And so are you, should I choose it. Now toss the boy out, he's surplus to our requirements."

"I said no," Kedgewick took a lumbering step toward Spires.

Spires pulled a dagger from his waistcoat, but before he could use it, the giant snatched it from him and used it to sever a chain from Spires' throat. A tiny key gleamed at its end. Kedgewick lifted it, and then, with a long, leaden sigh, he fed it into the lock in the porthole in his chest.

"What are you doing, you fool?" Spires demanded."I'm the only one who knows how to maintain the clockwork. And that's all that's keeping you alive!"

"Indeed," Kedgewick said. "And how you've used that against me. But your *gift* of life isn't worth the price you demand."

He clutched the photograph to his chest and lumbered back to the trapdoor. His feet teetered on the edge and the wind ruffled his hair as he reached up into the porthole. There was a terrible snapping sound and gleaming pieces of clockwork rained around Kedgewick's feet and fell into the darkness below.

"No!" Jake cried as Kedgewick reached further into the porthole in his chest and a hideous sound filled the air. Ashen faced, the giant toppled, fell through the trapdoor, and was snatched away by the screeching wind.

CHAPTER SIXTY-TWO

"I f you want a job done," Spires sighed as he grabbed an umbrella from a stand in the corner, and jammed it into the steering wheel, "then you must do it yourself." He flipped a lever and turned to Jake. "There, the craft can fly itself while I finish the job." He grabbed his knife from where it lay on the floor and advanced on Jake.

Jake stepped away until his back struck the wall.

"Have no fear," Spires said. "I take no pleasure in ending lives. I'll make it quick for you."

"No!" Jake flinched as Spires grabbed his shoulder and brought up the knife.

"Hold still, child."

"Please!"

"Stop fighting. Your pain will soon end." Spires twisted Jake's hair, exposing his throat.

"Unhand him!"

Jake glanced past Spires as the Professor sat up, his bleary eyes fixed on them. He climbed to his feet, his usually kindly face baleful below the flashing lights.

Spires swiped his knife at him, but the Professor sidestepped and seized Spires' wrist before giving it a sudden twist.

"Damn you!" Spires cried as his knife clattered to the floor.

"The controls, Jake!" Professor Thistlequick called as he continued to grasp Spires' wrist, holding him in place. "Take the wheel and steer us back to London! Then we'll-" The Professor's words were cut short as Spires seized him around the throat, his eyes filled with a murderous fire.

Jake rushed at Spires but was almost thrown from his feet as the entire craft thundered and shook.

"Fly us, Jake. Quickly!" the Professor called, his words half strangled.

The craft shook again and distant cries came from the hull. The sound of the children's distress was enough to jar Jake. He raced to the wheel and gazed out to find the ship descending toward a forest, its jagged treetops reaching up like brittle wooden fingers.

Jake yanked the umbrella free and grasped the wheel. It jolted in his hand as the craft tipped further and a terrible screeching filled the cockpit. "I can't stop it!"

"Pull... the wheel... toward you!" Professor Thistlequick cried as he fought to free himself from Spires. "Turn it..."

The entire wheel shook as if it had a life of its own. Tiny cracks filled the cockpit windows as they continued to dive, the sound of their descent almost deafening.

"We're going to crash!" Nausea flooded Jake's stomach. "I don't know what to do!"

"Steer!" the Professor gasped.

Jake glanced back as Spires pulled Professor Thistlequick up and punched him twice in the stomach before shoving him at the trapdoor. The Professor only just managed to veer away at the last second and his eyes grew wide as they focused on the windows. "Do something, Jake!"

Jake's fingers shook as he grasped the wheel.

They were seconds from crashing. The wheel rattled and spun. "I can't...."

You Jake Shillingsworth will never h'amount to h'anything.

The memory of Silas Grumble's mocking words was enough to break the hypnotic hold of the fast approaching trees. "You're wrong!" he shouted. "I will!" He wrenched the wheel with all his might. It shuddered, but as he pulled it back the craft climbed a little.

The treetops continued to surge toward them and Jake dimly heard the Professor cry out. He pulled the wheel back with all his might sending the entire craft shaking with such force it seemed it was about to break apart. But then the nose tilted, and with a heavy rumble, the ship began to climb once more.

Stars gleamed through the spider web of cracks in the glass.

They were ascending.

Jake glanced back to find Spires clinging to a bank of machines, while the Professor gripped the edge of the trapdoor to stop himself sliding back. Jake pushed down on the wheel and the craft began to even out. As soon as it did, Spires let go of the machines and lunged at the Professor.

"No!" Jake cried, and spun the wheel, sending Spires' thudding to the floor. He landed heavily, his fingers reaching out and grasping the other side of the trapdoor. He and the Professor stared at each other, and for a moment they were utterly still, as if frozen like statues.

As the craft began to thrum and jitter, Jake pulled the wheel back and tried to keep it steady. They shot through the air until the sprawling golden web of London stretched below.

Jake gazed down, mesmerized by the city until a low thunk came from the bank of machines behind him, and suddenly the ship began to pick up speed again.

Another rumble shook them and they dipped down. Jake turned as Spires advanced on the Professor, his eyes murderous once more.

"You should know showing mercy is always worthless," Jake shouted, echoing the words Spires had spoken on the rooftop all those nights ago. He twisted the wheel before Spires could strike, sending him sliding down through the trapdoor.

Professor Thistlequick fell to his knees and reached down through the trapdoor. "I've got him!" he called. "Keep her steady!"

"You've got to help me! Now!" Jake cried.

The Professor's face was almost purple with exertion. Beads of sweat glistened on his head as he continued to hold Spires through the trapdoor.

"No!" Jake cried as the levers on the bank beside the wheel began to slide of their own volition. The craft lurched further and began to pick up speed.

The levers wouldn't move, no matter how firmly Jake pulled them. A terrible screeching din filled the air. It was coming from the wings...

London's lights grew brighter as they screamed toward the city. "I can't slow it!" Jake cried.

The looming buildings grew in size in the cockpit's windows and a heady scent of chimney smoke filled the air.

Everything turned black with smoke and for a moment it was like they were soaring through the clouds again…

… and then the smoke faded and a colossal building appeared through the grey haze.

Big Ben.

They were going to smash right through it!

CHAPTER SIXTY-THREE

The Professor flinched as searing pain shot through his arm. He gritted his teeth. Screaming would only expend valuable energy.

It felt as if his arm was about to be torn from its socket as he gripped Spires' wrist.

He'd have to let go, and soon.

The lights alongside the Thames glinted below. The river wasn't the best of landings for Spires, but better that than the hard frosty streets.

Suddenly, the river vanished and they soared over chimney stacks and a glistening cobbled road. Professor Thistlequick held his other hand out to Spires. "Take it!"

Spires' eyes held no fear as he stared back. Then, he glanced down at the moonlight shimmering over the manmade pools of water below his dangling feet. He gazed back at the Professor. "Take your filthy hand off me."

"You won't make it. Just-"

Professor Thistlequick cried out as Spires raked his nails across the Professor's wrist, tearing at his soft flesh.

"I said release me!" Spires cried and smashed his knuckles into the Professor's wrist.

Professor Thistlequick howled, and as Spires struck again, he finally let go and watched in horror as Spires plummeted away. His eyes never left the Professor's as he fell in silence, arms outstretched, his stare filled with malice and spite.

And then the craft roared onwards, and he was lost from sight.

Professor Thistlequick rolled over and nursed his arm, which felt like it had been clamped in a vise. He closed his eyes and allowed himself a long breath, until Jake's panicked cry cut through the tumult.

CHAPTER SIXTY-FOUR

"I can't slow down!" Jake screamed as the ship careened toward Big Ben. He yanked the wheel but it barely turned, and a grinding squeal came from the control panel.

"Damnation and mustard!" Professor Thistlequick cried as he seized the wheel. "Pull with me, Jake. One, two..."

The clock tower was so close Jake could see the minute marks upon its face.

"Three!"

They pulled together.

Jake's arms shook as his gaze remained glued to the clock tower.

"Pull right," Professor Thistlequick shouted. They yanked the wheel and with inches to spare, the craft shot past the tower, its wings scraping the stone. "We've got to land!"

They soared over the House of Lords, and banked right, the fins screaming through the air as the craft descended. They were so close to the ground Jake could see the people lining the street below, their faces stricken with terror.

The craft swept down Whitehall, mere feet from the carriages below. Nelson's Column hurtled towards them, the lions at its base coming fast into view. "How-"

Jake's words were snatched away as the craft shook harder than ever. Deep cracks splintered through its windows and a terrible keening sound issued from its fin-shaped wings. Jake's stomach flipped as they lurched down, careening past the Column, descending into Trafalgar Square.

Whump!

The craft scraped across the ground and smashed into a fountain, sending jets of water into the air. "No!" Jake's head struck the wheel. A whine rang through his ears and tiny white stars glittered before his eyes.

He watched numbly as the Professor stood and staggered to the control panel. He thumped his hands into the buttons, sending great hisses of steam billowing around them as the jaws of the giant fish opened.

Professor Thistlequick shouted, but Jake couldn't hear him over the hum of engines and the screams and cries coming from the square. Jake limped across the craft, grabbed the Professor's arm and led him to the trapdoor. Together, they jumped into the rubble below.

Thankfully, the only casualty of the crash appeared to be the fountain. A crowd formed around them, their faces filled with horror. And then, one by one they glanced up as HMS Watcher roared overhead, its searchlights lighting the scene.

Jake shuffled forward and fell to the ground. He lay with his back to a plinth, closed his eyes, and sunk into a deep, dark sleep.

. . .

HE AWOKE TO VOICES. Slowly, he opened his bleary eyes. Trafalgar Square still teemed with people and heavy flakes of snow fell around them, turning the unoccupied ground crisp and white. Jake shivered, and pulled the blanket someone had draped over him tight around his neck.

"What's wrong with them? Are they diseased?" A well-to-do lady demanded of a nearby police officer. She was gesturing at Adam and the boy from the engine room as they stood before the fountain, staring ahead with blank faces.

Jake scoured the crowd for the Professor, but there was no sign of him. The craft still smoked and rumbled as it rested in the square like a great brass fish out of water. It emitted a low drone and trembled as a police officer and Inspector emerged from its belly. They raised their truncheons and began to push the crowd back.

"Are you alright son?" a ratty-face man asked Jake, as he handed him a mug of steaming tea.

"I think so."

The man nodded to the craft. "Were you in that thing?"

"Yes." Jake's head felt numb and sleepy and he had to fight to keep his eyes open.

The man gave the crowd a furtive glance as he pulled a notebook from his pocket. "I work for the Times. Tell you what, son, you give me your story, in your own words, and I'll give you a pretty penny. Just as long as it's my exclusive. Right?"

"H'exclusive my shoe!"

Jake gasped as cold grasping fingers seized his wrist. He looked up to find Silas Grumble towering over him, his coat barely hiding his stained long-johns.

"I don't know what damnable lunacy you've h'involved yourself in this time, boy," Grumble said. "And I don't care neither. I've worn my fingers to the bone trying to keep the Crow ship-shape while you've been mooning about London." Grumble wrinkled his nose and gave the craft a distasteful glare. "So you left my gainful h'employment for that! Japes, midnight larks, and who knows what other hokum!"

Silas Grumble yanked Jake to his feet and cursed at the journalist. The ratty face man shook his head, before making a beeline for Adam and the other kids gathered before the ship. "Come, boy," Grumble said. "Step lively, before the police detain you, and rob me of what is mine."

CHAPTER SIXTY-FIVE

Jake didn't fight. He didn't even protest. He simply let Silas Grumble drag him through the snowy streets as exhaustion enveloped him like a thick swaddling blanket.

Silas Grumble continued to mutter to himself as they made their way to St. Giles, but Jake barely heard him. He was numb and hypnotized by the softly falling snow.

"Did you hear me?" Grumble's fingers dug into Jake's shoulder blades. "You think you can run out on me, do you boy? Think you're free to go gallivanting far and wide?"

"I wasn't gallivanting. I was trying to save Nancy, and-"

"What, you and that posh friend of yours?" Grumble barked. "That bearded fiend who came to the Crow in the guise of a gentleman? The warlock who put you under his spell and stole you away, only to forsake you? No doubt he's returned to his gilded mansion by now. Yes. I can almost see him reclining there, draped in a fine silken dressing gown, drinking brandy and feasting upon pheasant hearts and roasted deer tails. He won't spare a thought for you, boy. Not a single consideration. Unlike me, who ventured out in this blizzard to save you. Yet again! You're in my debt, Jake Shillingsworth, and you'll pay it by serving in the Crow until the day you die. Do you hear me?"

Jake flinched as Silas Grumble squeezed the tip of his ear. "Yes, I hear you, Mr. Grumble."

"Good. And don't think you'll be enjoying the leisurely tasks I offered you before. No, there'll be no taking the air and flitting across London delivering messages. Your duties will be pot cleaner, mud scraper, spud scrubber and serving whelk." Silas Grumble paused to wipe his eyes. "I gave you a livelihood, and you dragged my good intentions through the gutter. You harpooned my generosity with a... with a harpoon! I've paid more than a monetary cost to keep you under my roof, Shillingsworth. It's been my life's work, my duty, my penance! To spend these long cold weary days with your strange little face and uncannily mismatched eyes. To suffer the slings of your stories and serpent words. Do you hear me?"

Jake nodded dully. All he wanted to do was lie down and close his eyes.

Finally, they stopped outside The Tattered Crow. Silas Grumble threw the door open and shoved Jake inside.

The bar was full of people, smoke, and a din of slurring voices. A single limp Christmas bough hung from a rafter beside a few shriveled tendrils of mistletoe. Other than that, nothing had changed.

"Clear the tables, boy," Grumble ordered. "And scrub the pots. And when you've finished, attend to the water closets, for I've seen cleaner slaughterhouses. After that, you will return to me for further instructions. And no shirking, or I'll fetch my shirking stick, Christmas Day or not!"

Jake began to clear the tankards and trays of ash as the murmur of low rasping voices grew like a tide in the smoky heat.

I'm home, he thought. *Back where I belong.*

~

IT WAS dawn by the time Jake finished cleaning. His fingers felt raw, his eyes were blurred, and his feet burned and ached.

Silas Grumble, following his yearly Christmas tradition, was already drunk. The tip of his nose was ruddy red, the veins in his face like tiny red worms. He held up his special yuletide tankard, which had been decorated with a sprig of holly, and drained the ale. "Merry..." he burped and grinned at the customers along the bar. "Merry." He hiccoughed and waved his hand, as if trying to catch a fly. His face soured as he gazed at Jake. "Merry to everyone but him, the Judas goat. Come here boy. You've h'evaded me long enough. Come and collect your Christmas clip around the ear, you little maggot!"

Jake barely heard Grumble as he stared out the window, wondering where Nancy and Adam were, and if they'd recovered from their strange malady. Everything felt unreal, like the last few days had been nothing but a fever dream. Jake took a deep breath. He was home alright, back in the rancid place of smoke, threats and bruises.

"I said come here!" Grumble growled. "Timmy turncoat!" He gestured to the drunks at the bar. "He forsook the good ship Crow, and all who sail in her. Left us high and dry without a serving whelk. Mutinous pustule that he is!" Grumble wiped the drool from his lips, and fixed Jake with a red-eyed stare. "Now come and receive your festive punishment. And then, and only then, can you repair to your room to lurk and fester as you please."

Jake almost went to Silas Grumble.

Almost.

But as he thought of his friends, and everything that had happened, he clenched his fists. "No."

Grumble lunged, knocking his festive tankard across the bar. It fell and shattered on the floor. "Vandal!" he screamed. "Wastrel! Waster! Scandalous article! Come and get what's coming to you!"

The men at the bar laughed and nudged each other.

"No." Jake clenched his fists. His eyes stung with tears of anger. "I won't. Don't ever raise a hand to me again. Not if you want to keep it."

"What?" Grumble spluttered. "Are you threatening me, boy? Me, your master and liege?" He clambered onto the bar, sending tankards and glasses flying in all directions. His hands shook as he snatched the air, tumbled, and fell heavily to the floor.

Jake walked to the front door and opened it. He was almost through when a hand shoved him, sending him sprawling across the ice.

"The streets it is then, boy!" Grumble filled the doorway. "I won't suffer your grotesquerie for another moment." He stabbed a finger at Jake. "I always told you you'd h'amount to nothing." He roared as he lunged through the door.

Jake tried to get away, but he slipped and fell upon the icy ground.

"Out with bad rubbish and odorous drear!" Grumble kicked a chunk of ice at Jake, but then he stopped and wavered, his eyes focusing on something behind Jake. "You!" he snarled.

Jake caught a glimpse of bottle-green from the corner of his eye, and then a voice rang out. "Good morning, Jake. Fancy seeing you down there!"

"What do you want?" Grumble demanded. "Fiend! Ogre of means! Everything was fine until you arrived in your shiny shoes!"

Professor Thistlequick stooped and helped Jake to his feet. He straightened Jake's torn shirt, before turning to smile at Silas Grumble. "At first glance it almost looked as if you were bullying my young friend. But I'm sure you were merely treating him to a caper in the snow. How festive of you. May I wish you a very Merry Christmas, Mr. Grumble!"

"You may not! Christmas be damned!" Grumble spat into the street.

"A charming turn of phrase, Mr. Grumble," the Professor said. "But perhaps my assessment was wrong. Perhaps, when I saw you hurling Jake from your door, you were actually dismissing him from his position in your venerable establishment?"

"Are you mocking me?" Silas Grumble's eyes narrowed further.

"No." Professor Thistlequick held up a gloved hand. "I'd never dream of mocking a gentleman such as you, sir. I was merely enquiring as to whether Jake's dismissal from your Inn is a permanent affair?"

"It certainly is! I never want to see the little ratpig again. He broke my Christmas tankard, and deserted the Crow in her hour of need! The boy's nothing but a moper, shirker, and skiver! The streets are welcome to his rickety bones and unpleasantly colored eyes."

"Well, that's fortuitous." Professor Thistlequick brushed the snow from Jake's shoulders. "But to be quite clear, you've definitely dismissed Jake from his duties at The Tattered Crow?"

"That's correct." Grumble grasped the doorframe as he sought to steady himself. "He can go and linger like a welt upon London's backside! An abrasion in the streets. Pestilent flotsam!" Silas Grumble wiped the saliva from his lips and flicked it at Jake. "Snakeweasel!"

"Well then, Jake." Professor Thistlequick offered his hand to shake. "Now Mr. Grumble has so kindly freed you from your indenture, I wondered if you'd be interested in working with me? I might not be able to pay much, but Mrs. Harker has given me permission to offer you the spare room. Admittedly it's a squeeze, but at least there's no fungus on the walls or holes in the ceiling. And I can recommend the food, especially the Sunday roast. What do you say?"

Tears filled Jake's eyes, turning the street into a white, watery blur. "Really?"

"Really." Professor Thistlequick shook his hand. "Now may I suggest we leave? Come, the Penny Farthing awaits."

"Hang on!" Silas Grumble staggered after them. "You can't take the boy. He belongs to the Crow."

Professor Thistlequick kept walking. "You just dismissed him from his duties, Mr. Grumble. You were most clear on the matter."

"No! I've changed my mind!"

Professor Thistlequick clamped his hands over his ears. "I can't hear a blessed thing. Can you Jake?"

Jake held his frayed sleeve over his ears. "Nothing at all."

"Come back, boy. Come back at once!" Grumble slid across the cobbles, his face split with fury. "That's an h'order!"

Jake climbed onto the seat as Professor Thistlequick placed his foot on the pedal and swung his leg over the frame.

"Come down from there!" Silas Grumble was almost upon them when the Professor threw back a lever.

A cloudy plume of steam engulfed the street and a great hiss filled the air as the bicycle's long, leathery wings unfolded. One clipped Silas Grumble, sending him flailing across the road where he landed in a bank of snow, his furious red face bright against the soft white glow surrounding him. He barked something indecipherable before collapsing into the snow. Then, his hand rose, his fingers clawed, before falling with a heavy thud.

The bicycle's wings kept the Penny Farthing steady as Professor Thistlequick cycled down the icy street. As Jake glanced up, the great grey-white clouds above unleashed another fall of snow, but the bitter, wintry weather couldn't keep the beaming smile from his face.

CHAPTER SIXTY-SIX

J ake sat before the fireplace wrapped in the folds of a dressing gown Mrs. Harker had found for him. It was at least two sizes too large, but perfectly comfortable.

His fingers were as wrinkled as prunes as he held them before the glowing coals and yawned contentedly. He'd never bathed in so much hot clean water in his life. Nor would he have ever imagined the row of mechanical ducks that had sailed around the tub scrubbing the tips of his toes. Indeed the bath had been incredibly relaxing until the moment Happiness had half sunk a claw into his chest.

Jake took a deep sniff, savoring the aroma of cooking wafting from upstairs.

"Here you go." Professor Thistlequick appeared with a glass of what looked like sour churned milk.

"What's that?" Jake wasn't sure he liked the look of it.

"A posset. It's warm spiced curdled milk. A most popular drink in medieval times and a perfect tonic for dark winter days."

Jake chanced a sip. The posset had a rich, creamy taste and

held a hint of lemon. He drained the glass and let out an almighty burp. "Sorry!"

"Not at all. But please refrain from such outbursts at the dinner table. Mrs. Harker has a nervous temperament, and has been known to faint at far less." Professor Thistlequick smiled. "Can you smell that symphony of joy rising from the kitchen? Goose, potatoes and other such roasted wonderments."

Jake's stomach rumbled. It felt like he hadn't eaten for weeks. And then he gazed past the towers of books to the door to the spare room. "Are... are you sure I can stay here?"

Professor Thistlequick eyes twinkled. "Entirely. But listen, this isn't charity, Jake. I'll need your assistance in return."

"With what?"

"Well, Mrs. Harker's tired of being a test subject for my experiments. She's convinced she almost lost her sight the other week due to one of my studies, and as for the instance of the furious shrimp..." Professor Thistlequick stopped. "I see my paltry effort at humor isn't quite working."

Jake shook his head. "No one's ever helped me before. Not without me paying for it in one way or another."

"I understand. Especially considering your former master's ill treatment. If master's a word that can be ascribed to such a revolting individual. Listen Jake, you can teach me as much as I can teach you. I've no head for business, but I believe you have. My mind's filled with fluff, clockwork, dust and ephemera, while yours is as sharp as a knife."

Jake nodded. "If you say so."

"Good. I've been thinking of finding an assistant for some time now. To take errands, fetch materials and help me turn a penny rather than throwing them down the drain. In return

I'll give you bed and board, and teach you how to read and write. If you'd like?"

"I... yes." Tears pricked Jake's eyes. He wiped them away.

Professor Thistlequick coughed and gazed studiously into the fire. And then he straightened his back and clapped his hands. "Very good," he blustered. "Very good indeed! So that settles it. At least as far as your living arrangements are concerned. But we still have other matters to attend to and loose ends to tie up, such as the vile Mrs. Wraythe. And the fact that I'm not exactly on the best of terms with the police for now. They wanted to question me further in connection with the great flying fish that crashed into Trafalgar Square."

"Did they come here?" Jake asked and cast a nervous glance to the window.

"No, I went to see them while you were sleeping to ensure your friends are in good care, and they are. I also dropped off a compound that I'm confident should act as an antidote to whatever agent Mr. Spires used to put his victims into their stupor. It should alleviate the physical effects at least, although who knows what other sorcery he used. Still, the authorities should be able to help, and the effects should wear off now that the doses are no longer being administered."

"I'd like to see Nancy, and Adam myself."

"And you will. But you should probably go alone considering I'm a wanted man for now. I probably wouldn't have gotten away from the police station if it hadn't been for a well-placed flash bang and a handful of-" Professor Thistlequick glanced up as four loud thumps shook the ceiling. "Huzzah! A signal to bliss. Dinner is served."

Professor Thistlequick adjusted the bow tie he'd put on for the occasion. "Now I've told Mrs. Harker you'll be dining in your dressing gown, at least until we find you new clothes.

She kindly agreed not to laugh at you. Not too much, anyway." Professor Thistlequick scooped Happiness from her cushion. "Ready, Happiness?" She purred loudly and blinked slowly. "This is the one day of the year Mrs. Harker permits Happiness to dine with us. She even sets her her own plate. So come, let us feast on what might well be the eighth wonder of the world."

~

It didn't take Jake long to clear his plate of buttered peas, goose and golden roasted potatoes. Professor Thistlequick filled Jake's plate with another helping of meat and gravy, while Mrs. Harker beamed with a satisfied smile. Happiness sat beside Jake, her paws resting on the tablecloth as she ate a sausage wrapped in bacon.

"This is heavenly, Mrs. Harker." Professor Thistlequick produced a small corkscrew from his pocket, along with a tiny key. He affixed the corkscrew to a bottle of wine and wound it with the key. Clockwork whirred, the corkscrew began to rise, and then it popped as it broke away from the dusty bottle. Professor Thistlequick set the corkscrew down, pride glinting in his eyes.

"Is that one of your inventions?" Jake asked.

"It most certainly is."

"It doesn't really solve any problems," Jake said, "does it? I mean you could just pull out the cork with a normal corkscrew, couldn't you?"

"He has a point" Mrs. Harker said, as she poured herself and the Professor a glass of wine.

"You see!" Professor Thistlequick clapped his hands as he beamed at Jake. "You're as bright as a button. Had you have been around when I came up with that harebrained idea, you'd have saved me days of work."

Professor Thistlequick filled Jake's glass from a bottle of Mrs. Harker's homemade blackberry cordial. "Now," Professor Thistlequick said. "May I propose a toast. To Christmas, and roast dinners. And friends, new and old. And to new ventures, mistletoe and Happiness."

Happiness looked up, her nose coated in gravy. Jake chuckled. Soon they were all laughing as the Professor's nose wobbled and he brayed like a crazed donkey.

THE SNOW FELL in great white flakes, adding to the thick blanket covering Primrose Hill. Everything was perfectly white and still, but for a single figure standing upon the summit holding a spyglass to his eye. It was trained upon a cottage and a window filled with warm flickering candlelight.

The man smiled as he watched the Professor raise a glass of wine to a doughy faced woman and the boy with the mismatched eyes. "To Jake Shillingsworth," the man raised an imaginary glass. "And Professor Thistlequick. And to this cursed city of bones and rust. And to tomorrow, and nightmares, and new beginnings."

Mr. Spires lowered his spyglass as a raven flew down from a nearby tree and hopped across the snow. "And to portents," Mr. Spires said. "And all they may bring."

He pulled his coat tight as he trudged through the snow.

There was so much to do, and such little time.

THE END

A PREVIEW OF THE BOOK OF KINDLY DEATHS BY ELDRITCH BLACK

THE BOOK OF KINDLY DEATHS

Chapter One

On a desk in the room with the stained glass window sat a book.

It was a thick volume with a worn and cracked black cover revealing a golden symbol; a slim rectangle within two circles that sparkled and flickered as if teased by ghostly fingers. Voices whispered from inside the book, a few human, a few not. As their distant howls and cries grew louder, the book rocked with such force that it flew into the air and hovered.

When it thumped back onto the desk, the thick fountain pen next to it leapt into the air like a tiny brass salmon. As it clattered down upon the desk, a spark shot from the pen's nib, playing over the book and sending its pages flying open.

One by one, the pages flipped, faster and faster, an animated blur of neat blue writing seeming to jump with the book as its dusty pages turned.

Beyond the room with the book and the stained glass

window, the room that had no business being there, the dark, sprawling house was silent.

Like a cat, tensed and still and waiting for its prey to make a move.

The man in the old-fashioned suit awoke. He took a deep breath and filled his lungs, his eyes wide with the exertion as he muttered at the dull ache in his borrowed joints. He had no idea how long he'd lain on the cave floor. How many days and nights had passed in that black and dreamless sleep? He glanced down at his clothes, fussily wiping spots of mildew from his cuff with long, thin fingers.

All he knew, as he scrubbed, was that he felt a terrible yearning for the book. And that it had fallen from his grasp many, many moons ago.

He walked, taking large strides, stretching the ache from his long legs as he went. At the cave's entrance, the remains of its original occupant stared lifelessly, its large, curved teeth yellowed in its broken skull. He kicked the bones as he passed. Whatever creature they'd belonged to hadn't dared confront him, not even in his deep, dreamless sleep.

Beyond the cave, a small graveyard. More bones.

One of the graves stood empty, a smashed coffin lid beside a dark hole. The grave where he'd found his new body. The man's flesh was still weaving itself together as he raised his mottled hand, shielding his eyes from the soft, insipid daylight.

He climbed the hill above the cave, and the farther he got, the more treacherous the ground became. He began to slide and slip, throwing out his hands and grasping at tufts of brown grass. He splayed his fingers, remembering how strong his previous incarnation had been, allowing the memory to give him the strength he needed to continue.

Eventually, he made it to the summit and looked out over a body of cloud-gray water. Far in the distance, a string of twinkling lights strewn across the horizon drew his eye to the mainland. He shook his head, fighting to control his voice. It was a struggle to speak and would be until the body he'd dug up was fully his to occupy. "When...I?" he asked, the words ragged and guttural. He tried to swallow. "When... am...I?" He pointed a pale white finger toward the coast. "Whenever...am. I...been tricked."

∼

Eliza Winter stood in her grandfather's garden for the first time in six years.

Flowers towered above her, the few petals left on their stems curled, dead and withered. She stamped her feet against the chilly January day while her parents fussed around the car, removing bedding, blankets, and backpacks.

Eliza would have offered to help, but as she spotted the agitation on her mother's face, she thought better of it. She gazed along the path, at the tufts of grass glittering with frost, remembering how her grandparents, Tom and Susan, had always kept the garden so pristinely tidy. Eliza wondered what they'd make of it if they could see its state now.

She glanced up at the wide, sullen sky with sadness as she thought of the people who had lived here. The people she'd barely known.

The house reared before her, taller and darker than the other houses on the street. As her gaze fell upon the small tower jutting from the side of its sloping roof, Eliza recalled standing in its room as sunbeams filtered through all four windows. A stark contrast to this drab and bitter winter's day.

She looked past the tower to the chimneys, tall stacks of dark-red bricks, and wondered when smoke had last risen from them.

Three months? Three years?

Her mum had only told Eliza of her grandfather's disappearance a few days ago. And while no one knew exactly how long Tom had been missing, Eliza got the feeling her parents weren't expecting to see him again.

"Miss Winter!" She jumped at her father's voice. He grinned, balancing a large bag on his head and swaying across the pavement like a clown. Behind him, her mother threw worried glances at the neighbors' windows.

"Miss Winter," her father repeated as he tossed her a ring of keys. "Open up, would you? And get the kettle on. Before we die of thirst and hypothermia."

Eliza forced a smile and walked through the garden. As she neared the house, she glanced at its windows and was relieved to find them empty.

The man in the well-tailored suit hiked down the hill, a grim sense of purpose in his crane-like strides. His eyes were set on those distant lights, an unpleasant sneer playing over his thin, cracked lips.

A cliff yawned below him, and again he let the memory of his old body fill this new, borrowed vessel. It may have been a worn old thing, he thought as he looked at the bones he'd stitched together, but it would suit this world. He slithered over the edge of the cliff and wove his way down the rocks like a spider, his gnarled fingers grasping the crevices and cracks. Eventually he stood on a shore, the sea breaking over the dark-green pebbles and rocks at his feet.

The man in the old-fashioned suit took a deep breath, fixed his eyes on the coast across the sea, and stepped into the icy waters.

Eliza walked up the steps leading to the tall, looming red front door and did her best to ignore the knocker. It was just as she remembered it. Just as ugly and just as strange. A vile brass gargoyle with a malevolent grin. Eliza tutted, glancing into its mocking eyes. "It's just a door knocker."

But still her hands trembled as she lifted the key.

"Come on, you're twelve years old, not six!" she chided herself.

The phantom of a forgotten memory crossed her mind. A ghost of an event that had occurred the last time she was at this house. Although the recollection was fleeting, she still felt an icy sting of dread.

In the distance, her parents' voices jarred her, her mother's irritation slicing through Eliza's thoughts, lending her the strength and certainty to reach up and unlock the door.

The book on the desk leaped and flipped, and the stained glass window above the desk shuddered as a strange, pungent breeze wafted through the cracks in its ancient glass.

Far below, in the house, beyond the hidden room, a lock turned.

As the front door opened, the book crashed back down upon the desk, its cover shut, its pages silent.

—————————————————————————————————

The Book of Kindly Deaths is out now!

THE CLOCKWORK MAGICIAN IS NOW AVAILABLE ON AUDIBLE!

You've read the book, now experience this spooky adventure in audio. Each of the character & monsters has been brought to life by Hannibal Hills' stunning narration.

Visit https://eldritchblack.com/audio-books to hear a sample now!

BOOKS BY ELDRITCH BLACK

The Book of Kindly Deaths
The Clockwork Magician
Krampus and The Thief of Christmas
Spooky Stories

The Pirates of Penn Cove
The Day of the Jackalope
The Island Scaregrounds
The Mystery at Ebey's Landing

Short stories (Collected in Spooky Stories)

The Night of the Christmas Letter Getters
The Mysterious Case of Spring-Heeled Jack
The Ghosts of The Tattered Crow
One Dark Hallow's Eve
Three Curses for Trixie Moon
The Festival of Bad Tidings

AFTERWORD

Thank you for reading The Clockwork Magician! I hope you enjoyed Jake and the Professor's adventures. If you have a moment, please consider leaving a quick review online. Even a couple of sentences would be appreciated!

All the best,

Eldritch

ABOUT THE AUTHOR

Eldritch Black is an author of dark, whimsical spooky tales. His first novel 'The Book of Kindly Deaths' was published in 2014, and since then he's written a number of novels including 'The Clockwork Magician', 'Krampus and The Thief of Christmas', 'The Pirates of Penn Cove' & 'The Day of The Jackalope'.

Eldritch was born in London, England and now lives in the United States in the woods on a small island that may or may not be called Weirdbey Island. When he isn't writing, Eldritch enjoys collecting ghosts, forgotten secrets and lost dreams.

Connect with Eldritch here:
www.eldritchblack.com
eldritch@eldritchblack.com

Made in the USA
Middletown, DE
06 August 2022

70348928R10215